ARMENIAN FOLK-TALES
AND FABLES

Armenian Folk-tales and Fables

Translated by
CHARLES DOWNING

Illustrated by
WILLIAM PAPAS

OXFORD UNIVERSITY PRESS

OXFORD   NEW YORK   TORONTO

Oxford University Press, Walton Street, Oxford OX2 6DP

Oxford New York Toronto
Delhi Bombay Calcutta Madras Karachi
Kuala Lumpur Singapore Hong Kong Tokyo
Nairobi Dar es Salaam Cape Town
Melbourne Auckland Madrid

and associated companies in
Berlin Ibadan

Oxford is a trade mark of Oxford University Press

© Charles Downing 1972
First published 1972
First published in paperback 1993

A CIP catalogue record for this book is available
from the British Library

ISBN 0 19 274155 1

Printed in Great Britain
on acid-free paper

To Friedel

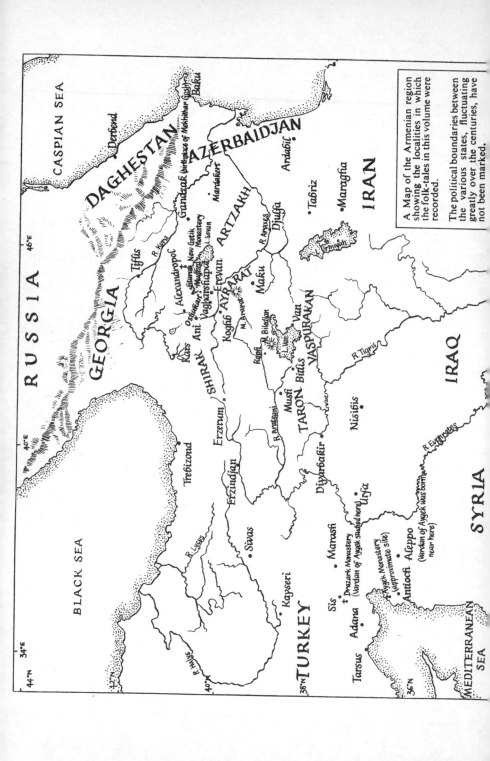

CASPIAN SEA

RUSSIA

DAGHESTAN

AZERBAIDJAN

GEORGIA

IRAN

Derbend

Baku

Gandzak (birthplace of Mekhithar Gosh)

Ardabil

Tabriz   *Maragha*

Mardakert

R.Kura

Tiflis

ARTZAKH

R.Araxes

Urmiyah

Djulfa

Maku

Alexandropol   *New Getik*
Sitavuk *Haghbat Monastery*
Osakan *Mughni*   L.Sevan
Ani   *Vagharshapad*
SHIRAK   *Erevan*   AYRARAT
Kars   Koghb
M.Aragatz
M.Avatd

Erzerum

BLACK SEA

40°E

46°E

44°N

34°E

M.Biledian
L.Van
Van
Rapi   VASPURAKAN

R.Araksani

Mush   Bitlis
TARON

R.Tigris

Trebizond

Erzindjan

Nisibis

IRAQ

Diyarbakir

R.Lycus

Sivas

Urfa

R.Euphrates

SYRIA

Kapseri

(Vardan of Aygek was born near here)

Sis   *Marash*
† Drazark Monastery
(Vardan of Aygek studied here)

TURKEY

Tarsus   *Adana*   † Aygek Monastery
(approximate site)
Antioch   *Aleppo*

R.Halys

MEDITERRANEAN SEA

38°N

36°N

40°N

42°N

A Map of the Armenian region showing the localities in which the folk-tales in this volume were recorded.

The political boundaries between the various states, fluctuating greatly over the centuries, have not been marked.

CONTENTS

FABLES

Foreword

The remote land of Armenia, unfamiliar to most Englishmen, seems a long way to go for a story, and a few words of introduction may be useful. The narrators of the tales here presented dwell, or dwelt, in a mountainous region surrounded by Russians, Turks and Persians, with Georgians, Kurds and Circassians in neighbouring villages or quarters of the town. They belong to a country that has been known to history for more than three millennia. The Book of Genesis relates how Noah's Ark, as the waters of the flood subsided, came to rest, not 'on Mount Ararat' as is commonly misstated—the Armenians call this *Mount Masis*, a name (*Masios*) used by Greek geographers to denote a range to the south-west—but 'upon the mountains of (the land of) Ararat', i.e. a country known to the ancient Assyrians as *Urartu*. This ancient name (for *Urartu* and *Ararat* are synonymous) is perpetuated by that of the central Armenian province of *Ayrarat*, the source of some of the folk-tales included in this volume. The Urartians differed in race and speech from the Armenians, who speak an Indo-European language akin to those spoken by the ancient and more recent immigrant inhabitants of the British Isles (Celtic, English, Gypsy, Urdu, Greek, etc.). The Armenians invaded the region of Ararat after the Urartian kingdom, exhausted by Assyrian and Cimmerian attacks, fell to the Medes in 612 B.C. In the course of time, Persians, Greeks, Romans, Parthians, Arabs, Mongols, Turks and Russians turned the region into a battlefield on many occasions, but the Armenians have managed to survive, as a nation, to the present day. They were converted to Christianity from various Iranian and pagan sects at the turn of the third and fourth centuries.

At the beginning of the fifth century St. Mesrop invented their very distinctive alphabet, and an extensive written literature began. Before that, tales and songs were current among them, passing from mouth to mouth, some of which were recorded by their ancient historian

Moses of Khoren. It is to such oral tradition that the folk-tales in this volume belong. They are not the work of men of letters, deeply versed in classical learning, or sophisticated poets of court and church, but they, and their proverbs, show that imagination and wisdom are not the sole preserve of priests and princes, and that the peasants too may observe the universe, and not necessarily from the bottom of a well. The folk-tales were taken down, in their original rustic dialects, greatly divergent from the standard literary languages of Armenia, by scholars, largely in the nineteenth and early twentieth centuries, before the massacres of 1915–1921 wiped peasant, proverb and patois from Turkish Armenia, leaving virtually only the Armenians of Russia and Persia to perpetuate native Armenian culture. The narrators of these tales were simple labourers, vine-dressers, millers and so forth, men (and the occasional woman) who had heard the stories from their grandmothers and grandfathers, and would recount them, seated around the communal hearth during the long, rigorous, idle Armenian winter evenings, to their own children and grandchildren, while the smoke curled up through the chimney hole in the roof, the surviving cattle stirred in the adjoining room, and the snow swirled round the icy windows and skylight (for 'the villages in [parts of] Armenia, are built partly under ground . . . the greatest part of [the houses] being lighted by apertures at the top', see below, p. 155); or the more skilled among them would relate them in town and village coffee houses and taverns to anyone who chose to listen. They who had long lost their native aristocracy and had been for centuries under foreign rule, and whose national identity was largely preserved by the Armenian Orthodox Church, would tell of kings and princes, priests and veziers, God and Satan, the Virgin and Beelzebub, witches and werewolves. They had yarns to beguile the fancy or to curdle the blood, stories to lead the imagination into the high mountains or deep into the dark, menacing forests, tales in which for the most part the good triumph and the evil perish. The story-tellers, some of whom display an individual narrative skill of a high order, such as Hakob Hadloyan, who figures prominently in this volume, drew on several sources of inspiration, including the tales of surrounding peoples such as Kurds, Persians, Turks and Arabs. Of these tales the Armenians would often have direct knowledge, for on the cultural crossroads which is Armenia many languages were current. Hakob Hadloyan, for example, is known to have spoken Kurdish and Turkish as well as his native Armenian, and a merchant, never happy to lose a customer for the want of a few foreign phrases, would have a smattering of many more. Armenian vernaculars are full of Turkish, Kurdish, Persian, Arabic and Russian loanwords, and the full flavour of the ethnic and linguistic complexity of Armenian village life may be tasted only in the original versions of the tales, where Arabic expressions like 'Ya Rabb!' (O Lord!), 'Yallah!' (Be quick!),

'Imshi!' (Be off!), etc., fall from the lips of Armenian princesses and peasants. Any English version of such tales is bound to sell them short: 'Poetry,' said the American poet, Robert Frost, 'is what gets lost in translation.' It is hoped, however, that something of the Armenian reality, or unreality, will strike through. Although, as in folk-tales in any language, many themes will be recognized as common to those of many nations (the heroine of *The Red Cow*, and to some extent Arevhat, or Sunbeam, of *The Fair Maiden Sunbeam and the Serpent Prince*, are clearly Cinderella types, for example), many details in these Armenian tales will appear unfamiliar: English rulers do not have a special official, the *milchi*, to put out their enemies' eyes; English dragons never have nits. The stranger the tales, however, the better it must be, for it is not the aim of any story-teller, Armenian or otherwise, to relate *only* those stories which everybody knows, however strong may be the desire, satisfied by Armenian exponents of the art as by others, to hear the old, familiar tales yet again retold.

Collections of fables in which animals mirror human behaviour in order to illustrate a moral precept or an item of practical statecraft are by their nature more the concern of sophisticated authors, priests, philosophers, and political theorists, rather than of imaginative but simple peasants, whether their name be unknown, as in the case of the Indian collection called the *Pañcatantra*, or as famous as that of Aesop, La Fontaine and Krylov. The Armenian fables included here are no exception, being largely the work of two medieval monks, Vardan of Aygek and Mekhithar Gosh, whose motives are plainly didactic. The animal stories upon which they draw can often be traced, like those of La Fontaine, to earlier collections: some Armenian fables can be traced via Syriac and Iranian to India, while others, like those under the name of Olompianos, ascend to Aesop, for whom Olompianos is probably only another name. While the Armenian fables are illustrative of human behaviour the world over, thus readily understood, the same blend of familiarity and unfamiliarity displayed by the folk-tales will be found again in the examples of a more primitive and basic folk art included in the volume, namely the proverbs (it is, of course, difficult to trace the evolution of literature with any certainty, but these succinct formulations of workaday wisdom must rank with myths invented to explain natural phenomena like thunderstorms; war cries and work chants; and campfire accounts of heroic deeds, as the creative nuclei whence folk-tales, fables, epics, lyric poems, and novels derive). Armenian proverbs reflect the usages and beliefs of a society which, while basically Christian, differs greatly from our own, following what might be called a general Middle Eastern way of life, predominantly Muslim, already evident in the folk-tales (a description of forms of this may be found in the chapters on Anatolia and the provinces in R. Lewis, *Everyday Life in Ottoman Turkey*, Batsford, 1971). Many Armenian proverbs are variations of items of an almost universally current practical wisdom. In England, 'when the cat's away, the mice will play'; among the Armenians, readier to break into songs and dances than we, they, with more discrimination, 'dance the saraband'. That 'a man cannot clap with one hand' is known in Armenia and China. Some proverbs are perhaps better understood with the help of a little local knowledge: 'A donkey which has been to Jerusalem forty times will still be a donkey' reminds one that the pious Armenian Christian longs to visit the Holy Land once in his lifetime and acquire the title of *mahtesi* 'pilgrim',[1] as the pious Muslim longs to visit Mecca. In the case of this and other proverbs, however, imagination will serve as well, perhaps better, than knowledge: to understand 'An ox breaks a leg in Daghestan and there's trouble in Koghb' one needs no map to know that the two places mentioned are not particularly close together.

The tenth-century Armenian historian John Catholicos protested that his work did not consist of 'mere tales culled from the lips of old men'. On the whole, this one does. The reader must judge for himself whether it is the worse for it – even for the historian, who may find in such folk material details of the everyday life of a people neglected in weightier accounts of the deeds of rulers and their ministers.

[1] From an Arabic form *maqdisī* (dweller in *or* visitor to the *Beitu 'l-Maqdis* 'House of Sanctity', i.e. Jerusalem).

Note on Armenian Idioms

Armenian tales, like those of all other nations, abound in set expressions, and those occurring in the tales selected for this volume have often been translated literally at the risk of seeming unfamiliar to English ears. The form of address 'Man of God!' means little more than 'My dear man!'. The greeting 'Light to your eyes!' normally accompanies glad tidings, but occasionally expresses the hope, upon the announcement of the contrary, for better fortune. The common formulae 'May I die for (*lit.* unto) your soul *or* your sun (i.e. your life under the sun) *or* your head!' assert a readiness to sacrifice one's life for the person addressed, and express reverence and affection. 'May I die for (*lit.* unto) your feet' appears to be basically a request to the person addressed to use his feet to come to one's aid, and accompanies urgent supplications. Armenian tales normally begin with a phrase such as 'There was, there was not, there was a king', a formula, common in Russian tales, which is sometimes retained in the translations below, and sometimes replaced by its English equivalent, 'Once upon a time . . .' As in Turkish tales, the hero 'goes a long way, or goes a short way' towards his destination, the Armenian narrator occasionally remarking that 'only God knows the longness or shortness of his journey'. There are other typical Armenian expressions in the translations to follow, but it is hoped that, though strange, they will be readily intelligible.

FOLK-TALES

Princess Radiant

Once upon a time there was a young man, and though he was in no way ill-favoured in his person, he seemed to have no luck whatsoever, and however so many times his old mother, a widow, went the rounds of all the families with marriageable daughters to dispose of, not a single one of them would accept her son for a husband. The parents of the girls would only laugh in her face, and ask:

'Do you really think that your miserable son is a fair exchange for our fine daughter?'

Well, some time passed, and the young man sank into deep despair. He could not eat, he could not drink, he could not sleep. Soon he was nothing but skin and bones, his body wasted away like an old, threadbare rag. His mother could see that he was eating his heart out with grief, but what could she do about it? You cannot sue for a girl's hand by force! So the youth sat and wept with frustration, and cursed his ill fate.

But for every ill, they say, there is a remedy, and one day the young man said to himself:

'You poor fool, what binds you to this place? Girls have not disappeared entirely from the face of the earth! There will be many others elsewhere. Let us go and see what blind chance may have in store for us!'

So he put a loaf of bread in his knapsack, and set out along the highway. He went a long way, he went a short way, and then he felt weary, and sat down to rest a while at the side of a well, intending to drink of its water, and then go on his way. As he stooped to drink, he sighed a great sigh.

'A-a-a-akh!' he sighed.

'What is the matter?' suddenly exclaimed a voice. It was clearly that of a girl, but there was no one there to be seen.

'Oh!' cried the young man. 'Who said that?'

'It was I,' said the voice. 'I asked you what was the matter.'

'Who are you?' said the young man. 'I hear a voice, but see no one!'

'Have you never heard of me?' replied the voice. 'I am called Lusaghen, Radiant, daughter of the King of the Waters. I live with my papa and mama in this well. As soon as I saw you, I fell madly in love with you. It was love at first sight. Go quickly, tell your mother to come and ask my father, the King, for my hand in marriage on your behalf!'

'If it is like that,' said the young man, hesitantly, 'just show yourself for a minute, and let me look at you!'

'I cannot do that,' said the voice. 'You will understand later why I cannot.'

The young man was bewildered. He plunged his head quickly into the well, and peered beneath the surface, all round. But there was neither man nor beast to be seen. He heard only the soft rippling of the water.

'By Allah!' he cried. 'My eyes and ears have deceived me! For what man ever heard a person who could speak, or utter sounds, and yet was nowhere to be seen? Alas, blind Fate! why do you play tricks with me? Let me get up and go on my way!'

'Dear friend,' said the maiden Radiant's voice from the pool. 'I am not deceiving you. Go back home, and you will find your walls and roof made of gold and silver, and bread and all manner of provisions on your table. If you do not find this to be so, then I have indeed deceived you. But if you find it to be true, then tell your mother to come to my father, the King, and ask for my hand on your behalf. Go, see, and believe.'

So the young man returned the way he had come. When he arrived home, he saw that all that the voice had told him was now true! The walls and the roof of the house were indeed made of gold and silver! Gate and gable, all was changed beyond recognition, and the table groaned under the weight with all manner of provisions fit for a king!

'Mother!' he exclaimed. 'Who has transformed our house like this? Who has covered the table with all that food?'

'For the life of me, I know not!' replied his mother. 'I went outside, heard a voice—and there was only a voice to be heard, and nothing to

2

be seen!—a voice which said: "Walls and roof, turn ye to gold and silver! Table, deck thyself with food!" Then I looked round, and the house was completely changed! "Can this be our house?" I said to myself. "Is that our table?" That is how it all happened!'

'I know it is true, mother!' said her son. 'All this is the doing of the Princess Radiant! She lives in a well, by a spring. You can hear her voice, but there is nothing else to be seen. She told me to come back and ask you to visit her father, the King of the Waters, to ask for her hand on my behalf!'

'May I lay down my life for her!' exclaimed the good woman. 'Do you think I should go straight away?'

'I do, mother,' said the young man. 'Go now. Perhaps my luck has changed.'

He explained to his mother how to get to the well, and she rushed out of the house, ran up to the water's edge, and called down:

'Princess Radiant, may I die at your feet! I am the mother of the young man you wish to marry. Tell your father that I have come to ask him for your hand and to take you back with me as my daughter-in-law!'

No sooner had she spoken, than a tall, imposing figure began to rise slowly and majestically from the well. The old woman beheld a handsome old man, with a crown of gold on his head, clad in purple robes, with eyes as green as glass, with a beard that looked as if it had been carved from green marble, and bearing a staff of mother-of-pearl in his hand. It was the King of the Waters.

'Greetings, gossip King!' said the old woman.

The King smiled benignly.

'May naught but good befall thee!' he said. 'But I have not yet given your son my daughter's hand in marriage, and you already call me gossip?'

'Well, will you give me your daughter, so that I can take her to my son?' said the old woman.

'Not yet,' said the King of the Waters. 'I *shall* give your son my daughter's hand, but only on one condition.'

'What condition, gossip King?' said the old woman.

'If your son can retrieve from my enemy, the King of the Forest, the chest of clothes he stole from my daughter, with the result that she has nothing to wear and dare not venture out of this well, naked as she is, then I shall give her to him to be his bride. If he can't, I shan't! Go back home, where you will find a fully harnessed horse standing in your yard, ready for your son's journey. His saddle is of mother-of-pearl, his bridle is of silver, his horseshoes are of gold, and a fine steel sword hangs from his saddle!'

The old woman went back home, and behold! there in the yard stood a richly accoutred horse, with a saddle of mother-of-pearl, a

3

bridle of silver, horseshoes of gold, and a fine steel sword hanging from the saddle. There could be only one like him in the whole world! Joyfully she told her son what the King had said.

'My boy,' she said, 'your father-in-law, the King, will give you his daughter on one condition, namely, that you go and retrieve from his enemy, the King of the Forest, the chest of clothes he stole from his daughter. If you don't, he won't. What do you say, my son?'

'What can I say, mother?' said the young man. 'I have never ridden a horse, or wielded a sword! What can I do?'

By God's command, the horse opened his mouth and spoke.

'Fear nothing,' he said. 'I shall keep you firm in the saddle. But the King of the Forest is of a most grotesque and fantastical shape, and if any man's eye fall on him, his heart will stop beating right away. As soon as you pick up the chest, he will seek to terrify you. But however much he may roar, "Creature of clay, look behind you, and whatever you ask for, I shall give", you must pay no attention, and not look back. If you do, you will be turned into a tree of the forest!'

'Very well!' said the young man. 'If that is how it is, let us be on our way!'

The young man leapt on to the back of the horse, and galloped away until he came to the forest. Now in this forest, but do not breathe a word of it to him, all the trees were in fact grotesquely enchanted human beings. Their heads were like wicker-work baskets, their feet were all twisted and tangled roots, and their faces were as black as niggers'. No sooner did they set eyes on the young horseman, than they began to roar and moan and dash their branches furiously against each other, so that the whole forest seemed to be shaken by a violent earthquake. Their King, who towered above them like a lobster with a thousand claws and feet, thrashed about him in a frenzy.

'Seize him! Seize him!' he roared. 'It is an age since last I tasted man's flesh! Catch him, trees! Catch him!'

The sight and sound of the rustling, roaring trees struck terror into the heart of the young man, and he almost turned back. But his horse encouraged him.

'Do not be afraid,' he said. 'It is all but empty sound and fury. Ride on!'

The youth summoned up his courage and urged the horse forward. His sword flashed in his hand, and he laid about him on all sides. Leaves and branches scattered around him, until at last his sword thudded down on the back of the King of the Forest's neck, sending his head one way, and his body the other. When the forest trees saw that their King was slain, they fell suddenly silent. The youth dismounted, picked up the chest which had been hidden in the undergrowth, leapt back into the saddle, and galloped off as fast as he could. As he went, the trees began to roar and moan again.

4

'Look back, look back!' they cried. 'If you fail to look back, you will turn into a tree!'

The youth nearly dropped the chest and almost did look back, but his horse bade him be of good heart, and he galloped on until he came to the well. There he called down into the depths of the water:

'Princess Radiant, daughter of the King of the Waters, I have brought back your clothes. Come out, dress yourself, and let us be off!'

At these words, the King of the Waters emerged from the well, approached the young man, and embraced him warmly and kissed him on the forehead. Then he shouted back down the well:

'Daughter, put your head out of the water! The young man has brought your clothes back! Come out, and put some clothes on at last!'

The princess, her cheeks burning, poked her head up out of the water.

'If you will turn your backs, I shall put my clothes on,' she said.

The King and the young man turned their backs, and Princess Radiant stepped out of the well, and dressed. And there before the young man stood such a wonderfully beautiful fairy maiden, that if you saw her, you would be as one bewitched, unable to touch a morsel to eat or a drop to drink. She came up to the young man and put her arms round him, and kissed him, and when she had received her father's blessing, she swung herself up on to the horse's croup, and rode behind the young man back to his house.

When the young man's mother beheld her beautiful daughter-in-law, she almost went out of her wits with admiration, and rushed from one quarter of the village to the other, announcing to all her family and to all and sundry the news of the wedding of her son.

'High and low, wives and maidens, come in your droves!' she shouted. 'Tonight is the wedding, all green and red, all bright and beautiful, of my son and the Princess Radiant, daughter of the King of the Waters!'

Of course, those girls who had declined to marry the widow's son were too ashamed to go to the wedding, and they slunk off to sulk in a corner and beat their heads against the wall. But all the others came, and for seven days and seven nights, to the noise of pipes and drums, the wedding feast went on.

And as they met with their hearts' desire, so may we also!

Lusagheni heqiath, told in 1908 by the farm-labourer Hakob Hadloyan in the village of Koph, province of Taron, printed for the first time in *APT*, X, no. 1.

The Mocker Mocked

I don't know who and when and where exactly, but once upon a time there was a King of a land in the East who had the habit, when he had finished his work for the day, of seating himself at the window of his pavilion to watch the people passing by. One day he looked out and caught sight of a most weird and fantastical little old woman scurrying past his window, so comical indeed that, unable to restrain his mirth, he burst into a gale of loud laughter, so strong that it threatened to split his sides.

'Never have I seen such a ridiculously hideous old crone, I do declare!' he laughed. 'She must be some sort of she-devil, one that haunts the bottom of a well!'

The poor old woman heard this, but paid no attention to it and went on her way.

Well, one day, one week, one month, the King was again seated at his window when he caught sight of the old woman again. As soon as he saw her, up went the loud hoots and guffaws, and he laughed and laughed until the old woman finally lost all patience and came to a halt beneath his window.

'Laugh away! laugh away!' she cried. 'We'll soon see which of the two of us laughs last!'

So saying, off she went.

Now don't say anything, but that old woman was a sort of free-lance witch, one able to take on any shape or form she wished. One day she might appear as a fine-grained angel, another day as some monstrous devil, or I don't know what. She could assume thousands of different shapes and sizes, and could turn the ugly into the beautiful, and the fair into the repulsive; she could make the brainless clever, and the intelligent stupid.

Well, now we know everything about the old woman, so there's no need to repeat it. Enough is enough. So this silly King proves incapable of giving up his bad habit, and the more he sees the old woman, the louder he laughs, until one day he touches the old woman to the quick. Unable to bear the ridicule any longer, she changes her shape and form, turns into a pretty girl, and goes to see the Queen.

'Your Majesty,' she says. 'I am as dust beneath your feet. My husband has died, leaving me with many little ones. Could you not employ me as your maid, perhaps? I should come early in the morning, see to

6

everything, and go back home in the evening. Thus I could earn enough to afford to keep my children with me.'

'Well, why not?' said the Queen. 'It just so happens I need a servant. You seem a pleasant, well-favoured body. You may bathe me, and comb my hair. It's my day of the week for a bath, so let's go now.'

They went to the bath-house. The Queen had a good wash, then came out of the water. The witch took her comb and began to comb her hair, and no sooner did her hand touch her, than the Queen turned into a hideous old woman, so hideous, indeed, that the devil himself would have been terrified out of his wits! When the Queen looked in the mirror, she gave herself such a fright that she screamed out loud.

'King! King!' she yelled. 'Come quickly!'

At the sound of her voice, the witch vanished.

The King ran up, looked, and saw that his wife's nose had grown to an enormous length, that her lips hung down to her bosom, that her hair was as tangled as tree-roots, and that her face was of such a colour, you might well have thought that someone had shovelled ashes from the stove over it. In a word, she was of all ugly women *the* most ugly.

'Wife, what has happened to you?' cried the King.

The Queen explained as best she could.

'A pretty young woman came along and asked me to employ her as a maid. When I had taken my bath, no sooner did her hand touch me, than I changed into the hideous monster you see. Do something!'

'What can I do, wife?' said the King.

'Find that woman!' snapped the Queen.

Not knowing which way to turn, the King stood rooted to the spot. There were about a million women in the city, who could know which one had acted as the Queen's maid? Ah well, to work! Let us get on with it. So let them remain, while we return to the witch.

As soon as the witch returned home, she changed her shape again, and reassumed her first fantastical guise. Her conscience began to prick her, however, and in the end she got up and went to see the King. She came up to the door of the pavilion, but the guards would not let her pass.

'Clear off, you horrid old creature!' they cried. 'Our pavilion does not need the likes of you in it!'

So saying, they thumped and shoved and shouted, so much that the noise reached the ears of the King.

'What is it, my lads?' said the King.

The guards pointed to the old woman.

Stupid he may have been, but for once a glimmer of sense passed through the King's head.

'Leave her alone!' he said. 'Let her come in!'

He led her into the pavilion, sat himself on his throne, and placed the old woman in front of him.

8

'What is your wish?' he said.

'Your Majesty,' said the witch, 'I am the old woman you are always laughing at. Can you see how your mockery has rebounded on to your own head? If you want to know, I am the one who turned your wife into an ugly old woman. Are you still laughing?'

'Ah, woman!' said the King. 'If you will, your good fortune shall follow mine. Turn my wife back to what she was before, and I shall give you your weight in gold!'

The witch laughed.

'What are you laughing at?' said the King.

'What then? Shall I not laugh, when it is my turn?' mocked the witch. 'Listen to me, King! When you laughed at me, I thought to myself that there could be no one more stupid in all the lands of the East. What you do to others shall fall on to your own head. I am sorry for your wife, not for you. Call her, and I shall turn her back into the pretty woman she was before. And from henceforth a little good sense shall dwell in your head, and you will not be so ready to laugh at people in future!'

The witch reached out her hand, and the hideous Queen turned back into a beautiful lady. And before the King could say a word, the witch vanished. From that day forth, they say, that King never again made fun of the faults of others.

Or tsitsgha, ur vren kë tsitsgha, literally, 'He who laughs, at him shall others laugh', told *c.* 1900 by the illiterate labourer Manuk Avdalian in the village of Koph, province of Taron, and published for the first time in *APT*, X, no. 8.

The Power of Love

A young man was intending to get married, when suddenly Death appeared and stood in front of him.

'You shall die on your wedding day,' he said.

Petrified with fear, the young man could not utter a single word. He wandered sadly off until he came to the foot of Mount Biledjan. He looked up and saw an old man with a white beard seated upon an aery throne, a staff in his hand. The old man's face shone with a bright light.

'Why are you so pale, boy?' asked the old man. 'Where are you going?'

'I'm running away from Death,' replied the young man. 'I'm in grave trouble, that's for sure!'

The old man smiled grimly, nodded his head and stroked his beard.

'Nobody has ever yet managed to escape from that mangy bag-o'-bones, sure enough!' he said. 'But I'll tell you something: his beard is firmly in *my* grasp, and *I* tell him when to take the soul of such and such a man, or shorten the life of such and such another, or lengthen that of such and such another.'

'Who are you then, grandfather?'

'They call me Time.'

'If you have such power, let me fall at your feet and beg you to save me! You can see that I'm still very young, and full of vigour. Why does he encompass my downfall? What have I done to him?'

The old man was moved.

'For so long as you remain terrified of Death, you will flee him, and remain for ever homeless,' he said. 'So walk one hundred paces to my right until you come to a wild plum tree. There you will find a well with water as limpid as the eye of a crane. Drink of that water, and the taste shall rid you of your fear, and the spirit of fortitude shall rise within you. Then go your way, and God be with you.'

The young man kissed the old man's hand, thanked him, found the well, drank the magic water which rid him of his fear and inspired him with fortitude, and went on his way. He marched on and on, until he came to a city built at the edge of a great sea. Here he settled for a few years, earned himself a small fortune, and then made his way back home to his mother and father. No sooner had he crossed the threshold, however, when, hey presto! there stood Death in front of him!

'So you thought you'd escape me, did you?' said Death. 'Who can

extricate himself from my clutches, pray? It's all up with you now! Come on, hand over your soul!'

The young man's mother darted in between them.

'Why do you kill my young son?' she cried. 'If you must have some-one's soul, take mine!'

Death started to tug at her soul, till it began to leave her feet and move up through her windpipe. The old woman could not stand it for long.

'Help, Death is ravishing my soul!' she cried.

Death relaxed his grip.

The young man's father darted forward.

'Do not kill my only son, the pillar and light of my house!' he cried. 'If you must have someone's soul, take mine!'

Death started to draw his soul till it left his legs and moved up past his tongue. The old man could not stand it for long.

'Help me, son! Death is robbing me of my soul to save your life!' he cried.

Death relaxed his grip.

'I cannot blame them,' said the young man. 'There is no need for them to suffer for my sake. But since you are here, let us go to the house of my betrothed. If she is not prepared to sacrifice up her soul for me, then most gladly will I surrender my own!'

So Death and the young man went to the house of his intended bride. As soon as the girl saw the young man, Death had no time to set to work, before she ran up, threw her arms round the young man's neck, and kissed him warmly. So close was their embrace, it seemed they were but one body and soul.

'Ho there!' shouted Death. 'That's enough! I've no more time to waste. Tell me what you wish to do!'

'What do *you* want?' asked the girl.

'I am here to take your young man's soul!' said Death.

'If you must take someone's soul, take mine!' said the girl.

Death began to tug at her soul, till it slowly came away at the tips of her toes and the roots of her hair.

'Why are you torturing me so?' cried the girl. 'If you want my soul, take it at one go! Let me only first kiss my betrothed, as I yearn to do, and then do as you will!'

Death snatched away the girl's soul with one sharp tug. No sooner had he done so, however, than he began to marvel at her great love and devotion, and being unable to dismiss the young man and the young woman from his mind, he relented, and he gave her back her soul, and left them together, and went on his way. The young man and his betrothed returned home in great joy. For three days and three nights the wedding festivities continued, and they achieved their hearts' desire.

Three apples fell from Heaven: one for the bride, one for the bridegroom, and one for the white-bearded old man, who was, is, and ever shall be, until the End of Time. Amen.

Siru heqiath, literally, 'A tale of love', told in 1915 by Hakob Hadloyan in the village of Bardav, Badnotz region, province of Taron, and printed for the first time in *APT*, X, no. 5.

The Thieving Daughter-in-Law

There was once a newly-wed bride and her mother-in-law. They kept a large sack of chick peas in that household, and it so happened that the daughter-in-law was very fond of chick peas. One day she stole some of them, secretly boiled them and ate them. One, two, five, ten days passed, and when the mother-in-law looked, she found that the sack of chick peas was only half full.

'First they're there and then they're not!' she muttered to herself. 'This is the work of our daughter-in-law.'

But if the mother-in-law was a cunning old devil, the daughter-in-law was not less so. She quickly divined the thoughts that were passing through her mother-in-law's head.

'What shall I do, for goodness' sake?' she asked herself. 'How shall I prevent her suspicions settling on me?'

One day when she was sweeping out the house, she found a single chick pea lying on the floor. She picked it up and ran to show it to her mother-in-law.

'I've found a cornikin, pippikin, with a catling's snoutikin!' she cried. 'Nanny, for goodness' sake, what is it?'

When the mother-in-law heard that, her suspicions faded.

'May coals of fire fall on my head!' she said to herself. 'How could I have thought of blaming our poor daughter-in-law? How should she think of stealing the chick peas, when she does not even know what a chick pea is?'

> *Gogh harsë*, first noted down in Vagharshapat, province of Ayrarat, between 1876 and 1891, details of the narrator being lost; *APT*, II, no. 47.

King Zarzand's Daughter

Once upon a time there was a poor peasant. Every day and all day he would go from door to door asking for work, offering his labour for hire, while his wife stayed at home making little linen handkerchiefs and towels. Thus, between them, they managed to scrape a bare living for themselves and their only son, whose name was Zurab.

One day Zurab's father fell under a cart while labouring in a field, cracking his skull and breaking many of his bones. After lingering on, more dead than alive, for more than a month, he died.

Zurab was only four years old when this happened. His mother, supplementing her meagre income from her linen handkerchiefs and towels by cleaning out the stables of this neighbour and that, or churning their milk, earned enough bread and butter and yoghurt to enable her to keep her son with her.

A few years passed, and then a plague fell upon the village. Twenty-five or thirty of the few inhabitants died of it, there being no doctor in the village, or any medicine. Zurab's mother was one of those who died, leaving him a complete orphan. One of the neighbours, a well-to-do farmer, the owner of many sheep and cattle, took Zurab into his own house, on the one hand because he felt sorry for the bereaved child, and on the other hand because he realized that, though now only nine years old, he might, if he fed him well, be able to pasture his sheep and cattle for him. The orphan's mother had dwelt in a miserable little hut, and since this was of no further use for anything, he had it pulled down, and annexed the land to his garden.

Zurab's guardian possessed four or five young calves, and every morning Zuro (for so they called him, by way of abbreviation, after the death of his mother) would lead these into the fields for pasture, and then bring them back in the evening. The boy was clearly one to keep his eyes open.

When Zuro was twelve, he was entrusted with the task of pasturing the young lambs as well. Zuro the Orphan was not big for his age—'one and a half span, as much scarab as man', as they used to say in our village—but, Heavens! he already possessed the strength of his father, or any grown man. Whenever there was a free-for-all among the village children, Zuro would tackle and overthrow all the boys four or five years older than himself.

It chanced one day that a wolf crept silently up to the little group of lambs in the field to which Zuro had led them to graze. At the time Zuro was sitting down to his lunch, blissfully unaware of what was happening. Suddenly the wolf seized one of the lambs and darted away with it, but finding his way barred by other shepherds and their dogs, he doubled back, to find himself face to face with Zuro the Orphan. Before the wolf had time to change direction, the boy moved like a flash of lightning, held the wolf down with his knee and grasped him by the throat. In a twinkling the wolf lay throttled and limp on the ground. When the shepherds saw this, they all spoke at once.

'What is this?' said one. 'Shall we call you Zuro the Wolf-strangler?'

'Are you a Bear, to hug like that?' said another.

'No, he is an *Aslan*, a Lion!' shouted others, and from that time forth Zuro was known as the Orphan Aslan.

Aslan reached the age of twenty-one, and his master appointed him shepherd to look after his flock of sheep. Aslan was completely fearless. In the summer evenings, when the flock, as is the custom in that season of the year in these parts, had spent the day grazing on the green hillside, the shepherd would lead the sheep down from the hill and shelter them in a cavern in a valley three versts[1] away from the village. He would guide them into this natural sheepfold, station his dogs outside the gate, while he himself would lie across the entrance to the cave, his back resting against one post and his feet against the other. Thus, with his loaf of bread and jug of water hanging from the wall above his head, he would fall asleep and slumber in peace.

One day Orphan Aslan suspected that something was wrong. He could have sworn that someone had helped himself to his bread and water in the course of the night. He gave the matter great thought.

'But no,' he said to himself, 'I must be mistaken. The dogs are lying outside, the sheep cannot get at my satchel, so who could have done such a thing?'

A few days passed, and his master's wife gave him a whole round of *baghadj* or unleavened bread and four eggs as his day's rations. Zuro did as he usually did: he put the loaf and the four eggs in his satchel and that evening hung them up over his head. In the morning he woke up to find that half the loaf and two of the eggs had gone.

'Whether there is anyone to do it or not,' he said, '*someone* or *something* comes at night and takes half shares in my food!'

All the following day Aslan was ill at ease, and he kept glancing at the sun as it crawled across the heavens, waiting impatiently for darkness to fall, so that he could drive the sheep to the fold and find out who was so rash as to come during the night and steal half of his rations.

Eventually it grew dark, and Orphan Aslan gathered his sheep together and led them from the green hillside down to the cave in the

[1] A Russian measure of distance, 1 verst being equal to 3,500 English feet.

valley. There he pulled his felt *kulab* or shepherd's cloak up over his head, and pretended to sleep, keeping a good lookout from under the cloak. It suddenly occurred to him that the unknown thief might be an evil demon!

'If it is, so be it!' he said to himself. 'I shall recite the prayers my mother taught me, and the demon will crawl back to Hell!'

A long time passed, and nothing came. There was not the slightest sound or whisper. The deep silence continued, and Aslan's eyelids grew heavier and heavier in spite of himself, and he was about to fall asleep, when his ears caught a faint rustling sound. All drowsiness vanished!

And then . . . what did Aslan see? Blessed were the eyes that beheld such a vision of delight! There before him stood a beautiful maiden of sixteen or seventeen—but no! not a mere maiden! She was a houri, a gazelle-like creature, a fairy princess, one who might so command the Sun in the heavens: 'Trouble not to rise, O Sun, for my own radiant countenance shall illumine the Earth! Where'er I shine, men shall forget to eat and to drink, to stand and stare in amazement at my wondrous light!'

If he who now listens to this tale be himself a young man, let him swallow hard, and keep a grip on himself!

When Aslan saw her, his wits almost flew from his head. He yearned to leap up and embrace the maiden there and then, and it was all he could do to restrain himself.

The girl took his satchel from the nail, drank some water, broke off her chosen portion of the loaf of bread, and made to return through the wall of the cave whence she had emerged.

But now Aslan already held his arm round her neck!

'Where are you going to, my pretty maid?' he said. 'Are you my lucky star?'

The girl turned round and plaintively entreated the young shepherd to release her.

'Let me go!' she cried. 'I shall bring you no luck! You will only place yourself in terrible danger!'

'Dispose of my life as you will!' exclaimed Aslan. 'There is nothing on this earth that I am afraid of! Stay with me, and be my beloved!'

His tender words tore at the maiden's heartstrings.

'Hear me!' she said. 'Far away, across seven mountains, there dwells a mighty king by the name of Zarzand, or 'Terror'. All other kings tremble at the mere sound of his name. That king is my father. Four or five years ago (I have lost count exactly) seven kings banded together, declared war on my father, and marched against him. My father drew up his own army and sallied forth to do battle with his enemies, leaving my two brothers behind to look to the affairs of state. Just then, however, in these days of great confusion, the three-headed giant demon Tapagöz arrived with six of his brothers, attacked my brothers, and seized me and carried me off with them. My brothers managed to draw up something of an army, and they marched out to do battle with the six devs. For ten days they struck and counter-struck, and by the eleventh day four of the demons were utterly destroyed; but my elder brother perished also. On the thirteenth day another dev and my younger brother were killed, and our armies were greatly depleted. And when my brothers were no more, our soldiers abandoned the struggle and scattered, and returned to their homes.

'The giant Tapagöz, who was the eldest of the demons, lifted me up and brought me back to his own country. When we arrived at Devils' Castle, as they call it, Tapagöz said to me: "Girl, you have no lord and master. What would I not give to be your husband! If you obey me sensibly, I shall treasure you like the light of my eyes!" I did not want a dev for a husband, and I refused to accept him as my betrothed. For forty days the giant pleaded with me. He fell at my feet, trying to talk me round, and he sighed sigh upon sigh. But I only told him "I do not want you!", and kept to my word. On the fortieth day Tapagöz went completely mad. He foamed at the mouth, and the one eye in the top of his head bulged as large as a water-melon. He fell to the ground, and pounded on it with his fists, all the time calling out my name: "Simizar, my darling Simizar!"[1]

'The ogre's mother, a hideous old woman, ground her teeth and scowled darkly at me, and longed to tear me to shreds when she saw the suffering I was causing her son, but she was too afraid of him to dare do anything to me.

'The dev remained in this mad state for three days. Then he regained a certain sanity, resumed his entreaties and supplications for another forty days, and then went mad again. After three more days he came to his senses again, called his mother, and said, "Take this man's whelp out of my sight. But take care, do her no harm!" The giant's old dam was a witch, past mistress at all manner of sorcery. I do not know what she did exactly, but in the wink of an eyelid I found myself immured in this cave. The old woman picked up a green wand, struck the rock-face with it three times, and cried, "Rock, receive within you this daughter of a king, and keep her until such time as the swallows may tell her rescuer how to release her. Then, and only then, when he shall strike you three times, open, and give her to her lord and master. In the meantime, you shall open once a day, at midnight, and let her walk abroad!"

'That, then, shepherd,' concluded the princess, 'is the tale I have to tell. Leave me now, and let me return to my dark and dismal niche in the cold stone. If you really love me, as you say you do, go and find the swallows who know how I may be freed from my prison!'

[1] The girl's name is Persian and means 'with cheeks of silvery hue'.

The young man released the princess, and stood deep in thought.

The next morning, at break of dawn—may its goodness and gladness shine on you also!—Aslan gathered his sheep together and drove them straight to his master's door. When he saw all his sheep returning from the fields long before the summer pasturage was at an end, he was astonished. Aslan asked his master to pay him the wages due to him, declaring that he no longer wished to be a shepherd. His master strove hard to dissuade him, but there was nothing for it: Aslan received his wages, and took to the road.

Once outside the village, he stopped. The road branched out in three different directions, and he was unsure which one he should take. As he stood and thought deeply, he remembered a prayer of his mother's, and he said first the Lord's Prayer, and then prayed silently to himself: 'God of my dear father and mother,' he said, 'I shall shut my eyes and throw my staff into the air. I beg and beseech you, cause it to fall on the right road!'

So saying, Aslan hurled his staff into the air. When he opened his eyes, he saw that it lay on the middle of the three paths. He strode off along it. He walked and he walked, little or much only God knows. Just as dusk was falling he came to a village. It was not an Armenian one, but he had nowhere to stay, no one to turn to, so where else should he go? Somehow it seemed to him that he might find there the swallows with the knowledge to teach him how to release Simizar from her stone prison.

Aslan wandered from this house to that, looking hard for a swallow's nest under the eaves. He passed by many houses, and saw none. All at once, however, on the outskirts of the village, he came to a small cottage, and as he looked, he saw a swallow emerge from the doorway, and then fly back in again.

'By Allah!'[1] he said, 'perhaps my luck is in! If I go and ask at this house, perhaps they will have a place for me to stay the night, until we see what path God will open up for me.'

As luck would have it, the door of the house was open. Aslan went in, looked about, and saw an old woman lighting a candle.

'Greetings, grandmother!' he said. 'I wish you well.'

'Greetings, all good is from God!' replied the old woman. 'I am at your service.'

'Grandmother,' said Aslan, 'I am a stranger in these parts, and have no friend or acquaintance here. Could you perhaps give me shelter for the night?'

'Hospitality to a guest is a sacrifice to God,' said the old woman. 'Come in.'

The old woman fed the young man on bread and everything she had

[1] Such exclamations are used also by Christians in regions where Islam is dominant.

at hand, and when it was bedtime, she prepared a couch for him, and retired to sleep on her own.

Aslan could not sleep.

'Lord God,' he said to himself, 'are these swallows those that can teach me how to save Simizar, or have I still a long way to go to find them?'

As he was pondering on this, and brooding on that, his eyes closed, and he fell asleep.

At the first light of dawn Aslan got up and went to look at the swallows' nest. They were bustling about, and chirping merrily.

'Dear God,' prayed the young man, 'can you not grant me the power to understand the language of birds?'

At this, one of the swallows gave a chirp, and it suddenly seemed to Aslan that he understood something of what was being said. He strained his ears and listened.

'Wife,' said the male swallow.

'What is it?' said the female.

'Do you know the young man? It seems to me that I have seen him somewhere before. Ah! I have it! When we used to go to the cave to collect worms and things, he used to throw us some crumbs!'

'You are right,' said his wife. 'It is Orphan Aslan. He has come to ask our advice on how to rescue Simizar, who is held captive by the dev.'

'It is a good thing he came now, before we left for warmer climes!'

'Aslan has only to do as follows,' said the female swallow. 'When he bids farewell to the mistress of the house, he must kiss her hand three times, and three times must he say "Thank you, good grandmother!" Then the old woman will tell him what to do to rescue the princess.'

When he heard this, Aslan was beside himself for joy.

Just as the sun was rising above the horizon to the prayers of the faithful, Aslan dressed rapidly, saw that the old woman had put her clothes on, and went up to her.

'Grandmother,' he said, 'I must make haste and be on my way. Give me your hand, that I may say farewell, and go.'

And he kissed the old woman's hand three times, and said 'Thank you, good grandmother' three times also.

The old woman kissed the young man on the forehead.

'Bravo, dear Orphan Zurab,' she cried. 'You really are a Lion, an Aslan, among men. God will grant your every wish, never fear!'

And the old woman gave Aslan fourteen hazel nuts, two walnuts, a small bottle of water, and a handful of flour wrapped in a cloth.

'I know the road you are to take,' she said. 'Devils' Castle is seven days' journey from here. Put the fourteen hazel nuts in your pocket, and eat one every day. When you have gone a short distance from this village, sit in a ditch at the side of the road and crack open the two walnuts. You will then have everything that is necessary for your journey. When you arrive at the devs' palace, Devils' Castle, that is, which is in fact a well seven poles deep, you will see the giant's mother seated at its mouth, keeping watch. Take the bottle of water I have given you, fill your mouth with it, and creep up and spit it out into her face. This will render her unconscious. Go down into the well, where you will find the giant Tapagöz fast asleep, due to wake up in three days' time. At the bottom of the well you will see the green wand resting in a pool of water. Pick it up, and climb out of the well with it. What you are to do with the flour, should the need for it arise, someone will be there to tell you. I wish you a safe journey!'

No words can describe Aslan's happiness! He walked a short distance from the old woman's village until he came to a ditch by the side of the road. He took out one of the hazel nuts, cracked it, and ate it. It was as though he had eaten a whole sheep! His hunger of the past two days vanished, for in his worry he had eaten little. He took out one of the walnuts and cracked it. And guess what he saw then! A well-shod horse, strong enough to bear a blacksmith! A horse, do I say? It was a creature of fire and air, and had wings invisible to mortal eyes! It wore a silver saddle on its back. It stationed itself smartly in front of the young man, and waited. When Aslan saw the horse, he was so overjoyed, he hardly knew what he was doing.

Aslan took the other walnut and cracked it, and out of it came a spear tipped with the finest steel; a sword which would cut through wrought iron; a shield—well, I say a shield, but a man could take up his abode under it; and a suit of clothes, but what clothes! what clothes! they beggared all description!

Aslan leapt into the saddle as though anxious to fly to the ends of the earth in the space of an hour. But there was no deviating from the old grandmother's instructions: Aslan journeyed on for seven days, and finally reached Devils' Castle.

Aslan followed the old woman's instructions to the letter. He put the giant's mother to sleep with the water, went down into the well, took the green wand out of the water and put it under his cloak, and then leapt on to Tipi's back—Tipi, or 'Snow-storm',[1] was the name of his horse—and galloped away shouting 'Simizar's cave, where art thou? I am on my way!'

Aslan journeyed on for three more days, and on the fourth, towards evening, he heard a muffled clattering sound behind him, and wheeling his horse round, he saw a mighty cloud of dust coming along the road. It was the giant and his mother, hard on his heels!

By God's command, Tipi suddenly spoke in a human voice.

'Throw the flour into the air!' he cried.

Aslan threw the flour into the air, and the wind spread it all around

[1] In Turkish.

him. There and then, in the twinkling of an eye, a great forest stood between him and the giant and his mother, a forest with undergrowth so thick that a bird could not have flown between the branches of the trees. Aslan travelled on, while the devs entangled themselves in the forest.

So, coolly and calmly, Aslan continued his journey for two more days. Only one more day and he would arrive at Simizar's cave. Aslan's heart beat fast, and he longed to be with his beloved. Suddenly, however, his ears picked up another faint clatter behind him. He turned round and again saw the giant and his mother pursuing him furiously. Again the horse spoke.

'Do not be afraid,' it said. 'Let us stand and fight!'

When he had made the necessary preparations, Aslan stood his ground and waited for Tapagöz to catch up. As soon as he drew near, the giant let fly a punch that would have lifted the boy's head off his shoulders and dashed it against the rocks, perhaps just leaving the larger part of an ear intact. But Aslan stepped aside, and the force of the blow carried the giant forward, and he slipped. Aslan came up behind him and with one blow of his sword struck off one of the giant's heads. The dev made to come at the boy again, but the horse lashed out with its hooves and dealt him a kick that threw him off balance. Aslan wheeled round, and slashed at the second of the giant's heads with his sword. It fell forward, dangling uselessly on his chest. Only the giant's middle head remained. Seething with rage, the giant gathered up a huge boulder and threw it, whoosh! straight at the boy's head. But Aslan parried with his strong shield, and the rock smashed itself to pieces and fell to the ground. Aslan then drew the shield high up on his arm, grasped his lance in both hands, and hurled himself at the giant. With all his strength he thrust the lance into the one eye in the top of the giant's head, and the heavy steel point went right through his brain and came out at his occipital. The giant reeled, and fell down dead.

By now, however, the giant's mother was catching up on him! Aslan reined his horse back on to the road leading to the cave, and saw in front of him, spread right across his path, an enormous lake! There had been none there before, that he knew, and now forty bushels of wheat scattered over its surface would never have covered it. The divinely inspired horse spoke again.

'That is the spittle of the giant's mother, intended to cut off any escape from her son. She has turned herself into that duck there, swimming on the lake. Quick, pluck three hairs from my mane and throw them on to the surface of the lake!'

The shepherd quickly plucked three hairs from his horse's mane and threw them on the surface of the lake. They immediately formed themselves into a bridge, and Aslan galloped safely across.

And so he reached the cave where Simizar was imprisoned safe and sound. He dismounted, ran to the rock wall of the cave, struck it three times with the green wand, and cried three times in succession:

'Open up, wall of rock! Make way for the daughter of a king!'

The rock split asunder, and Simizar came forth and rushed into Aslan's open arms. But her great happiness was too much for her, and she swooned and fell to the ground. Aslan gave her water from his flask and tugged lightly at her ears, and slowly, very slowly, she regained consciousness.

For one hour and two days they rested in the cave, and the shepherd told the princess everything that had happened to him since they last met. They made all the preparations necessary to travel to the capital of Simizar's father's kingdom. Then Aslan said:

'Simik, my dear, I am not your real rescuer, and it would be a wretched thing to forget who that really is. The old grandmother really saved you. Wherever we go from now on, she must come with us.'

Simizar gladly accepted this proposal. Aslan led out his horse, sat Simizar on the saddle with him, and crying, 'Grandmother, where are you? We are on our way!', they set off. They arrived at the old woman's house at nightfall. She was happy to learn of Simizar's escape, and especially happy when she heard that they were going to take her back with them and look after her as though she were their own mother.

The following day the old woman gathered her few possessions together, and they all set off. The old woman would not let Aslan put Simizar and herself on the saddle of the horse and walk on foot himself.

'*You* shall sit on the horse,' she said, and drawing a small wheeled carriage from her bosom, she blew it up, and sat on it. And the magic carriage rolled merrily along close behind the horse.

Our travellers journeyed on and on, whether a great way or a little way we do not know—only God knows what is great and little—and they finally came to the border of King Zarzand's kingdom.

Now just there, on top of a high mountain, a castle stood, guarded by a powerful army under the command of a general, ready to prevent any possible enemy from crossing the border.

The general was now standing on the watchtower beside his lookout when he noticed the three travellers approaching the frontier and about to set foot on the soil of his country. He swiftly despatched ten of his men to stop them doing so. Aslan wanted to fight, and cross the border by force, but Simizar sought to dissuade him.

'For one thing,' she said, 'these men belong to my father's army; and for another thing, there are six mountains behind this one that we shall have to pass. If we fight our way across every one of them, it is possible that you will receive a mortal blow in one of the battles. And what for me would be the sense of living without you?'

The old woman was also ill-disposed to fight their way through, and persuaded the ten men to return to their general.

'We shall withdraw and refrain from setting foot in your country for as long as you are not agreed to let us do so,' she said.

When the soldiers had marched away, the old woman untied the shawl around her head and spread it out on the ground.

'Remain seated on your horse,' she said. 'Let the horse stand on the shawl, and it will carry you all through the air to the King's capital. I shall sit on it in my carriage, and thus may we arrive at our destination without actually setting foot on the soil of the country.'

'No, mother!' said the horse. 'You and my lady shall sit on the shawl, and Aslan shall remain in my saddle. God has given me wings to fly with, and I shall use them to fly him to the capital.'

And with that, he extended his wings, and they all flew off together and descended on the outskirts of King Zarzand's capital city.

Aslan desired to go straight to the royal palace to tell the King that his daughter Simizar was there, but the girl would not allow it.

'The sons of our Grand Vezier were hoping I would favour one of them,' she said, 'and if they know that it is you who have rescued me and brought me back, they will kill you.'

'You stay here and rest a while,' said the old grandmother. 'I shall go and do what is necessary.'

Simizar gave the old woman a small portrait of her mother in a golden frame.

'If they should not believe what you say,' she said, 'show them this picture, and sing them my mother's favourite song which I used to sing for her, namely, "My father is the mightiest of men, My mother is the sweetest of all women". If they will not let you in, you only have to sing that song under my mother's window.'

The old woman went off, and sat on the suitors' stone outside the palace. (This is the stone at the door of Armenian houses upon which those who come to ask for the hand of the daughter of the house on behalf of a would-be husband take their seat.) A servant hurried from the palace.

'What do you want, old woman?' he asked.

'I have come to ask for the hand of the King's daughter for my son.'

'But the King has no daughter any more!'

'Yes, he has!' said the old woman. 'Take me to the King, or to the Queen.'

The King was informed of what was happening.

'Who knows what she means?' he sighed. 'It must be some old woman driven out of her mind by grief.'

The old woman saw that they were not prepared to let her into the palace, so she raised her voice and began to sing the song the princess had taught her:

> *'My father is the mightiest of men,*
> *My mother is the sweetest of all women.'*

The song floated into the air. The Queen heard it in amazement, and swiftly sent a messenger to fetch the old woman to her.

'Why were you sitting on the suitors' stone?' she asked.

'I have come to ask for the hand of your daughter for my son,' said the old woman.

'I no longer have any daughter,' sighed the Queen. 'But that song you sang used to be sung to me by the poor daughter I once had, and was my own favourite song. How do you come to know it?'

'Your daughter taught it to me herself, your daughter Simizar, and she gave me this picture to show you also,' said the old woman. And she related to the Queen everything as it had happened.

As soon as she heard the good news, the Queen fainted right away, overcome with joy. Her handmaidens crowded round her, the King hurried to her side, and between them they brought her round. When they heard from the Queen that the Princess Simizar was alive and well, the entire court set out in a fleet of cabs and carriages to bring Aslan and Simizar to the palace.

King Zarzand and his Queen were overjoyed to see their long-lost daughter again, and they arranged a great ball, to celebrate the forthcoming wedding of the Princess Simizar and the Orphan Aslan.

While the necessary arrangements were being made, the grooms came from the royal stables, and spoke to Aslan.

'For the past two days a mosquito has been flying about the stables, and it will not leave the horses in peace,' they said.

Aslan wanted to go and see what the matter was, but the old woman would not let him.

'I shall go,' she said.

The old woman took two sprigs of narthex and went to the stables and set them alight. The mosquito disappeared immediately.

The old woman was given a good room and a servant all to herself, and she was held by everyone in great esteem.

That same night the old woman crept quietly out of her room when everyone was asleep, quietly opened the door of Aslan's bedroom, stationed herself a few paces from the door, and sat down and waited. In her hand she held an iron rod with three prongs at one end and a short handle at the other.[1]

Just past midnight she heard a faint rustling sound. This was what she was waiting for. A large, black, scaly snake was crawling along the ground in the direction of Aslan and Simizar's beds. Swiftly the old woman struck out with her iron weapon, piercing the snake right through the top of the head, just where the single eye of a Tapagöz

---

[1] Perhaps a sort of fork, or rake.

would be. The vile creature gave a fearful scream, writhed in agony, and then sank lifeless to the ground. Aslan and Simizar were startled out of their sleep by the snake's scream, and the old grandmother related what had happened. The snake was in fact the giant's mother, and it was she also who had been flying round the stables in the shape of a mosquito, waiting for a chance to attack them, before she was finally driven away. Now she had sought to do a mischief to the young couple in the guise of a snake.

The King and the Queen were delighted and relieved to hear how Aslan and Simizar had been saved from the venomous bite of the snake. They spent a great sum of money, and sent out hundreds of invitations, and the wedding festivities went on for seven whole days, and seven whole nights. And so Aslan married his beloved Simizar.

As the King himself was very old, he abdicated his throne in favour of the shepherd, and named him King Orphan Aslan.

And as they achieved their hearts' desire, may you achieve yours also!

Zarzand thagavori aghdjikë, recorded in 1940 by Hambardzum Ter-Vardanian of the village of Mahmughdjugh, province of Shirak, and printed for the first time in *APT*, IV, no. 7. Details of the narrator are lacking.

Kush-Pari

Once upon a time there was a King, who had three sons. When he grew old, he went blind. Doctors came and went in droves, but they could not restore his sight. The King finally summoned his eldest son.

'You must go and find a cure for my blindness,' he said.

'Where must I go to find that?' said the prince.

'You must ride to the place where no horse's hoof has ever trod,' said the King. 'Fetch me some soil from that country, and it will cure me.'

His son went away, led his horse from the stable, mounted it, and rode away. For six whole months he journeyed, and finally came to a wild and deserted place. There was a spring there, and above the spring stood a withered tree.

'Heavens!' said the prince. 'The tree is growing by a spring, and yet is completely withered. There is no shade where I might shelter from the sun and sleep!'

He threw his felt cloak over a branch of the tree, lay down in its shade, and went to sleep.

When he woke, he saw that the tree had put forth green leaves. Large apples hung from its branches, each a pound in weight. The prince filled a saddle-bag with the apples, and filled five or six skins with water from the spring.

'I shall take these to my father the King,' he said. 'No horse's hoof has ever trodden this ground, that is certain!'

And so saying, he started back home.

In six months he had arrived at the palace. The courtiers ran to tell the King that his eldest son had come back.

'Akh!' sighed his father. 'What is that to me? He set out empty-handed, and empty-handed he has returned.'

The prince came and greeted his father.

'Welcome back, my boy!' said the King. 'How far did you go?'

'Father, I have been to a place on which even your forefathers never set eyes,' replied his eldest son.

'Tell us where you have been, boy,' said the King, 'and we shall see.'

'I rode out until I came to a spring . . .' began the prince.

'Say no more,' said the King. 'I'll tell you. You came to a withered tree. You slept in its shade, it put forth green leaves and bore apples.'

'That is right, father!' said the prince, in amazement.

'I was there, my son,' said the King. 'I set out one morning, drank

28

tea there, and was back here for supper. Nothing you have brought from there will restore my sight.'

The King summoned his second eldest son.

'My son, now you must go,' said the King.

'Father,' said the second son, 'if my elder brother could not bring you a cure for your blindness, how shall I?'

'There is nothing for it,' said the King. 'Go you must.'

His second son went away, led his horse from the stables, mounted it, and rode away. After six months, he came to the withered tree.

'My elder brother has been here,' he thought.

He continued his journey for another three months, and finally came to a high hill. The summit of the hill was covered with amber. There were many diamonds there also, and all manner of precious stones.

'If my father had been here,' said the prince, 'these stones would now be gracing his counting-house'; and filling both sides of his saddle-bag with the jewels, he started back home.

When he arrived back at his father's palace, after a year away, the courtiers ran to tell the King.

'Light to your eyes, O King!' they said. 'Your second son has returned!'

'Akh!' sighed his father again. 'He has come back, but empty-handed.'

The prince came and greeted his father, kissing his hands. His father welcomed him back, and kissed him on the cheek.

'Well, my boy,' he said, 'how far did you go?'

'Father, I have been to a place which seven generations of your forefathers have never seen,' said his son.

'Tell us where you have been,' said the King, 'and we shall see.'

'I came to a high hill . . .' began the prince.

'Say no more,' said the King. 'You have brought back a collection of precious stones, jewels, pearls, and such-like, have you not?'

'That is right, father,' said the second son.

'Go and fetch your saddle-bag,' said the King.

They undid the saddle-bag—and found that all the stones were nothing but coloured glass!

'Go away, boy!' said his father. 'May God be good to you! Send me my youngest son!'

The youngest prince came and stood before the King.

'What is your command, father?' he said.

'As your father, I command you to go in search of a cure for my blindness.'

'Father, I am too young. I have not even been outside the palace yet. Where should I find a cure for your blindness?'

'You must go all the same, my son,' said the King. 'There is no other hope for me.'

The young prince demurred, went to his garden, lay down, and fell asleep.

He had a dream. Someone came and said:

'Why are you lying there, sound asleep, young prince?'

'What should I do?' said the prince. 'My father has ordered me to go and bring him a cure for his blindness. I have never travelled. I do not know which way to turn.'

'Prince,' said the vision. 'Go to your father, and say: "Give me the ring from your finger, the sword from your side, and the horse you ride. Then I will go and do as you ask." '

The dream faded, and the young prince awoke, went to his father, and said:

'Father, give me the ring from your finger, the sword from your side, and the horse you ride, and I shall go and do as you ask.'

The King was overjoyed, embraced his son, and kissed him on both cheeks.

'You are my brave little son,' he said. 'I know that you will bring me the cure.'

The next morning the King rose, gave his son the ring on his finger and the sword at his side, and commanded his *muhtar*, the Royal Groom, to saddle and harness his horse for the prince.

The prince mounted the horse, and rode off. He went the way his father told him. In the morning he drank a glass of tea in the palace, at noon he was eating his lunch under the withered tree, and towards evening he arrived at the high hill. As he passed beyond the hill, he suddenly saw two suns, one in the sky and the other on the ground.

'What sort of country have I come to?' he said to himself. 'There is one sun in the sky, and another on the ground!'

He urged on his horse towards the second sun, and found that it was in fact the feather of a bird, a golden feather which shone as bright as the sun in the sky. He dismounted, picked it up, and tucked it in his turban.

'Prince,' cried his horse, 'throw that feather away!'

'Why should I throw it away?' said the prince.

'That feather will be the cause of much misfortune.'

'How can a mere feather be the cause of much misfortune?' mocked the young prince.

The horse repeated his warning three times, but the prince would not listen.

'Very well,' said the horse. 'On your head be it!'

So the prince kept the feather in his turban, and rode on. Eventually he came to a city, ruled by a King. The King's ministers hurried to their master to inform him that a young man was riding towards the city, and that there was one sun in the sky, and another on his head.

'Bring the young man to me,' commanded the King.

They brought the young prince to the King.

'What manner of man are you?' asked the King.

'I am a stranger here. I am travelling through these parts,' replied the prince.

'What is that sun you are wearing in your turban?' said the King.

'It is a feather. I found it on the road and picked it up.'

'Let me look,' said the King.

As soon as he took the feather in his hand, the King was enraptured and enthralled.

'Thank you,' said the King. 'You can leave now.'

The young prince withdrew. The King hung the golden feather on the wall and could not take his eyes off it. If anyone from that time forth came to seek audience of him, he would say, 'I have no time! Go away!'

One day someone stole some chicks belonging to an old woman, and she came to the King to sue for justice.

'Go away, old woman!' sighed the King. 'I have no time for you.'

The old woman saw that the King's whole attention was absorbed by the golden feather hanging on the wall, and she said:

'That is only a feather you are gazing at, O King. What would you do if you saw the bird it belongs to?'

The King turned round.

'What?' he said. 'Who could find that bird for me?'

'Why not the young man who found the feather?' said the old woman. 'Let him who found the feather find the bird.'

The King summoned one of his ministers.

'Go and find the man who brought this feather,' he said, 'and bring him to me.'

They found the young prince in the inn, and brought him to the King.

'Ah!' thought the young man. 'When the King took the feather from my hand, he went out of his mind, and forgot to pay me anything for it. Now he intends to pay me. But what shall I do with the money?'

The young prince came before the King, bowed his head seven times, crossed his hands on his chest, and bowed again.

'Do you know why I have summoned you, young man?' said the King.

'How can I know, Your Majesty?' said the prince.

'You must go and fetch me the bird this golden feather belongs to,' said the King, shortly.

'I am a stranger here, Sir!' protested the prince. 'I have never been in this country before. How do I know where to find the bird?'

'*I* don't know where you will find it,' said the King. 'I only know that if you do not fetch it to me, I shall chop off your head!'

The young prince withdrew, went back to his inn, and began to weep. When he had wept his fill, the horse spoke:

'Now that you are crying your eyes out, you may remember that I told you not to pick the feather up, because no good would come of it. Now you know that I was speaking the truth. And this is not the end of it. You will soon be in far greater trouble.'

'What shall I do, dear horse?' wept the prince. 'May I die for your legs and hooves! I have got into trouble. Help me out of it!'

'Do not worry, prince,' said the horse. 'Lie down and sleep. I will help you tomorrow morning!'

The prince lay down, but by the time dawn came, he had not slept a wink. He rose early in the morning, groomed and fed his horse, and sat down to eat a little food.

'Where shall we go?' he asked the horse.

'Let the reins hang loose,' replied the horse. 'I shall take you where we have to go!'

The prince gave the horse its head. The horse galloped on, a little way or a long way only God knows, until they came to a forest.

'Do you know what forest this is?' asked the horse.

'How should I know what forest it is?' said the prince.

'They call it Wasteland Wood,' said the horse.

The prince dismounted.

'Loosen my girth and take the bit from my mouth,' said the horse. 'Look! Do you see that large tree in the middle of the forest, the white poplar?'

'I see it,' said the prince.

'Under that tree there is a white marble bathing pool,' said the horse. 'Dig a hole near by, and hide in it. Today is Friday. Every Friday a Houri-Pari, a nymph of Paradise in the shape of a bird, comes to the pool to bathe. She will take off her feathers, place them beside the pool, and then bathe. When she has finished, she will come out of the water, and put on her clothes. You must do nothing until she has put on her feathers and rises to unruffle them. While she is still so engaged, you must steal quietly up, reach out your hand, and grasp her firmly by the legs. Keep a tight hold on them, and bring her back here!'

The young prince went to the marble pool under the white poplar tree, as the horse had instructed him, dug a hole near by, and hid in it. A wonderful golden human-headed bird appeared, radiant as the sun. It removed its golden feathers, then its clothes, and a beautiful nymph came into sight. She stepped in the pool, washed herself thoroughly, came out, put on her clothes, then her feathers, and had just begun to smooth them, when the young prince came out of his hiding-place, stretched forth his hand, and caught her by the legs.

'What do you want with me?' cried the Pari. 'Let me go! You will bring disaster upon your house if you take me into it!'

32

'May I die for your good name and for your feet, good bird!' said the young prince. 'I am still young. It is my eager wish to take you to the King, for if I do not, he will chop off my head!'

'On your head be it!' said the bird. 'As soon as I have the opportunity, I shall send you to a place whence you shall never return!'

The young prince picked up the bird, carried it to his horse, and rode back with it to the King.

The King took the golden bird, as he had its feather, and was again enraptured. 'Thank you,' he said. 'You can go now.'

And again the prince received no payment for his services.

He withdrew and returned to the inn. The King placed the golden bird in a cage and hung it on the wall. He became utterly absorbed in the bird. But though the King dearly desired to hear it sing, the golden bird would neither sing nor talk, but kept its beak tight shut. Nothing the King did was of any use.

'Whatever you wish for, I will give you, beautiful bird!' he pleaded. 'If only you will talk to me.'

'May your house fall in, O King!' said the Pari. 'Underneath these feathers I am such a maiden, that if you went round the world from East to West, you would not find one like me. If you grant me my wish, I shall cast off my feathers and become your queen, and you will be a king that all other kings shall envy!'

'Make your request!' said the King. 'Whatever you desire, I shall give you!'

'What I desire is the presence of my maidservant. She is a prisoner of the Red Dev somewhere between the Black Sea and the White Sea,'[1] said the Pari. 'Bring her to me, and I will be your queen!'

'How shall I fetch her, fair bird?' said the King.

'The young man who succeeded in bringing me from such a far distant place,' said the Pari, 'will surely be able to find my maidservant!'

'Ho there!' cried the King. 'Summon that young man to my presence, forthwith!'

His servants found the young prince, and called him out of the inn.

'Brothers,' complained the prince, 'it's like living on hot bricks here! But I'll go with you and see what the King wants now.'

So the young prince went and stood before the King as before, folded his hands across his chest, and bowed. The King returned his greeting, and said:

'Young man, do you know why I have summoned you?'

'How can I know, Your Majesty?' said the prince.

'I have summoned you,' said the King, 'that you may sail to the land

___

[1] No reference to Russia or the *Beloe More* (White Sea) is intended. If not wholly fictitious, the White Sea, in Anatolian terms, would refer to the Mediterranean, in Turkish *Akdeniz* (White Sea).

between the Black Sea and the White Sea where a maiden languishes in the hands of the Red Dev. Find her, seize her, and fetch her here!'

'How shall I cross the seas?' protested the young man. 'How can I sail the Black Sea and the White Sea, and overcome the Red Dev, and fetch the maiden back here?'

'Don't bother my head with such questions!' said the King. 'If you fetch her, you fetch her. If you do not fetch her, I'll chop off your head!'

The young prince withdrew, and bursting into tears, returned to the inn.

'Well?' said the horse. 'Now what has happened?'

'How can I tell you, good horse?' wept the prince. 'May I die for your feet! The King—may his house fall in!—says I must go to the land between the Black Sea and the White Sea where a maiden languishes in the hands of the Red Dev, fight him for her possession, and bring her back to the King!'

'Do not cry, prince,' said the horse. 'God is merciful. Show some backbone! But for the present, lie down and sleep!'

That night the young prince managed to sleep a little. He rose early in the morning, groomed and fed his horse as before, ate a couple of slices of bread, and led his horse from the stable.

'Where shall we go?' he asked the horse.

'You do not need to know,' said the horse. 'Let the reins hang loose, and whither we must go, thither shall I take you.'

The prince let the reins hang loose, and the horse galloped off—a little way or a long way God only knows—until they came to a seashore.

'This is the Black Sea,' said the horse. 'How are you going to cross it?'

'How should I know?' said the prince, helplessly.

'Are you aware of the special powers of that sword which you have girt about your loins?' said the horse.

'No,' said the prince, 'it has never left the scabbard since I girt it about me!'

'That sword of your father's,' said the horse, 'is made of pure lightning. Take it out of the scabbard, place its hilt against your forehead, and point the tip out to sea. A path will open up through the water. When you get to the other side, you will observe a thin spiral of smoke rising from a cave. Knock at the door of the cave, and say: "Come out, dev, and fight!" The dev will say, "Come in, let us eat together!", but you must not go in. Repeat your challenge three times, and the dev will then come out. Draw your magic sword, and strike him with it. His head will fly off and plunge to the centre of the earth. Then you must take the maiden by the arm, and swing her on to my croup behind you. Point the tip of your sword at the sea again, the waters will open, we shall ride across with the girl, and you may then give her to the King.'

The young prince did as the horse instructed him: he passed through the sea, slew the Red Dev, captured the maidservant, and brought her to the King.

'Thank you,' said the King. 'You may go now.'

The young man withdrew, and this time also received no recompense for his pains.

'Kush-Pari,' said the King, 'is this the maid you were asking for?'

'It is,' said the bird. (Kush-Pari, or Fairy-Bird, was her name.)[1]

'Well,' said the King, 'I have brought you what you desired. Now cast off your feathers.'

'May your house fall in, O King!' said the bird. 'If I take off my feathers and you see me in my true shape, you will drop down dead!'

'What shall I do, then?' said the King.

'This is what you must do,' replied the bird. 'On the shore of the Red Sea live forty mares, creatures of pure blue fire. Fetch them here, bathe in their milk, and you too will become a Houri-Pari. Then we shall be able to live together, and our children shall be Houri-Paris, too.'

'Who can bring back these forty fiery mares?' said the King.

'Who should bring them back?' said the Pari. 'He who brought me here, and brought my maidservant here, he shall fetch the forty mares!'

'Ho there!' shouted the King. 'Run and find that young man before he departs, and fetch him quickly to me!'

The servants hurried away, and found the young prince eating his dinner.

'Come with us,' they said. 'The King has summoned you!'

The young prince ran to the King, bowed his head, crossed his hands on his chest, and waited.

'Do you know why I have summoned you, young man?' said the King.

'How can I know, Your Majesty?' said the prince.

'I have summoned you,' said the King, 'to go to the Red Sea, find the forty fiery mares that dwell there, and bring them back to me, so that I may milk them and bathe in their milk.'

'How shall I find them?' protested the young prince. 'I am only one man! How shall I alone bring back forty fiery mares?'

'Don't bother my head with such questions!' said the King. 'If you fetch them, you fetch them. If you do not fetch them, I'll chop off your head!'

The young prince withdrew, and again bursting into tears, returned to his horse.

'Now why are you weeping?' said the horse.

'If I have not cause to weep, who has?' said the young prince. 'The King—may his house fall in!—has sent me to fetch the forty fiery mares that dwell by the Red Sea!'

[1] Turkish *kush* 'bird'; Persian *pari* 'a winged spirit', usually Englished as *peri*, a Turkish form.

35

'Cry no more!' said the horse. 'Any harm that comes of this venture will come to me. Nothing will happen to you. Go to the King and say: "Give me forty camel-loads of wool for the forty fiery mares, forty loads of felt, and forty loads of leather, and send them to the shores of the Red Sea". When he has done that, I shall go and fetch the forty mares.'

The young prince went back to the King, and did as the horse had instructed him.

'Very well,' said the King. 'I shall dispatch the bales to the Red Sea all through the night!'

The prince returned to his inn. The King saw to the necessary preparations for his journey, and by morning all the bales stood on the shores of the Red Sea. The young prince mounted his horse, and rode off.

As they approached the Red Sea, the horse spoke:

'Prince,' he said, 'there are not forty fiery mares dwelling by the Red Sea, but only thirty-nine. One is my mother, thirty-eight are my sisters, and I myself am the only son. Owing to an act of disobedience I fell into your father's hands, where I have remained for thirty years. "My son!" my mother said. "If you ever fall into my hands, I shall tear you to shreds!" When we arrive on the shore of the Red Sea, I shall lie down. First of all you must cover me with the bales of wool, then the bales of felt, and then the bales of leather. Then withdraw a long way off, and hide. I shall neigh softly, the surface of the sea will rise, and a fearful storm will rage, but do not be afraid. My mother will emerge from the sea, and while my sisters huddle together and weep, she will fly at me and try to tear me to pieces. First she will tear off the leather, but you must say and do nothing. Then she will tear off the felt, but still you must say and do nothing. Then she will tear at the wool, but by the time she has torn off half of it, she will be exhausted, and pause to stretch herself. At that moment you must run up, thrust your foot in the stirrup, and leap on her back. Hold very tight, for she will soar up in the air, high into the sky, and try to make the friction of the air burn you up. Then you must slip under her belly. She will then descend from the sky and plunge towards the centre of the earth, but you must quickly climb on to her back again, and hold on as tight as any devil. Then whip her hard under the belly until her milk comes out of her nostrils. Then once you say, "I am your master!", she will go wherever you shall direct her. My sisters and I will follow you.'

The young prince followed the stallion's instructions. He covered the horse first with the bales of wool, then with the bales of felt, and finally with the bales of leather. Then he withdrew a long way off, and hid. The horse neighed softly, the surface of the water rose, and a fearful storm began to rage. The mother of the fiery mares emerged from the sea, and while the stallion's sisters huddled together and wept, she flew at her son and strove to tear him to pieces. She tore off the leather, and

36

the prince said and did nothing. She tore off the felt, and the prince said and did nothing. Then she began to tear at the wool, but when she had torn only half of it off, she became exhausted, and paused to stretch herself. The young prince then ran from his hiding-place, placed his foot in the stirrup, and leapt on to the mare's back. The mare shot up into the air, high into the sky. The wind whistled round him, and the friction seared his skin. The prince slid quickly down under the horse's belly, and it began to plunge down out of the sky again in an attempt to shake him off or crush him against the ground. It dived straight towards the centre of the earth, but the young prince climbed up into the saddle again, and held on tight, like the very devil. He took his whip and lashed her under the belly, until he saw milk coming out of her nostrils. Then he cried, 'I am your master!', and immediately the mare quietened down, permitting him to guide her in whatever direction he wished. And so the young prince rode back, followed by the stallion's sisters and the stallion himself, and he tethered all the mares in the royal stables. Then he went to see the King.

'I have fetched the mares, Your Majesty,' he said. And remounting his stallion, he returned to the inn.

'Well, King!' said the Pari. 'Milk the mares, and bathe in their milk.'

'Who shall milk the mares?' said the King, helplessly.

'O King—may your house fall in!—why did you permit the young man to withdraw?' said the bird. 'He can milk the mares!'

The King dispatched messengers to tell the young man to come and milk the mares.

'Prince,' said his horse, 'take me with you when you go to milk my sisters. Before you do so, tie the ring you received from your father to a cotton thread, hang it in the middle of the vat, and lay your sword across the top. Let out the mares one by one, and milk each one separately over the vat. Then rise, undress, and bathe in the milk. Dress, pick up your sword, wipe it clean, and replace it in the scabbard. Then pull out the ring, wipe it clean, and put it on your finger. Then tell the servants to inform the King that he may come and bathe in the milk.'

All this the young prince did, and no harm came to him. But when the King came to the stables, undressed, and stepped into the vat, the milk immediately began to bubble and seethe, and the King was suddenly all boiled to a pulp! As his horse had previously instructed him, the prince threw what remained of the King, and his own clothes, down a well, clad himself in the King's robes, returned to the court and took his place on the throne.

Kush-Pari at once understood what had happened to the real King. She cast off her golden feathers, and turned into a radiantly beautiful maiden. She went up to the prince and put her arms round his neck.

37

'Everything I did was for your sake,' she said. 'Now you are the King, and I am the Queen.'

The people did not know what had happened, or what had not happened. When the new King had reigned for some months over his new kingdom, he suddenly remembered his father, and he burst into tears.

The nymph came up and saw the young man crying.

'Husband—may your house flourish!' she said. 'You have a wife like me, and though a commoner, you have become a king! What possible grief can there be in all the world to make you sit and weep like that?'

'Dear Queen,' said the young prince. 'May I die for your head and your sun! Is not my father a king? His eyes are bereft of sight. I came here to find a cure for them, and all I do is to sit about! I do not know whether my father is dead or alive! That is the reason for my tears!'

The beautiful nymph laughed and flung her arms round the young man's neck.

'Husband—may your house flourish!' she said. 'Your father is blind because he sought for ten years to capture me, though he could never catch me. That is why he has gone blind. I shall go to your father, cut his finger, and smear the blood over his eyes. Then he will immediately be able to see again. Let us go to your father's palace!'

The young man assembled his people, and ordered a great banquet to be held.

'Choose yourselves a good king,' he said. 'I must go to another land. It may be I shall return. But it may be I shall not return.'

So the people found a good man, and made him king. The young prince and his wife thanked them, dressed themselves in everyday clothes, and taking some money for the journey, they led the thirty-nine mares and the stallion from the stables. The princess mounted the stallion, the prince the oldest mare, its mother. The people insisted upon accompanying them for the first day of their journey, and then returned home, and with their grateful thanks ringing in their ears, the prince and his wife made their way towards his father's city.

On the outskirts of the city they met a shepherd.

'Go and greet the King,' said the young prince, 'and tell him his youngest son has returned.'

The shepherd hastened to the palace.

'Light to your eyes, O King!' he said. 'Your youngest son has returned!'

'What does he bring with him, shepherd?' said the King.

'He brings forty fiery horses, ethereally blue as the sky!' said the shepherd. 'And one radiantly beautiful woman!'

'Glory be to God!' cried the King. 'He has come indeed from a far distant land! When I myself thought I had gone a long, long way, I was in fact not far from home! Ho there! Give this shepherd a pot of gold!'

The young prince entered the palace, and kissed his father's hands. His father kissed him on the cheek. The princess made a cut in the King's finger, and smeared the blood over the old man's eyes. Straightway the King's eyes were opened, and he could see again! He rose and kissed his daughter-in-law on the forehead, took the crown from his own head and placed it upon that of his son.

'From henceforth you, my son, shall be our King,' he cried, 'and your wife shall be Queen!'

So they all met with their hearts' desire, and so may you all meet with yours!

Three apples fell from Heaven: one for the story-teller, one for his listener, and one for him who lends an ear.

Ghush-Pharin, told in 1913 by the illiterate vine-dresser, aged 51, Nerses, son of Karapet Ter-Minasian, of the village of Ashtarak, province of Ayrarat; *APT*, I, no. 2.

The Fair Maiden Sunbeam and the Serpent Prince

Once upon a time there was a King. One day he went out on to the balcony of his palace to take the air, when he noticed a mother snake in the courtyard below caressing her little ones and playing with them in the sunshine.

'Lord God!' cried the King; 'why have you not blessed me with a son? Would not I love him as much as that snake loves her children? Am I so inferior to her as not to deserve a little one such as she has?'

The gates of God's mercy opened. The Lord heard the King's prayer, and granted him his wish.

The King's servants rushed out on to the balcony to congratulate him.

'Light to your eyes, O King!' they cried. 'The Queen has given birth! But, you must know, to a little snake!'

'Praise be to God!' said the King. 'It is still a child. Such is God's will.'

The snake began to grow and to grow, until at the end of a week it had become a dragon.

The King named his son Odz-Manouk, that is, in Armenian, Serpent Child.

'Heavens!' said the counsellors, 'what shall we feed him on?'

For whatever they set before him, he would touch none of it. He roared and roared, crying for food, until the walls of the palace were in danger of collapsing.

One day the chamberlain's daughter came to look at the young dragon, and as soon as his eye fell on her, he seized her by the arm and gobbled her up. Then everybody knew what he wanted to eat.

The King commanded that henceforth maidens were to be sacrificed to his son, the Serpent Prince, at the rate of one a day. Each morning a troop of soldiers would scour the countryside for unsuspecting maidens, and when they found one, they would feed her to the dragon.

One day they came upon a beautiful maiden, with golden hair and as radiant as the sun, sitting under a tree. Her name was Arevhat, meaning a piece of the sun itself. We shall call her Sunbeam. The soldiers brought her to the King, who told them to take her to his son.

By this time the soldiers were too frightened of the dragon to open the doors of his chamber, lest he should escape, and they took Sunbeam up on the roof, and lowered her down through the skylight.

The maiden descended like a ray of sunshine into the dark chamber, and stood before the young dragon.

'God's light upon you, prince,' she said.

No sooner had she pronounced these words, than the dragon cast off its skin, and became a handsome young prince. He took the girl by the hand, and they fell in love.

Some time later, the King told the soldiers:

'Go and see if the Serpent Prince has devoured the maiden.'

When they went, they found that the dragon had disappeared, and that a handsome young man stood in his place.

'Why do you keep the doors bolted?' said the prince. 'Open them!'

They unbolted the doors, and ran to tell the King.

'The dragon has turned into a handsome young man!' they cried. 'He has not eaten the maiden Sunbeam! They are laughing and talking together!'

The King was overjoyed, and he ran to embrace his son. The Serpent Prince and Sunbeam stood side by side, and bowed to the King.

The King saw to his great satisfaction that his son was a well-built young man, and that Sunbeam was a beautiful and most modest maiden.

'What wish can I grant you, my son?' said the King.

'Long life to you, father,' said the prince. 'I wish to marry this maiden.'

The King arranged for the wedding to be celebrated at once, and the feasting went on for seven days and seven nights, and all drank to the health of the fair maiden Sunbeam and her bridegroom, the Serpent Prince.

After the wedding, the King summoned his new daughter-in-law.

'Daughter,' he said. 'Tell us who you are, and whose daughter you are.'

'May you enjoy long life, Your Majesty,' said Sunbeam. 'I am an orphan, and have neither father nor mother. I used to live with a step-mother. Every morning she would give me a bushel of wool, and say: "Take the cattle to pasture, spin this bushel of wool, and bring it back in the evening!" She would give me a piece of dry bread, and tell me to be sure to bring half of it back in the evening.

'One day I was sitting spinning on a rock on the side of the hill, when the rock suddenly opened, and my bobbin dropped from my hand and fell into the hole. As I bent down to look for it, I saw an old, old woman in a cave below.

' "Grandmother!" I said. "Please give me back my bobbin."

' "My child," said the old woman. "I am old and infirm, and cannot get up to give you your bobbin. Come down and fetch it for yourself."

' "Where is the door to your cave?" I said.

' "In the middle of the ravine," she said.

'So I went down into the ravine, found the door to the cave, and went in. I picked up my bobbin, but when I turned to go, the door had disappeared!

' "Where is the door, grandmother?" I said.

' "Come here, my child," said the old woman. "I have something to tell you. Afterwards I shall show you the way out."

'I went over to the old woman.

' "Fetch a broom," she said, "and sweep the floor of our house."

'I found a broom and swept the floor.

' "Child," said the old woman, "whose house is cleaner, mine or yours?"

' "Your house is cleaner, grandmother," I said. But it wasn't, being in fact very dirty.

' "Child," said the old woman again. "Sit down beside me, put my head on your knees, and brush my hair."

'I went and sat down beside her, took her head on my knees, and began to brush her hair.

' "Child," said the old woman, "whose hair is cleaner, mine or your mother's?"

' "Your hair is cleaner, grandmother," I said.

'There was a lot of moisture on the walls of the cave, which dripped down and formed a pool in the corner.

' "Child," said the old woman, "let me rest my head on your knees and sleep a little. When you see black water flowing, do not wake me. When you see red water flowing, do not wake me. But when you see yellow water flowing, wake me at once."

'The old woman went to sleep. I saw black water flowing, and said nothing. I saw red water flowing, and said nothing. Then I saw yellow water flowing, and I woke the old woman.

' "Wake up, grandmother," I said. "The yellow water is flowing."

'The old woman suddenly jumped up, seized me by the feet, and plunged my head into the yellow water. My hair became the colour of gold. The old woman opened the door.

' "Go now, good child," she said. "God be with you!"

'I came out of the cave, and went back to the cattle and sheep on the mountainside.

' "What shall I do now," I thought. "If I go home with my golden hair, my stepmother will beat me and tear my hair out!"

'I found a shepherd, and asked him to slaughter one of my sheep, keep the meat for himself, and give the sheep's stomach to me.

' "Very well, sister," said the shepherd, "I shall do you this favour." And doing as I asked him, he said:

' "Sit down, child. I shall prepare some fine *khorovats*, roast mutton on a spit, for us!"

'We sat down and ate the roast meat. Then I took the sheep's stomach, drew it over my golden hair, and remained sitting in the sunshine all day long, so that the skin might dry on my hair and disguise its colour. Then I led my cows and sheep back home.

' "You wicked girl!" screamed my stepmother. "Why haven't you finished spinning all the wool I gave you?"

'She gave me a few smacks, and then said:

' "I shall wash your hair now. Tomorrow is Sunday."

' "I do not want my hair washed!" I cried.

'My half-sister, my stepmother's darling, rushed forward and pulled my hair. The sheep's stomach came off, my hair tumbled over my shoulders, and shone like pure gold.

' "You wicked child!" shouted my stepmother. "What have you done to your hair?"

'I sat down and told her everything that had happened.

' "You immodest girl!" cried my stepmother. "Tomorrow you will take my daughter with you and show her the rock. Then she too will have golden hair!"

'The next morning, at break of dawn, she gave her daughter a bushel of wool and a piece of dry bread, and we led the cows and sheep to pasture. I showed my half-sister the rock, and she sat on it and began to spin. Suddenly the rock opened, her bobbin fell out of her hand and fell into the hole. When she bent down to look for it, she saw the old, old woman in the cave below.

' "Grandmother!" she said angrily. "Give me back my bobbin!"

' "My child," said the old woman. "I am old and infirm, and cannot get up to give you your bobbin. Come down and fetch it for yourself."

' "Where is the door to your cave?" said my half-sister.

' "In the middle of the ravine," said the old woman.

'So my sister went down into the ravine, found the door to the cave, and went in. She picked up her bobbin, but when she turned to go, the door had disappeared.

' "The door's vanished!" said my sister. "Where is it?"

' "Come here, my child," said the old woman. "I have something to tell you. Afterwards I shall show you the way out."

'My sister went over to the old woman.

' "Fetch a broom," she said, "and sweep the floor of our house."

'My sister found the broom and swept the floor.

' "Child," said the old woman, "whose house is cleaner, mine or yours?"

' "Our house is cleaner," snapped my sister. "Yours is filthy!"

' "Alas, my child!" said the old woman. "I am very old, and who is there to sweep the floor for me? But sit down beside me, put my head on your knees, and brush my hair."

'My sister sat down beside her, took her head on her knees, and began to brush her hair.

44

' "Child," said the old woman, "whose hair is cleaner, mine or your mother's?"

' "My mother's hair is much cleaner!" said my sister. "Yours is quite disgraceful!"

' "Child," said the old woman, "let me rest my head on your knees and sleep a little. When you see yellow water flowing, do not wake me. When you see red water flowing, do not wake me. But when you see black water flowing, wake me up at once."

'The old woman went to sleep. The girl saw yellow water flowing, and said nothing. She saw red water flowing, and said nothing. Then she saw black water flowing, and woke the old woman.

'The old woman suddenly jumped up, seized her by the feet, and plunged her head into the black water. My half-sister became as black as night, and a horrid fold of black skin hung from her forehead.

'The old woman opened the door.

' "Go now, child," she said.

'My sister saw that the door was open, and she picked up her bobbin, and returned to me.

'I was horrified. She had become so hideous.

' "What has happened to you, sister?" I cried.

' "I don't know," she said. "The old woman plunged me into some black water, and I came out like this."

'We got up and went home, and as soon as my stepmother saw what had happened to her daughter, she picked up a stick and beat me, and then threw me out of the house. I came to a field, sat down beneath a tree, and wept. Then your soldiers came and captured me, and led me away.

' "Where are you taking me?" I asked.

' "To the King's son," they said.

'And that, Your Majesty, may you enjoy long life, is how I came to be here,' said the beautiful maiden.

Arevhat ev Odzmanuk, told in 1912 by the illiterate peasant, aged 66, Avetis Grigorian, in the village of Ashtarak, province of Ayrarat; *APT*, I, no. 17.

The Nightingale Hazaran[1]

There was and there wasn't, there was once a King, and this King decided to build a magnificent church. For seven years his men built. The church was finished, and the bishop consecrated it, when suddenly a great wind blew. The King was gasping for breath, when the storm just as suddenly died down again, and in front of him stood a hermit.

'Long life to you, O King!' said the hermit. 'You have built a fine temple, but there is one thing missing.'

The wind blew fiercely, and the hermit disappeared.

The King ordered the church to be demolished, and his men began again. For another seven years they worked, and there again stood a magnificent church, more beautiful than the first. The bishop consecrated it, the King knelt to pray, when a mighty wind suddenly blew through the nave. The hermit stood again before the King.

'Long life to you, O King!' said the hermit. 'You have again built a fine church, but there is one thing missing.'

Once again the King ordered the church to be demolished.

'This time,' he said, 'we shall build for nine years. There shall not be its like on earth.'

It was built. It was consecrated. The King knelt to pray. A tempest blew through the church, and again the hermit stood before him.

'Long life to you, O King!' said the hermit. 'Your church has not its like on earth. It is a pity that there is one thing missing.'

The King was desperate. He seized the hermit by the arm.

'This is the third time you make me destroy my church,' he said. 'Tell me, what is missing?'

'The nightingale Hazaran,' replied the hermit, and disappeared.

The King returned to his palace. He had three sons.

'I must acquire the nightingale Hazaran for my church,' he said. 'But how shall I find it?'

'We shall find it,' said his sons. And they mounted their horses and rode away.

After a month they came to a place where the road forked in three directions, and there they stopped, undecided what to do.

A hermit approached them.

'Where are you going, my brave fellows?' he said.

[1] Persian *Hazârân*, literally 'thousands', 'the bird of a thousand songs', the nightingale.

'We are looking for the nightingale Hazaran,' said the princes. 'But we do not know which road to take.'

'He who takes the first road,' said the hermit, 'shall return. He who takes the second road may return, or may not. He who takes the third has little hope of returning.'

The eldest brother took the first road, the widest; the second brother took the middle road; the youngest brother chose the third road, the narrowest.

'Why have I little hope of returning?' asked the youngest brother.

'It is a road beset with hazards,' said the hermit. 'You will come first to a river. The mistress of the nightingale Hazaran has cast a spell on it and polluted it, and none will drink of its waters. To pass it, you must drink from it, and say, "Ah! The waters of life!" Thus you will cross the river. Then you will come to a flower. The sorceress has changed it into a thistle, but you must pick it, smell it, and exclaim, "O flower of paradise!" As you go on, you will come to a wolf and a lamb tied to posts near each other; in front of the wolf lies a heap of grass, in front of the lamb a piece of meat. You must give the grass to the lamb, the meat to the wolf. Farther on you will come to a pair of huge gates; one side will be shut, the other open. You must shut the open side, and open the shut side. As you go through, you will behold the mistress of the nightingale Hazaran. For seven days she sleeps, for seven days she wakes. If you are able to do all the things I have told you, you will bring back the nightingale Hazaran; if not, you will not return.'

The eldest brother journeyed along the wide road until he came to a palace.

'Why should I look for trouble?' he said. 'I shall offer my services to the lord of this palace, and live a quiet life.'

The second brother journeyed along the second road, crossed over a hill, and beheld a splendid palace, which shone as bright as any beacon. He dismounted and tethered his horse, went into a pleasant garden and sat down on the soft, green grass. Suddenly he spied an enormous black Arab walking between heaven and earth. The Arab swooped down on the prince, struck him with his whip, and turned him into a small round stone, which rolled under a garden seat.

The youngest brother journeyed along the third road, and as the hermit had foretold, met with the river, the flower, the wolf and the lamb. He entered the palace, and saw, lying on a divan, a maiden as fair and graceful as a roe-deer. The nightingale Hazaran fluttered out of his cage, alighted on the maiden's bosom, and began to pour out a thousand lullabies. The maiden fell asleep, and the prince quickly grasped the nightingale, kissed the maiden on the cheek, and made his way back along the narrow road.

The maiden awoke after seven days, and suddenly saw that her nightingale had vanished.

47

'Gates, seize him!' she cried.

'God go with him,' said the gates. 'He closed our open side, and opened our closed side, and gave us great relief.'

'Wolf and lamb, seize the thief!' cried the maiden again.

'God go with him,' said the wolf and the lamb. 'He gave grass to the lamb, and meat to the wolf.'

'Thistle, stop him!' cried the maiden.

'God go with him,' replied the thistle. 'You turned me into a thistle. For him I was a flower of paradise.'

'River, stop him!' she cried.

'God go with him,' said the river. 'You turned me into a noxious stream, but for him I was the waters of life.'

The maiden leapt on to her horse.

In the meantime, the prince had come to the end of the road, where he found the old hermit waiting for him. He inquired after his brothers.

'They have not come back,' said the hermit.

The prince entrusted the nightingale Hazaran to his care, and galloped up the wide road. When he came to the large city, he went to the inn for a meal. There was his elder brother, working as a servant. He told him of the success of his mission, and took him back to the crossroads, where he left him in the care of the hermit. Then he went off in search of his other brother. Like him, he came to the palace which shone like a beacon. He dismounted, and went into a garden to lie on the soft green grass. Suddenly the huge black Arab swooped down upon him.

'Who said this grass was free for you to sit on?' said the Arab, and aimed a blow at the prince with his whip. But the prince was too fast for him and, wrenching the whip from the Arab's grasp, he struck him with it instead. The Arab was immediately turned into a stone.

'That is what must have happened to my brother,' thought the prince, and began to whip at the stones at his feet. The stones were suddenly transformed into human beings, who began to make off in all directions. He struck the last stone beneath the bench where he was sitting, and his brother appeared and made to run away.

'Don't run away, brother,' he called, and telling him of his successful mission, he accompanied him also to the crossroads. Here the three brothers took the nightingale Hazaran from the hermit, and made their way home.

On the way they came to a well, and being thirsty, they lowered their youngest brother down into the well so that he might hand them up a bowl of water. While he was still down the well, the eldest brother said to the second brother:

'If he comes with us to tell our father the King what happened, how shall we look?'

48

So they left their youngest brother down the well, and brought the nightingale to their father.

'Our younger brother has perished,' they said. 'But we have brought you the nightingale Hazaran.'

The King placed the nightingale in the church, and not only would he not sing, he barely breathed.

Soon afterwards the maiden came riding up to the King.

'Who was the brave youth who took my nightingale?' she said.

'We took it,' said the two brothers.

'What did you encounter on the way?' asked the maiden.

'Nothing,' said the brothers.

'You did not take it,' she said. 'You are liars and thieves.'

And she seized them, and their father the King, and threw them into a dungeon. Then she seized the whole town and began to rule over it herself, vowing that they should never again be free until she had seen the brave youth who had taken the nightingale.

In the meantime some harvesters had drawn the young prince out of the well. When he came to the King's palace, he saw neither his father nor his two brothers; but the townsfolk told him what had happened, and the young man went straight to the dungeon, and released his father and two brothers. As they left the dungeon the maiden came upon them.

'I am the mistress of the nightingale Hazaran,' she said. 'Are you not afraid?'

'I am he who took the nightingale Hazaran from you,' said the prince. 'Why should I be afraid?'

'What did you encounter on the way?' said the maiden.

The young man told of the river, the thistle, the wolf, the lamb, the gates, and all that he had seen and done.

'And while you were sleeping, I kissed you on the cheek,' he concluded, 'and now I claim you as my bride.'

The maiden held him to be worthy of her, and consented, and they were married in the King's magnificent church. And how the nightingale Hazaran sang there, pouring out a stream of a thousand melodies! How he sang!

Three apples fell from Heaven, one for the story-teller, one for his listener, and one for him who lends an ear.

Recorded in Turkish Armenia, and first published by G. Sërvandztiantz, *Manana*; see *Acknowledgements*.

The Red Cow

There was once a man and his wife. They had two children—a boy and a girl, and one of their proudest possessions was a red cow. The husband was a shepherd, and one day, when he was out looking after the sheep his wife took sick and died. Well, life had to go on, and someone had to look after the household, so the man married for a second time. His new wife conceived a violent hatred for the two orphans, and would not lift a finger to look after them. When the shepherd asked why she neglected them, she replied that they were not her children: she had not asked for them, and it was not her place to look after them. Seeing that his new wife only tormented them if they remained at home, he took to sending them into the fields to tend his flock, to be out of harm's way.

One day the red cow, remembering past happiness and taking pity on the children, opened her mouth, and spoke:

'Do not worry or be afraid, little ones,' she said. 'I shall look after the sheep for you, while you go and play.'

And so the red cow took charge of the animals, watched over them during the day, and gathered them all together in the evening for the children to lead home. The stepmother would give the children a single slice of stale bread each morning to see them through the day, but when they sat down to eat it, the red cow would come up to them and give them some of her milk, so that the children, thriving on bread and milk, grew plump and pretty.

Eventually the shepherd's new wife gave birth to a daughter. Time passed, until the girl was ten years old, and her mother sent her with the other children to the fields to tend the sheep. She was an ugly and spoilt child, the spitting image of her wicked mother.

'Whatever it is you are eating out there to grow so fat,' she told the boy and his sister, 'mind you give some to my daughter!'

At the same time she gave her daughter four or five loaves a day, but with no instructions to share them with the others.

'Never mind,' said the red cow. 'The new daughter can drink my milk. But whereas it will taste sweet to you, it will be as bitter as gall for her.'

The stepmother's daughter grew ugly and scrawny, while the other two continued to flourish. The wicked woman was puzzled, and curious to know what was happening. She could not send her husband into the fields, he had grown too old and decrepit. She questioned her daughter.

'How is it,' she said, 'that you eat four or five loaves a day to the others' stale crust, yet they grow like weeds while you seem like to waste away altogether?'

'It must be that red cow,' replied her daughter. 'The milk it gives me tastes like ink, but the others say that theirs tastes sweet as honey.'

'Just wait till that animal comes back!' said her mother.

The next day the woman woke her husband early.

'You can see how our daughter is wasting away,' she said. 'I had a dream last night. A holy man appeared to me and told me that if I slaughter the red cow as a sacrifice to our daughter, she will greatly improve.'

'Slaughter the cow?' protested the shepherd. 'What shall we do for our yoghurt and buttermilk then?'

'That is as may be,' insisted his wife; 'but the red cow must be killed!'

And she nagged away so persistently, that the poor man finally gave in, and prepared to slaughter the red cow.

Seeing the pole-axe and large knives, the cow soon guessed what was about to befall her. She hung her head, and her eyes filled with tears.

'Why are you so sad, dear cow?' the children asked, when they came to feed her.

'Your cursed stepmother has contrived to have me slaughtered,' said the cow.

'No, no! We shall plead with her, kiss her hands and feet, and beg her to spare you!' cried the children.

'She would only beat you,' said the cow, 'and I could not bear that. It does not matter. But you must do as I tell you. When they cut my throat, you must smear your faces with my blood without anyone seeing you. Your faces will then shine as bright as cloth of gold. Then gather up my bones and hooves and hide them in the manger. They will serve you well later.'

The children cried bitterly.

'Do not cry, children,' said the cow. 'What is written on our forehead cannot be averted.'

'Who will look after us when you are gone?' wept the children.

'Come with me. There is an old woman who lives near here,' said the cow. 'I shall entrust you to her.'

The red cow led the children to a small cave in the mountains, and an old woman came out.

'Do you know that I am to be sacrificed?' said the cow.

'I know,' said the old woman.

'I am entrusting these little children to your care,' said the red cow. 'I beg you in the name of God, see that they come to no harm!'

52

'I shall,' said the old woman.

They returned from the old woman's cottage to the fields, where the red cow told the children to cut off one of her horns.

'When you are hungry,' she said, 'suck on it, and you will be fed. The old woman will look after you when you are in the fields with the sheep.'

The next morning the cow was slaughtered. The orphans secretly took a cupful of her blood, and taking it to their room, smeared it over their faces. Their faces glowed bright as a precious brocade, and their skin shone like the morning sun.

When their half-sister ate the flesh of the cow which had been sacrificed on her behalf, it tasted like straw. What the orphans ate tasted like honey, so sweet it was. After the meal, the boy and his sister gathered the bones and hooves together, and buried them in the bottom of the manger. Thereafter, every time they felt the pangs of hunger, they would go to the manger, suck on the cow's horn, and their hunger would vanish. Their stepmother stuffed her ugly daughter until she was fit to burst, but ceased to give the orphans anything to eat at all.

That winter the whole family was invited to a royal wedding. The stepmother dressed her own daughter in fine clothes and took her to the banquet, leaving the orphans all alone in the house. The voice of the red cow mooed from the cow-shed, whereupon the old woman came from her cave in the mountains, dug up the floor of the manger, and took out the most luxurious garments you have ever seen. She dressed the orphans in the finest silks, and led them off to the wedding.

When the wicked stepmother caught sight of them, she did not recognize them at all.

'Heavens!' she exclaimed. 'What it must be to have such beautiful children! If only the parents would marry their handsome son to my daughter!'

When the guests dispersed, the old woman took the children home, removed their magic clothes, and replaced their old rags. The children quickly climbed into bed. When the wicked stepmother arrived back, she woke the orphans.

'You're always sleeping!' she cried. 'If you had been at the wedding, what sights you would have seen! There were two beautiful children there, roughly of your own age, though they had nothing else in common. The girl wore silver slippers, the boy wore golden shoes. I cannot begin to tell you how marvellous they looked. The clothes they wore must have cost a million!'

'Why didn't you take us with you, mother?' they said.

'Oh, you would not have fitted in. You would have been in everybody's way, and got yourselves hurt.'

The next day the stepmother placed a large cauldron in front of the orphans, and threw a pint of millet into it.

'If you want to cry because I am not taking you to the wedding party, use your tears to soak this millet!' she said.

She dressed her own daughter up again, and departed for the continuing wedding celebrations. The old woman again appeared with the magic clothes, and the orphans too went to the palace. This time, when the guests were leaving and the old woman had come for the children, the girl stumbled as she was passing the pond in the prince's garden, and one of her silver slippers fell from her foot and dropped into the water.

'What shall I do, nana?' she cried. 'I have lost my slipper!'

'Leave it for now, child,' said the old woman. 'We must get back to the house before your stepmother gets back. If she finds you dressed like that, she will take your clothes away, and it will be all up with you!'

She took the children home, removed their magic clothes, and replaced their old rags. The children quickly climbed into bed. When the wicked stepmother arrived back, she woke the orphans.

'Are you sleeping again?' she grumbled. 'Those children I saw yesterday were at the party again today. They were splendid. But afterwards they seemed to melt into thin air. Like the flame of a candle, puff! they were gone!'

The following morning the King's son sent his horse down to the pond to drink. But do what they might, curse, kick or cajole, the grooms were unable to persuade the horse to approach the water. When they told the prince, he came down to the water's edge, spied a brightly shining object floating on the surface of the pond, and ordered his men to throw out a line and haul it in. When they retrieved the silver slipper, the prince contemplated it in silence for some time, then took it to his father the King.

'Your Majesty! father!' he said. 'Either you find me the girl who wore this slipper, or I shall do myself a grave injury!'

The King sent out messengers on horseback to all corners of his kingdom, commanding them to assemble all the female inhabitants of the country at his palace. All the women came, but the orphan girl was not allowed to go.

'What good would it do to take you along?' said her stepmother. 'My own daughter, yes! That's quite a different thing!'

So she took her ugly daughter to the palace again.

But the slipper would not fit her, or anyone else. When the King finally found out that there was one girl who had not been to the palace, he angrily rebuked the wicked stepmother for her disobedience and stupidity, and ordered her stepdaughter to be brought to the court forthwith. They put her foot into the silver slipper. It fitted as though she had been born with it.

'She must be mine!' cried the prince. 'I want no other!'

The King, the Queen, the ministers and the guests, all tried to persuade the prince to renounce his absurd decision. But he would not.

'She is the girl I shall marry!' he insisted.

They began to question the girl, to find out about her family and fortune.

'I live with my old father, a shepherd, my stepmother, my brother, and a half-sister,' she said.

'Hm! Where is the other slipper?' they said.

'I do not know. Only my old nannie knows that,' she replied.

The girl returned home, while her stepmother remained at the palace trying to persuade the prince to take her own daughter instead, while the others advised him to take neither. But he was a very obstinate prince, who knew what he wanted.

Back home, the orphan girl was summoned by the voice of the red cow.

'Send your brother to the prince, and tell him to come to the house this evening. The old woman will give you to him.'

No sooner said than done. That evening the prince came to the house, the old woman dressed her in her wonderful clothes, and sent her away with her prince. Another royal wedding began immediately.

After a few days, the wicked stepmother came to the palace, and asked the King if she could have the new bride to stay with her for two or three days. The King agreed. On the second day, the woman dressed her own spoilt child in the magic clothes, and locking her stepdaughter in a cupboard, took her daughter to the palace, passing her off as the new princess.

In matters like this, however, princes are no fools, and that evening the deception was discovered. The prince told his father what had happened, and the King was very angry. He ordered the wicked step-mother and her deceitful daughter to be bound together at the feet, and each to be tied by the hair to the tail of a fiery stallion. Then:

'Whip the horses!' cried the King. 'And off with their heads!'

Afterwards, the King commanded his scribes to write the full details of the crime on a piece of parchment, and attach it to the two heads, which he hanged in the public square for all to see.

Thus the orphans achieved their hearts' desire. So may you also.

Recorded *c.* 1914 in Maku, N.W. Persia; see *Acknowledgements*.

The Liar

Once upon a time there was a King of Armenia, who, being of a curious turn of mind and in need of some new diversion, sent his heralds throughout the land to make the following proclamation:

'Hear this! Whatever man among you can prove himself the most outrageous liar in Armenia shall receive an apple made of pure gold from the hands of His Majesty the King!'

People began to swarm to the palace from every town and hamlet in the country, people of all ranks and conditions, princes, merchants, farmers, priests, rich and poor, tall and short, fat and thin. There was no lack of liars in the land, and each one told his tale to the King. A ruler, however, has heard practically every sort of lie, and none of those now told him convinced the King that he had listened to the best of them.

The King was beginning to grow tired of his new sport and was thinking of calling the whole contest off without declaring a winner, when there appeared before him a poor, ragged man, carrying a large earthenware pitcher under his arm.

'What can I do for you?' asked His Majesty.

'Sire!' said the poor man, slightly bewildered. 'Surely you remember? You owe me a pot of gold, and I have come to collect it.'

'You are a perfect liar, sir!' exclaimed the King. 'I owe you no money!'

'A perfect liar, am I?' said the poor man. 'Then give me the golden apple!'

The King, realizing that the man was trying to trick him, started to hedge.

'No, no! You are not a liar!'

'Then give me the pot of gold you owe me, Sire,' said the man.

The King saw the dilemma. He handed over the golden apple.

Recorded in a village in the province of Ayrarat c. 1884; see *Acknowledgements*.

The Beardless, the Lame, and the One-Eyed Thief

There was once a merchant of Yerevan. When he lay dying, he summoned his son and said:

'My son, trade anywhere you wish, but vow to me that you will not go to Aleppo to trade.'

The father died, and they buried him; his son loaded his goods on his mules and began to trade in many towns. One day he came home, and said to his mother:

'Mother, I am going to Aleppo on business.'

His mother said:

'Son, your father made you vow never to go to Aleppo.'

Her son replied that there was nothing for it, he had to go. He made inquiries about what wares fetched a good price in Aleppo, and everyone told him that box-wood was very expensive there. He therefore loaded forty donkeys with this merchandise, said a prayer, and set off for Aleppo, where the wood was, in fact, worth a king's ransom.

He journeyed on, whether much or little God alone knows, until he came towards evening within sight of Aleppo. Outside the town there was an inn, and the servants came out and told him that the inns in the city would be shut.

'Unload your donkeys, spend the night here, and start out again for Aleppo early tomorrow morning,' they said.

When they had unloaded the merchant's donkeys, a lame thief hobbled up and saw that his entire stock consisted of box-wood; he stole one bale, filled the hearth of the inn with half of the wood and tossed the rest under the table.

When the merchants came together to dine, the lame thief asked the merchant from Yerevan what he had come to sell, and when he was told, he pointed to the box-wood now lying all about the place and said:

'We use that wood here for firewood, my poor fellow; it's like sending salt to Koghb. Never mind, I'll give you these seven pots of gold for your wood, so that you may cover your loss.'

The young man thought, and said to himself:

'If I take this gold and return home immediately, they will ask me what I saw in the city of Aleppo, and what shall I say? I'll go first to Aleppo.'

So next morning he entered the city of Aleppo, and turned this way

57

and that in search of someone who might tell him what he wanted to know. Finally, he saw an old man in a shop, and he went in.

'Greetings, friend,' he said.

'Greetings, a thousand greetings, stranger,' said the old shopkeeper. 'Where are you from?'

'From the village of Parp, near Yerevan,' said the young man.

'What business brings you to Aleppo?'

'I have come to look around,' said the young man. 'Tell me: would you have any box-wood?'

'How much would you want?'

'Half a hundredweight, or a hundredweight perhaps.'

'Goodness, brother, we do not sell it by the hundredweight here! In the whole town there will be only four or five pounds, and an ounce costs thirty piastres!'

'Alas!' lamented the young man. 'God is on high, you are down here. Help me!' And he told the old shopkeeper exactly what had happened, and how he had almost been cheated. When he had finished the old man said:

'My son, this is a tricky business. There are three thieves in league with each other, who cheat those who fall into their clutches. As to who might help you, the cook at the inn is the only man who can. Go and ask him for advice.'

So the young man returned to the inn, went into the kitchen, and asked the cook to help him.

'Get me out of this predicament,' he said, 'and I shall reward you well.'

'I shall work on your behalf,' said the cook. 'I'll tell you something that will certainly help you. When you go to your bedroom this evening, make a hole in the wall, and put your ear to it. The three thieves—one is beardless, one lame, and one one-eyed—will come and ask questions of Ne'er-say-good. When you hear what advice he gives them, act upon it.'

The young man did as the cook said, and soon found himself listening to the conference of thieves.

'Ne'er-say-good,' said the three thieves, 'a merchant from Yerevan has brought forty bales of box-wood, for which we have offered him seven small pots of gold. The forty bales will make us rich!'

Ne'er-say-good said:

'He's a Yerevan man, who has been everywhere. You know many tricks, but he knows seven times as many. Supposing he says, "I do not want gold, give me seven pots of fleas", what will you do?'

'May thy house prosper, Ne'er-say-good,' said the thieves. 'He'll never think of that.'

But he did. The merchant had heard everything, and the next morning he went to the landlord of the caravanserai, and asked him to summon the three thieves so that they might settle the price of his forty bales of box-wood and he might go home.

The landlord summoned the thieves and bade them pay the merchant.

'We owe him seven pots of gold for them,' they said.

But the merchant said:

'I have many farms and have no need of gold. My herdsmen are always sleeping, and my sheep and cattle get hurt. Instead of seven pots of gold, I want seven pots of fleas to keep them awake: four pots of females, three pots of males.'

There was nothing for it. The thieves went off to Aparan to collect fleas. As soon as they caught one, and were wondering whether it was male or female, it jumped away. Seeing that they could not fulfil the contract, they returned to the inn. When the merchant had gone to inspect his wares, they found a man whom they bribed with a hundred piastres and a roll of linen.

'Wherever that Yerevan merchant goes,' they said, 'you go with him; when you know all about him, come back and tell us.'

This the man did. He introduced himself to the merchant and became his drinking companion. It was not long before the young man, taking the other to be his friend, had told him all about himself, where he was from, who his father had been, and so on. Then the man went and related everything to the three thieves.

The next day the merchant met the one-eyed thief in the street.

'Good morning, Martiros,' said the one-eyed man. 'How is your mother; how is so-and-so, how is this one, how is that one?'

The young merchant, somewhat surprised, stopped in his tracks.

'God be praised,' continued the one-eyed thief. 'I have been looking for you, and now I have found you. Many years ago when you were born, you had only one eye. I took one of mine, and gave it to you.'

Then the thief ran off to the magistrate, and said:

'When the merchant Martiros was born, he had only one eye, and I took out one of mine and gave it to him. He has kept it ever since. But now I am old and weak, and need it. I beg you to recover my eye from him and restore it to me.'

The magistrate summoned the merchant, and asked him if he knew the one-eyed man.

'Apparently he lived in our house once,' replied the merchant, 'but I do not recognize him.'

'He says that one of your eyes belongs to him,' said the magistrate. 'Now he wants it back.'

The merchant asked for one day's grace, and went to see the old shopkeeper in Aleppo, whom he asked for help.

'If anyone can help, it will be the cook,' said the shopkeeper.

So he went again to see the cook, and asked him for advice.

'Listen again tonight at the hole in your bedroom wall,' said the cook. 'The lame, the beardless, and the one-eyed thief will consult Ne'er-say-good. Act on what he tells them.'

That night the three thieves again consulted Ne'er-say-good and told him of the trick the one-eyed thief had played upon the merchant.

'Now let us see how he will get out of that, then,' said the one-eyed thief.

But Ne'er-say-good said:

'He is from Yerevan. You cannot get the better of him.'

'But what can he do? Now that he knows they are going to put one of his eyes out, he will flee and leave his wares behind him.'

'There is one thing he could do,' said Ne'er-say-good, and told them, and, unbeknown to him, the merchant.

The next day, again confronted with the one-eyed man, the merchant said to the magistrate:

'Very well, I am prepared for you to take one of my eyes out; but to prove that it really belongs to this man, you must take his one eye out also, so that they can be weighed together. If mine weighs the same as his, then give it to him.'

When he heard this, the one-eyed thief dashed out of the room, called his fellow thieves, the lame one, and the beardless one, and off they ran as fast as their legs would take them. Even today, if they hear someone breathe the name of Yerevan, they make themselves exceedingly scarce.

So, giving one bale of box-wood to the cook for his excellent advice, the merchant took his wares to Aleppo and sold them for an enormous quantity of gold, and then returned to his native land of Armenia.

And as his wishes came true, may your wishes also.

Three apples fell from Heaven, one for the story-teller, one for his listener, and one for him who lends an ear.

Recorded in the village of Parp in the province of Ayrarat and first published by E. Lalayan, *Margaritner*, vol. II; see *Acknowledgements*.

Worthless in Erzerum, Wealthy in Istanbul

In the city of Erzerum, in Eastern Anatolia, there once lived an Armenian family—father, mother, and only son.

The son was a lazy, good-for-nothing fellow, while his father was a skilled shoemaker, but one who received but few commissions, and remained very poor.

Well, the father died, leaving only one cow, his whole fortune.

What was the mother to do? How was she to make ends meet, with a worthless son like hers, who knew no trade, and had no inclination to soil his hands with work? The poor woman was reduced to selling the cow's milk to earn a little money to pay her way with. Every day she would scold her son.

'At least continue your father's trade!' she would say. 'Then we might be able to afford an extra crust of bread.'

But her son did nothing from dawn to dusk, and idled the livelong day away.

One day, however, a group of his friends came to see him.

'We are going to Istanbul,' they said. 'Why don't you come with us? We should make a fortune there.'

The son thought hard, then went indoors.

'Mother,' he said. 'Do you know what?'

'What?' said his mother.

'We are off to Istanbul with our neighbours. Business is good there. Get everything ready. We'll take the cow with us, and get out of this dirty hole. Perhaps Istanbul will make a man of me. You can't make anything of yourself in Erzerum, where only thieves flourish.'

'What are you saying?' exclaimed his mother. 'How can we go? And what should I get ready? We possess nothing in the world apart from the cow, and the journey would kill her. Let us sell her for shoeleather, since your father was a shoemaker, after all, and have done with it!'

'Mother! The world is not as bad as that! Anyway, we have already tried to sell the cow. Hurry, or they will go without us!'

Well, what could the mother say? There was clearly nothing for it. She got up and made a bundle of their belongings, while her son put a rope around the neck of the cow. Then they set off, joined their friends, and began the long journey to Istanbul. Mother and son bounced up and down and jostled from side to side as the cart trundled along the terrible roads of Anatolia, but the cow grazed on the grass of the fields and flourished, more or less. They finally arrived at the capital, where their old neighbours dispersed. The mother and her son found themselves a cave, and settled down. The son went out and wandered about, God knows where. Dusk fell, and he returned to the cave.

'What is there to eat, mother?' he said.

'What God has provided,' said his mother.

They ate their frugal meal, and lay down to sleep.

So it went on day after day. The son made no effort to look for work, or to find anything to do to earn a little money. When two weeks had passed, his mother had a word with him.

'It cannot go on like this,' she said. 'You brought me here. If business was supposed to be so good here, how is it you do nothing all day long?'

'Mother, this place is getting to be nothing better than a workhouse!' complained the son.

A few days later, however, when hunger was beginning to pinch, he said:

'Mother, I realize things cannot go on like this. I am going to sell the cow, and use the money to trade in the bazaar.'

His mother offered no objection. She fetched the cow, and her son put a rope round her neck and prepared to lead her away.

His mother's heart was in her mouth.

'Whatever you do, son,' she said, 'watch out that you are not cheated. The market-place is full of thieves!'

'Don't worry, mother,' said her son. 'With God's help, they'll never get the better of me!'

And leading the cow away, he made his way to the market-place, where he stood, and waited.

In front of him rose a large, opulent mansion. It so happened that this was the very headquarters of all the thieves and cheats of Istanbul, and when the leader of the gang looked out of the window, his eye fell upon the obviously green young man standing in the street holding a handsome cow. He summoned one of his men.

'Do you see that fellow down there, opposite the house?' he said, leading his fellow thief out on to the balcony. 'The one with the cow? Go and find a way of swindling him, and bring the cow back here!'

The thief slipped swiftly out, and sidled up to the young man.

'May God prosper you, sir!' he said.

'All good things are sent by God!' replied the young man from Erzerum.

'Is that heron for sale?' said the thief.

'What heron? What do you mean?' said the young man, in surprise.

'How much is the heron?' insisted the thief.

'Where do you see a heron?' stuttered the young man. 'This is a cow. A fat, handsome cow!'

62

'All right! all right! Just tell me what you *want* for your heron,' said the thief, soothingly.

'Go away!' said the young man. 'I have no heron to sell you!'

Expressing deep regret, the thief withdrew, and returned to his chief.

'It is no good,' he said. 'He will not be cheated.'

The gang-leader was furious. He shouted for his principal swindler, and led him to the balcony.

'Go and find a way of relieving that fellow there of his cow,' he said. 'Then we'll all have a fine feast tonight!'

The principal swindler went out into the square.

'May God prosper you, sir!' he said.

'All good things are sent by God!' said the young man.

'How much is that starling there?'

'They're a queer lot here!' thought the young man. 'Not the usual sort of customer at all! They could make a fellow lose his head!' And he cried: 'My cow is a *cow*! A *cow*! What is all this about a starling? If you want to buy my cow, say, "How much is your *cow*?" '

'You must be quite out of your mind!' said the swindler. 'That's a starling, not a cow! Never mind, tell me the price of your so-called cow, and I'll buy it!'

'I am not selling my property to the likes of you!' said the young man. 'So clear off!'

The swindler returned to the gang-leader.

'I failed,' he said. 'He's a tough one!'

The gang-leader tore his hair.

'Fetch me my fine fur coat!' he shouted. 'Now, watch me!'

He dressed himself smartly, and went out into the square.

'That's a fine quail you have there, my boy!' said the cheat of cheats.

The young man from Erzerum decided he might as well humour this one.

'It is, isn't it?' he said.

'How much would you be asking for it, then?'

'Well,' said the young man. 'I should not like to cheat a fine gentleman like yourself. Do you not know what a fair price for it would be?'

'I do know,' replied the trickster, 'but it is really up to you to tell me. I can see that you are a stranger to our city, however, so I'll tell you what. I'll take the quail with me now. You go to the covered market and ask the current price of quails. Then come to my house over there, and I'll give you five piastres more than the quoted price!'

When the cheat had taken his cow, and he had asked the price of quails in the bazaar, the young man realized that he had been well and truly swindled. But he went to the fine mansion, and asked for his money. The servants brought him his eight piastres, and he stood at the gateway and watched them slaughter his fine cow on the spot.

'What are you standing there for?' cried the servants. 'Clear off!'

'My late father gave me some strict advice. "Whatever you do," he said, "when you sell a cow, keep the tail." Please give me the tail, for the sake of my late father.'

The servants could not imagine any use for the cow's tail, and threw it to the young man. He took it straight away to a smith, and had it bound in leather, and studded with large nails. He hung it on his belt, and went home.

'Well, mother,' he said, 'you thought I should be cheated! I sold the cow to a man who passed himself off as a fine gentleman, but he has swindled me. Run quickly to our neighbours and borrow me some women's clothes!'

'What are you going to do, my son?' cried his mother. 'Verily, Satan has only to unfurl his banner, and you march after him!'

'No, no, mother, do not worry! You'll soon see!'

The mother went to her neighbours and borrowed some dresses. Her son bundled them under his arm, and went to the barber's.

'Take these clothes, shave off my moustaches, and disguise me as a girl,' he said.

'It will cost you a gold piece, effendi,' said the barber.

'Very well, I shall pay you,' said the young man.

The barber dressed the young man in the finest of the dresses, shaved him, hennaed his hair, and powdered his face. When he left the shop, anyone would have mistaken him for a very pretty girl.

He wrapped himself from head to foot in a white, half-transparent veil, and went and stood beneath the balcony of the mansion belonging to the chief of all the thieves and cheats of the capital city of Istanbul.

It was not long before the master of the house became aware of the pretty girl waiting idly in the street under his balcony, and struck with her beauty, he gallantly asked her to accept his hospitality.

'What a pity you did not come by a little earlier!' he said. 'We had a feast of fine roast meat. But if you like, I can offer you something to eat.'

He ordered his thieves to lay the table for them, and then go about their business.

When they were alone, the young man took out the heavily studded tail he had concealed under his clothing, and waved it in front of the swindler.

'Do you know what this is, agha?' he said.

'I don't know. It looks like the tail of a cow.'

The young man brought it smartly down across the swindler's shoulders.

'It is in fact a heron (*thud*)! a starling (*thud*)! a quail (*thud*)!' he cried, giving the man a fresh blow with every bird's name. 'A *heron*! a *starling*! a *quail*! A *heron*! a *starling*! a *quail*!'

64

And he whipped the swindler with the tail of his stolen cow until the man fell back on to the sofa unconscious.

The young man gathered together all the valuable objects he could find, and all the gold coins in the many coffers. Then he changed his clothes, and left the mansion.

'Mother,' he said, when he arrived home, 'I have brought these gold pieces and these silver vessels for you. The gentleman who bought our cow provided them, so you can see what a good man I sold the cow to. His conscience troubled him, and he said, "As God is my witness, I give these things to you!" '

Let us leave the son and his mother for a moment, and return to the mansion.

In the morning the thieves returned. They waited a long time, and hearing no sound from their master's apartments, they were puzzled.

'Our master is not such a heavy sleeper. God forbid that any danger should have befallen him,' they said.

They waited a while longer, and as there was still no sound from his room, they went in and found their master unconscious on the sofa.

'Agha!' they whispered. 'Wake up!'

Their master stirred with a groan.

'Euh! euh! euh!' he said.

'The master is still alive!' shouted the thieves. 'Bring some water!'

'Akh, akh, my friends!' moaned their bruised and battered chief. 'One may swallow insults, one may swallow death, but never should we have swallowed a morsel of that cow!'

The truth slowly dawned upon his men.

'Do you mean that that "girl" was really the owner of the cow!' they cried.

Their master only groaned.

Let them remain where they are, while we go back to the young man and his mother.

The following day, the young man secretly stationed himself under the swindler's balcony to find out whether he was alive or dead, and if alive, what his wants and desires might be. He listened attentively to all that was said in the room above his head.

'The doctors round here are no good!' said the master of the house. 'I still ache all over. Find me an English doctor!'

The truth of the matter was that he was so well known throughout the city of Istanbul as a cheat and a robber, that he was afraid a local doctor would poison him.

The young man ran to the barber's shop, gave the barber another gold piece, and said:

'Disguise me as an Englishman!'

The barber dressed the young man in a top hat and a frock coat, and transformed him into the spitting image of an Englishman. The young man collected a number of phials and bottles, filled some with the yolk of an egg, others with the white, and others with vinegar and similar substances, placed them all in a basket, and then walked through the market-place.

'I am an English doctor,' he called out. 'A good one. By Appointment to Her Majesty!'

One of the swindler's men heard him, and ran in to tell his master.

'Agha, there's an English doctor outside,' he said. 'If you like, I'll call him.'

'Call him, for God's sake!' said the swindler.

The 'English doctor' came and examined his patient.

'You appear to have been beaten quite severely,' he said. 'One wonders who would dare to do such a thing to you, but your wounds seem to have been caused by a large number of iron nails!'

The swindler was amazed at the accuracy of this diagnosis, and decided that this was a very good doctor indeed. He promised to pay him well, and said:

'What cure do you prescribe?'

'You need a bath,' said the doctor.

One of his thieves ran to the public hammam to ask them to clear it of other bathers and prepare it to receive their master.

'You can all come with me, men!' said the swindler-in-chief. The thieves were overjoyed, and were about to set off for the hammam, when the English doctor made an objection, pointing to the ragged garments in which they usually plied their nasty trade.

'*I* am not going anywhere with people dressed like *that*!' he said. 'They must make themselves more respectable!'

There was nothing for it. The gang-leader ordered them all to clothe themselves in fine silk robes, with silver sandals on their feet.

When they were all ready, they set off in splendid procession for the hammam, two of the thieves helping their aching master along. When they arrived, they led their master in and prepared him for his bath.

'I am afraid I shall have to bleed him,' said the doctor. 'He is bound to shout and scream and call for help when I cut into his veins, but take no notice. On no account try to come to his aid, or I may make a false incision and do him irreparable harm!'

'We understand,' they said, and went to the other cubicles to bathe on their own.

When the doctor was alone with his patient, he produced the heavily studded tail he had concealed under his clothing, and waved it in front of the swindler.

'Do you know what this is, agha?' he said.

When the swindler saw the cow's tail, his soul almost started from his body for fright.

The young man brought the tail smartly down across the swindler's shoulders.

'It is in fact a heron (*thud*)! a starling (*thud*)! a quail (*thud*)!' he cried, giving the man a fresh blow with every word. A *heron*! a *starling*! a *quail*! A *heron*! a *starling*! a *quail*!'

The swindler cried for help, but though his men heard him, they took care not to come. The young man whipped him with the tail of the stolen cow until the man fell to the ground unconscious. Then he gathered up all the fine silken robes and silver sandals belonging to the master and his servants, locked the door of the hammam behind him, and left. He sold the robes and the sandals, and took the money he received for them home.

'Look, mother!' he said. 'The gentleman who bought our cow gave this to me. He said, "As God is my witness, I give you all this money!" '

Let us leave the son and his mother, and return to the hammam.

When they had washed themselves thoroughly, the thieves realized that they had not heard any sound from their master for some time.

'We had better go and see how he is getting on,' they said. 'The doctor must have finished his treatment by now.'

They went to their master's cubicle and found him lying unconscious on the floor. He seemed to be in a worse state than before.

'Could that "doctor" have been the owner of the cow, too?' they asked each other.

They listened. They strained their ears. A faint murmur issued from the chief of the swindlers.

'Agha!' they cried. 'Speak to us!'

'Euh! euh! euh!' groaned their master.

'The master is still alive!' shouted the thieves. 'Bring some water!'

'Akh, my friends,' moaned their chief. 'One may swallow insults, one may swallow death, but never should we have swallowed a morsel of that cow!'

His men looked at each other. Their silk robes had gone. Their silver slippers had gone. They realized that they had been tricked. Then they discovered that they had been locked in the hammam. They hammered on the door, but a long time passed before a bath attendant arrived to let them out and one of their number could borrow some clothes to go back to the mansion and fetch them something to wear. When he returned, they dressed hurriedly, placed their aching chief on a litter, and carried him home.

When one and a half to two months had passed, it occurred to the young man to return beneath the balcony to see whether the swindler was alive or dead, and what his plans might be. He listened attentively to all that was said in the room above his head.

'Keep a lookout for me and tell me when you see a caravan leaving for Jerusalem,' he was telling his men. 'I intend to go on a pilgrimage, and shall stay in the Holy City for one or two years. My luck seems to have run out, and if I do not get away, that demon or whatever he is will come and bring another disaster on my head. If God wills that I return, I shall return. If not, so be it!'

Hearing this, the young man from Erzerum hastened to the bazaar, where he hired two camels and the robes and accessories of a camel-driver. He paid an assistant to ring a bell in the streets of the capital for a few days and announce, with a placard hanging from the camels' necks to the same effect, that a caravan of forty camels was about to depart for Jerusalem on a Christian pilgrimage to the Holy Land, that thirty-eight of them were already hired, and only two vacant camels remained. When the thieves heard the announcement, they ran to tell their master. The swindler arranged to hire both camels, one for him to ride on, the other to carry the two coffers of gold he was taking with him to cover his travel expenses. He set off with the 'camel-driver' to join the rest of the caravan, followed by his forty servants.

'The rest of the caravan stands some way off,' said the camel-driver. 'Why should your servants toil along after us? They will only have to make their way back when we come to the caravan. Send them back.'

'You are right,' said the swindler, and calling to his servants, or rather his band of thieves, he instructed them as follows:

'Continue to exercise our trade well. Look after my house in my absence. If I return, well and good. If I do not return in two years' time, divide up my property among yourselves, continue to dwell in my mansion, and say an occasional prayer for my soul.'

After riding alone with the camel-driver for some time, the chief of the swindlers asked him how much farther they had to go to join the rest of the caravan.

'We'll soon be there,' said the young man disguised as the camel-driver.

After a few more minutes, the swindler asked again where the rest of the caravan was.

'They are waiting on yonder hill!' said the camel-driver.

They continued until they came to the edge of a high cliff. The swindler looked all around him. There was no one in sight. The place was completely deserted.

The camel-driver took out the heavily studded tail he had concealed beneath his clothing, and waved it in front of the swindler.

'Do you know what this is, agha?' he said.

Just imagine the effect of this on the swindler! His blood ran cold, his liver burst! What could he do in that wilderness? He began to scream and shout, but who was there to pay any attention to him?

'You have roasted many victims, swindler,' thought the young man, grimly. 'Now it is my turn to roast you!' And aloud he said:

'Do you know what this is, agha? It is in fact a heron (*thud*)! a starling
68

(*thud*)! a quail (*thud*)! A *heron*! a *starling*! a *quail*! A *heron*! a *starling*! a *quail*!'

And he thrashed the evil swindler so vigorously that he finally tumbled down from his camel and gave up the ghost. The young man from Erzerum dragged his body to the side of the road, threw a handful of earth upon him, and returned to the city with the camels and the thief's possessions. Arriving back at nightfall, he changed back into his own clothes, and took the two coffers jingling with gold coins, and the two camels, back to his mother.

'Help me carry this gold into the house, mother!' he said. 'It is the final payment on our cow. The gentleman gave me these two camels also, but what shall I do with camels? I shall sell them tomorrow for cash.'

And so he did. He purchased a fine mansion, settled down in it with his mother, and began to lead a regular and respectable life. And thus did he who in Erzerum had not been worthy to be called a man become, in Istanbul, a very fine gentleman indeed.

Erzrumum mard cheghav, Stambolum agha eghav, told in the dialect of Erzerum. Nothing is known of the narrator. The tale was printed for the first time in *APT*, IV, appendix 1, no. 9.

The Illiterate Priest

Every morning at the crack of dawn the priest of a certain village would hasten to the church to recite the office, but by the time any of the congregation got to the church, he had finished and left.

'Father,' said the faithful, 'why are you not a little more patient? Wait till we are all there, then begin the service.'

'It is not my fault if you are always late!' retorted the priest. 'You will have to get up earlier!'

But try as they might, they could never get there in time. Their suspicions were aroused, however, and it soon occurred to them that the priest might not be able to read the service books, and was trying to hide this from them.

'It cannot go on like this,' said one of the faithful. 'Look, I'll pretend to die. You carry me to the church, and when our priest performs the last rites over my body, I'll keep my ears open. We'll soon see whether he can read or not!'

So the man pretended to be dead. They carried his supposed corpse in a coffin to the church, and laid it before the altar.

The priest crept into the church when none of the congregation was about, and began to recite, in his manner, the office for the dead.

Standing at the man's head, he said: 'From head to feet, alleluja-a-a, amen!'

Moving to the man's feet, he said: 'From feet to head, alleluja-a-a, amen!'

Moving to his right side, he said: 'From right to left, alleluja-a-a, amen!'

And moving to his left side, he said: 'From left to right, alleluja-a-a, amen!'

The 'dead man' saw that the priest could not read the office.

He raised his head in the coffin.

'That's not the right way to do it, father!' he said. 'Do it properly!'

The startled priest realized that the 'corpse' was not truly dead. He tightened his grip on the chain of his censer, and brought the vessel hard down on the man's head. One! two! three!—and the corpse really was a corpse!

The congregation rushed in, looked, saw the priest dripping with sweat, and cried:

'Father, for God's sake, what has happened?'

71

'You scoundrels!' cried the priest. 'You won't even give a man time to die properly! If it were not for me, he would never have given up the ghost.'

Angraget tērtērë, told by Ervand Thorosian, aged 63, of the village of Mughni in the province of Ayrarat, and recorded by V. Bëdoyan in 1939; *APT*, I, no. 48.

Loqman the Wise

There once lived in the region of Adana, in Cilicia, a young hunter who, at the time our story begins, had reached the age of fifteen years. One day, overtaken by a sudden downpour of rain, he took shelter in a cave, and much to his surprise, he found that he had strayed into the dwelling-place of the King of the Snakes, an aged creature with the head of a man and the body of a *vishap*, or huge serpent.

Affecting to pay no particular attention to the strangeness of this situation, the young man lit a fire, and prepared to dry out his wet clothes. While he was so engaged, the King of the Snakes reached out his right hand and placed his seal on the young man's back. Over the fire the young hunter prepared some *khorovats* or roast meat on a spit from the game he had shot before the downpour, and taking a small portion for himself, he offered the rest to the old King of the Snakes and the four other snakes who waited in attendance upon their ruler.

'You have given us food,' said the King. 'Now give us water.'

The young man took his goatskin, went to the spring, filled it with water, and returned. He hollowed out a hole in a rock and filled it with water. The four younger snakes came and drank.

'I am dying of thirst, my son,' said the King of the Snakes. 'What shall I drink the water in?'

The hunter fashioned a ladle out of a piece of wood and gave it to the King to drink out of.

Rain continued to fall for three whole days and three whole nights, and the young man was not able to leave the cave.

'Can you not devise a way to bring the water from the spring into the cave?' asked the King of the Snakes.

The young hunter set to, and working for six days, dug a channel from the spring to a basin he had prepared in the cave. Then he slaughtered a deer, made a fire, and cooked the venison on spits.

'Here is food for you,' he said to the King. 'Eat. I must go now, but I shall come back.'

'I hardly believe you will come back, my son,' said the old serpent. 'Leave me something as a pledge of your good faith.'

The hunter left his rifle, and went off. Soon he was back again, looking after the needs of the snakes and their King. When the time came for him to leave again, the serpent took a small stone, and gave it to the hunter.

73

'Take this stone,' he said. 'It is very precious. Do not show it to anyone. Wrap it in a blue cloth. At night it glows like fire. And inasmuch as you have given me food to eat and water to drink, I herewith adopt you as my son. But beware of undressing in front of strangers, for no one must see the seal I have placed upon your back.'

The hunter went away, sold the precious stone in France, paid his debts, built himself a large mansion, bought a flock of forty sheep, and again returned to the cave. He kissed the old serpent's hand, slaughtered the sheep, and richly entertained the snakes with roast mutton.

The old serpent took out another precious stone and gave it to the hunter.

'Never say a word about me to anyone,' he said. 'I am Shah-Mar, King of the Snakes.'

The young man kissed his hand, and when he was on the point of departing, the serpent lifted his finger, and four snakes appeared. They accompanied him to his mansion, two in front, two behind. When he arrived home, the hunter thanked them, and they licked his feet with their forked tongues, and returned to the cave.

Now in the meantime the ruler of Adana had fallen gravely ill. Terrible ulcers appeared all over his body, eating him slowly away. The best doctors were summoned to his bedside. A French doctor ordered two chickens to be slaughtered and cut in little pieces and placed upon his ulcers, and though this soothed them for the time it takes to smoke a pipe, they were soon as bad as before. When they took off the bandages, they found that the ulcers had consumed the pieces of chicken entirely.

The King was called Kayen, or Cain, and it was he who founded Adana, and the country was called Kilikia, or Cilicia, after him.

One of the doctors summoned to tend the King of Adana was a very knowing one. He examined the ulcers, and then said to the King:

'Sire, if I can get what I need, I shall have you up and about in no time. Give me three days.'

'I would give you a month, if it would do any good,' said the agonized King.

The doctor gazed into his crystal ball and learned of the seal of Shah-Mar on the back of the young hunter, whose name was Purto. The doctor told the King that if Purto could not be persuaded to bring Shah-Mar, the King would die.

They fetched Purto.

'Help me, save my life, my son,' said the King. 'Fetch me Shah-Mar!'

'You ask the impossible, Sire!' said the hunter. 'The snakes would sting me to death!'

The chief doctor was furious, and he ordered Purto to be tied to a stake and flogged. Purto shouted and screamed, but the doctor was relentless. He ordered the hunter's ears to be cut open and salt and

pepper rubbed in the open wounds. He had pieces nipped out of his flesh with pincers, and so tormented the young man that he finally undertook to fetch Shah-Mar.

On his way to the cave, Purto shot ten deer. He brought them to the cave, and did obeisance to Shah-Mar. The old serpent knew why the young man had come.

'You are my adopted son,' he said, 'and I cannot let you be tortured for my sake. It is too late to go now. Let us lie down and sleep, and we shall leave tomorrow morning.'

The next morning they set off, Purto in front, Shah-Mar behind. The other snakes made to go with them, but their King stopped them with a wave of his hand.

'Go back, my children,' said the King. 'As long as you continue to receive gifts from me while I am gone, you will know that I am well. For the rest, do as you like.'

The serpent and the hunter came to Mount Nauruz, which was covered with beautiful, sweet-scented flowers. Shah-Mar plucked one of the flowers and gave it to the hunter, commanding him to swallow it without chewing it. Then he picked five bunches of odoriferous flowers, and gave these too to Purto.

'Bring these flowers three times to the boil, then drink the juice,' he said. 'They will endow you with the ability to recognize the healing qualities of every herb and flower.'

Returning to his house with the serpent, Purto did as he was bid. He drank the magic potion, and then, as Shah-Mar now commanded him, he lay down to sleep. When he awoke, the serpent asked him:

'Do you feel the healing power within you, my son?'

'I now know,' replied the young man, 'that your head contains four brains: the two right ones are poisonous, the two left ones are beneficial and have healing qualities.'

Then Shah-Mar asked his adopted son to make him drunk on red wine seven years old, tie his hands, cut off his head, and bury his body in the ground. (You must know that it was the custom in that part of the world, when a snake was killed, to bury it in the earth, it being thought that if it remained on the surface, it would read the stars during the night, and bring itself back to life.) Shah-Mar reminded him to continue to send gifts to the other snakes, lest they learned of his death.

'If the other snakes hear of my death,' he said, 'they will destroy the earth!'

Shah-Mar drank the seven-year-old wine, and lost consciousness. Purto bound his hands together, cut off his head, and took out his four brains. Of these he prepared two concoctions, one poisonous, one healing, and then went to the King of Adana. The King commanded the chief doctor to examine the medicaments. Purto handed him the poisonous brew. No sooner did the wicked doctor put it to his lips, than he gave a fearful scream which echoed through the palace like the sound of a cannon, burst right open, and expired.

The King was thunder-struck!

'Is that how you were going to cure *me*?' he cried.

But Purto gave him the other medicine. The King drank it, and was completely healed of his sores. The hunter was appointed chief royal physician, and from that day forth they called him Loqman the Wise, the Father of Medicine.[1]

One of the snakes of Adana, however, chanced to find out about the death of Shah-Mar, and he told the other snakes. All the snakes assembled, and began to kill off the inhabitants of the country. When the King came to hear of it, he summoned Loqman, and asked him what to do.

Loqman made forty packets of Shah-Mar's liver, took the dead serpent's prayer-beads from his belt, and went to see the snakes. When they saw Shah-Mar's prayer-beads in Loqman's possession, they accepted him as their King, and made peace.

'As long as you continue to receive presents of Shah-Mar's liver, you will know that I, your new King, am alive and well,' he told them.

(And all the days of his life Loqman sent gifts to the snakes, while even today, in that region of Cilicia, the people, who are convinced that Shah-Mar's tomb still exists somewhere in the neighbourhood, put out gifts for the snakes every Sunday.)

The fame of Loqman spread far and wide. With the remedies made of Shah-Mar's brains he could raise the dead, and for seven whole years nobody died.

Now a certain woman was wont to go to Loqman's house every day to do the washing. One day, while she was bending over the tub, a handsome youth came up to her, put his hand in her pocket, took out a key, and went away. As the woman was leaving, Loqman's wife asked her who the handsome youth was.

'He's my son,' replied the washerwoman. 'He is deaf and dumb. I beg you, persuade your husband to accept him as a pupil! The doctor's secrets will be safe with him!'

Loqman's wife promised to try, and when her husband came home, she persuaded him to do as the washerwoman asked. The youth came and kissed the doctor's hand, and became his pupil.

When a month had gone by, Loqman said to his wife:

'Wife, I am convinced that that young man is neither deaf, nor dumb.'

[1] Loqmân, or Luqmân, the Wise is a legendary sage and physician celebrated throughout the Middle East, where he is 'by some said to be a son of Job's sister or aunt; by others, to have been a disciple of David; by others, a judge in Israel; while others declare him to have been an emancipated Ethiopian slave, and author of the fables current under his name' (F. Steingass, *A Comprehensive Persian-English Dictionary*, W. H. Allen & Co. Ltd., 1892).

And for fear of his secrets becoming common knowledge, Loqman tried to provoke the young man into leaving him with as many stratagems as he could think of. But the washerwoman's son was never seen to be anything but deaf and dumb, and survived all the doctor's attempts to catch him out. At the same time he faithfully carried out all his master's instructions. But Loqman was afraid, and tried to ensure that the young man remained in ignorance of his secrets.

The young man remained with Loqman for seven years.

One day Loqman was visited by a man from a distant country who suffered from intolerable pains in the head. Loqman shut himself and his assistant up with him in the shed, and gave him a potion to drink. The man lost consciousness. Loqman took his scalpel, lifted the top of the man's skull, and saw a black crawling thing with eight legs moving in the man's brain. Loqman took his pincers, but try as he might, he could not get a hold on the creature. He tried other instruments, and failed. In all his years as a physician he had never known such a case! For a long time his assistant watched his master's efforts impassively. Then he could stand it no longer. He forgot he was supposed to be dumb.

'Make the tongs red hot and then clamp them round the thing!' he shouted.

Loqman glanced at him grimly, but did as he said. The man was cured. As soon as the bandages were in place, the assistant took to his heels and vanished.

He went home, took three large cauldrons, and filled one with milk, another with wine. He crawled into the third, placing the cauldron with the milk under him, and the cauldron with the wine over him. There may he remain, while we return to Loqman the Wise.

The doctor searched everywhere for his assistant, but in vain. He cast spells, and learned that the young man was hiding somewhere between Red and White, presumably between the Red Sea and the White Sea. Loqman hired sailors to search the two seas and the land between them high and low, but there was no trace of his assistant. Finally he went to the young man's mother.

'I am old now,' he said, 'more than one hundred and four years old. I desire to talk to your son. Send him to me. I swear I mean him no harm.'

The washerwoman persuaded her son to come out of the cauldron, and took him to Loqman.

'You have caused me a great deal of worry, my son,' said the doctor. 'I am old now. After my death no one will know the secrets of healing, and my name shall pass out of men's minds.'

The young man kissed his master's hand, and they drank a cup of wine together. Since his assistant did not yet know that he could bring the dead to life and make old men young, Loqman told him:

'Put a large cauldron on the fire, and give me a potion to drink. When the water boils, throw me into it, and put the lid on. After forty hours, take me out of the cauldron, wrap me in cotton wool, and pour the drops from this phial into my mouth.'

The young man did as his master bade him, but when the time came to pour the drops into his mouth, the archangel Gabriel suddenly appeared and struck the assistant on his right hand, so that only one single drop fell into Loqman's mouth. This gave him some life, and he stirred slightly.

'Pour! pour! pour!' he murmured.

But then he died.

The assistant buried his master with Shah-Mar.

From that day forth, the young man could not live in peace with himself. Loqman's dying words rang constantly in his ears.

'Pour! pour! pour!' they said.

He took to wandering through the world, but the voice of Loqman the Wise followed him everywhere.

One day he chanced to visit a house in which there dwelt a bishop, a priest, two monks, and more than one hundred guests. He spent six days there without seeing anyone laugh or smile.

'Father,' the young man asked the priest. 'Why are you all so sad? If it is on account of me and my troubles, I shall leave.'

'My son, it is certainly not on your account. The lady of the house is in childbirth, and the child will not be born. She screams day and night in agony. We have called all the doctors, and none of them can help.'

'Why did you not tell me before, father?' said the young man. 'I can help her.'

And he went to the woman's aid. Using his knowledge of his master's skills, he cured the woman, and her child was born. The family's gratitude knew no bounds. They made him the child's godfather, and built him a splendid mansion. For the first time since the death of Loqman the Wise he slept in peace. He had not slept for twenty-five years, and now he slept for twenty-four hours on end, and the voice of Loqman the Wise was finally still.

He returned to his mother. She married him to a handsome girl, and the wedding feast went on for seven days and seven nights.

The minstrels recognized the bridegroom as the pupil of Loqman the Wise. They began to ask each other riddles.

'I have a riddle for you,' said the bridegroom.

'You are the pupil of Loqman the Wise,' said the minstrels. 'We cannot compete with you. We should lose our *saz*!'[1]

(For it was the custom in contests between minstrels for the loser to surrender his musical instrument to the winner.)

[1] The long-necked, small-bodied mandoline used by the Armenian *ashughs* or minstrels to accompany their songs.

'I do not want your *saz* or your money,' replied the young man. And he began to sing:

> *'What thing will water never wet?*
> *What thing on earth will never rust?*
> *What rolls and rumbles in the heavens?*
> *Who moans and groans beneath the dust?'*

None of the minstrels could solve the riddles. The bridegroom gave the answers:

> *'Water will run from the back of a duck.*
> *Gold will never turn to rust.*
> *Thunder rumbles in the heavens.*
> *And Loqman moans beneath the dust.'*

Recorded in Turkish Armenia *c.* 1900; see *Acknowledgements.*

The Wizard

Once upon a time a sick man threw his carpet bag over his shoulder and set off on a journey. He came to a spring bubbling out of a rock in the vicinity of a tall oak-tree, and when he saw how sweet and pure the water was with which a group of women were filling their pitchers, he suddenly felt very thirsty.

'Good women,' he said, 'could you let me have some of that water to quench my thirst?'

'You can turn to ashes first!' replied the women. 'Go away!'

But one woman took pity on him.

'Why will you not give him any water, neighbours?' she said, and letting him drink from her pitcher, she added: 'There will be a corner in our house to sleep in, brother, if you want to rest.'

'Why not?' said the man. 'I shall come.'

So he accompanied the woman home. When they arrived, her husband asked her who he was.

'Just a man,' she said. 'A guest.'

'Lay the table,' said the husband, 'and let us eat.'

'I only eat baby's flesh,' said their guest.

Now the wish of a guest is a host's command. The couple had only one baby, but this they fetched from its cradle, killed it, boiled it, and set it before their visitor. Then they all went to bed.

Early next morning, they heard a baby crying.

'Who can that be?' said the wife.

'How do I know?' said the husband. 'We had only one baby, and we killed him yesterday.'

They went to find the source of the voice, and there was their baby, crying in his cradle. Their guest was nowhere to be seen. Then they knew that their visitor was a wizard. He had reconstituted their baby from its bones, and had then departed.

The wizard continued his journey, and saw a man gathering brushwood.

'Hey, brother!' he cried. 'You won't get fat on that!'

'What can I do?' said the other. 'I am a poor man.'

The wizard turned the brushwood into a thriving vineyard.

'There, brother, eat, and prosper!' he said.

He continued his journey, and saw a man searching about in a grove of barren trees.

'Hey, brother!' he cried. 'What fine apple-trees you have there!'

He had turned the grove into an apple orchard.

'Prosper, brother,' he cried. 'Long life to you!'

He continued his journey, and saw a man humping rocks on his back.

'Hey, brother!' he cried. 'What a nice flock of sheep you have there!' He had changed all the stones into sheep.

'May you long benefit from them, brother!' he cried.

Not one of them guessed that the man was a wizard. The wizard travelled about for a whole year until he felt cured of his sickness, then said to himself:

'I'll go back now, and see what they are all doing.'

So he returned, and came upon the former hewer of rocks. He had slaughtered one of his sheep, and was having a feast.

'Could you spare a morsel for me?' asked the wizard.

'What?' said the man. 'Do you help me to look after the sheep?'

'No,' said the wizard. 'Give me a tiny morsel for charity's sake.'

The shepherd would not. The wizard made a gesture with his hands, and all the sheep turned back into stones.

He went on his way, and came to the apple orchard, where men were busy picking the fruit.

'Can you spare an apple for me?' asked the wizard.

'Don't show your face here!' said the orchard-owner. 'Clear off!'

The wizard made a gesture with his hands, and all the apples disappeared. The grove was completely barren again.

He went on his way, and came to the vineyard.

'Can you spare a bunch of grapes for me?' the wizard asked one of the workers.

'I shall go and ask the master,' said the man.

He went away and came back again.

'The master will not give you any grapes,' he said. 'He says you can perish first!'

The wizard made a gesture with his hands, and all the vines turned to brambles.

He went on his way, and came to the house where he had eaten the baby. The couple had not forgotten their hospitable ways.

'Welcome! welcome!' they said. 'What can we do? Our head and eyes are delighted to see you. It is as though the ground beneath our feet were green and crimson silk! Welcome!'

'You are good people,' said the wizard, 'and you manage your household well. From now on, four hundred gold coins will appear each night beneath your couch, and you will be very rich!'

Then he left them, and made his way home again.

Kakhardë, told in 1950 by the peasant woman Gyuli Avagian, of the village of Chaphar in the Mardakert region, province of Artzakh, Karabagh, and printed for the first time in *APT*, V, no. 65.

The Girl who Changed into a Boy

There was and there wasn't, once upon a time there was an old woman who had one daughter. Since she was an only child, the old woman dressed her daughter in boys' clothes, so that she could play with the neighbours' children.

Now one day the King's daughter got lost, and was found by the old woman's daughter, who took her to her mother, and said:

'I have found this little child. Let us keep her.'

So the old woman kept the girl.

The King ordered a proclamation to be made throughout the land, announcing:

'My daughter is lost. Whosoever shall find her may request of me what he will.'

This announcement came to the old woman's ears, and she informed the King that it must be his daughter who was living with her. One of the King's ministers mounted a fine mare called Lulizar[1] and came to the old woman's house to fetch the princess. The old woman's daughter went back with them, and on the way, Lulizar whispered to her:

'When the King asks you to make a wish, tell him you desire to possess me, and nothing else.'

When they came into the presence of the King, he embraced his daughter, and turning to the old woman's child, said:

'Make a wish, and I shall grant it.'

'Long life to Your Majesty,' said she. 'I should like to possess Lulizar.'

'Lulizar is worth my entire kingdom,' said the King. 'If I give her to you, I might as well give you my daughter too!'

And so he did.

The wedding feast lasted for seven days and for seven nights. It was not long before the princess realized that her husband was a woman like herself, and she ran to her mother, the Queen.

'A curse on you and your kingdom,' she cried, 'for marrying your daughter to a woman! He is a woman, as I am a woman! What shall I do?'

The Queen told the King.

'What shall we do?' said His Majesty. 'If we chop off his—her!—

---

[1] Persian, 'Pearly-face'.

head, it will not help much, and if we do not, our daughter will be very miserable. There is nothing for it. Let us send him to some place from whence he will never return.'

He called his 'son-in-law'.

'My boy,' he said, 'you must go and fetch me the brother of Lulizar.'

The 'husband' got up, went to the stables to find Lulizar, and burst into tears.

'Why are you weeping, girl?' said the mare.

'The King has commanded me to find your brother and fetch him back here!' she lamented. 'How can I do that?'

'Ask the King for a bottle of old wine and a bundle of wool,' said Lulizar. 'Then we shall leave together to find my brother.'

The girl followed his instructions, then led Lulizar from the stables, mounted, and rode off.

Eventually they came to the sea. Not far from the shore stood a marble fountain.

'Go over to that fountain,' said the horse. 'Empty the basin, block up the spout with the bundle of wool, and fill the basin with wine in place of the water. Then conceal yourself. My brother will emerge from the sea, gulp down the wine, and grow dizzy. Then you must run forward and leap on to his back. He will gallop towards the sea, but you must shout, "Whoah! your sister calls you!", and he will turn round and come over to me.'

The girl did as Lulizar told her. The sea-horse came out of the waves, sniffed the air, and drank the wine. When it grew dizzy, the girl emerged from her hiding-place and jumped on its back. The stallion galloped furiously towards the sea, but the girl shouted, 'Whoah! Whoah! your sister calls you!' Lulizar bounded up, her brother joined her, and they all returned to the palace, where the girl gave Lulizar's brother to the King.

When the princess saw that her 'husband' had come back, she blazed with anger.

'May you and your kingdom perish!' she cried. 'Rid me of that woman!'

The King summoned his chamberlain.

'He—she!—has come back,' he said. 'What must we do to get rid of him—her!—for ever?'

'Send her to the House of the Devs, Sire,' said the chamberlain. 'Let her try to collect the seven years' arrears of taxes they owe us. She will stand no chance of escaping from them!'

The King summoned his 'son-in-law'.

'My boy,' he said, 'the devs owe us for seven years' taxes. Go and collect it for me.'

The girl got up and went to find Lulizar in the stables, and burst into tears.

84

'Lulizar,' she wept. 'I am in your hands as you are in God's. The King has asked me to go to the House of the Devs and collect the taxes for the past seven years.'

'Do not cry,' said Lulizar. 'We shall collect them, never fear!'

The girl mounted her horse and they rode away. Eventually they came to the huge white marble gates of the House of the Devs. The gates were tightly shut.

'Tie my tail to the marble gates,' said the horse. 'I shall pull them open, and then you may go in and fetch the taxes.'

The girl tied the mare's tail to the marble gates, Lulizar pulled and tugged, and the dust flew up in clouds. Finally the gates burst open, and the girl slipped in. She suddenly found herself face to face with forty devs.

'Aha!' they chuckled. 'Our dinner has just walked in!'

'I don't know how you can sit there like that,' said the girl, 'when the King is about to confiscate all the marble in your quarry as compensation for your seven years' arrears of taxes!'

The devils rushed out to inspect their quarry. The girl looked rapidly around her, saw the seven years' arrears in a money bag hanging on a pillar, and had snatched it down, untied Lulizar, jumped on her back, and galloped away before the devs had time to collect their wits. Horse and rider returned to the palace, where the girl handed the King the seven years' arrears of taxes.

When the princess saw that her 'husband' was back again, she was furious, and ran to her father at once.

'Why do you not destroy that woman?' she demanded angrily.

The King once again summoned his chamberlain.

'She has escaped from the House of the Devs!' he said. 'What must we do to get rid of her for ever?'

'Sire,' said the chamberlain, 'your grandfather once had a valuable rosary which the devs stole and presented to their mother. Send her to get it back. She will never be able to escape from that old she-devil!'

The King summoned his 'son-in-law'.

'My boy,' he said, 'go and bring back my grandfather's rosary, which is now in the hands of the mother of the devs.'

The girl got up, went to find Lulizar in the stables, and burst into tears.

'Why are you weeping, girl?' asked Lulizar.

'The King has commanded me to fetch his grandfather's rosary, which is now in the hands of the mother of the devs,' she sobbed. 'How can I do that?'

'Do not worry, girl,' said the mare. 'God is great. We shall fetch the rosary.'

The girl mounted Lulizar, and they rode away, until at last they came to the castle which was the home of the mother of the devs.

The castle was built on a high mountain peak overlooking a deep ravine.

'When you enter the mother devil's castle,' said Lulizar, 'you will find her sleeping with her back propped up against a column. The rosary hangs on that very same column. At the first stroke of every hour, the rosary drops into her hands, and she begins to count her beads. When you see it begin to fall, snatch it away before it touches her hands, rush out with it, and leap straight out into the ravine. I shall be waiting on the road below, and shall catch you on my back.'

The girl went up to the castle, passed through the main gate, found the mother of the devs asleep against the column as Lulizar had said, and hid behind it. The hour struck, and the rosary started to fall into the she-devil's hand. The girl darted forward, seized the rosary as it fell, rushed out of the castle, and leapt straight off the edge of the wall into the ravine. Lulizar rose half-way up in the air, and caught her in her saddle. Awakened by the noise, the mother of the devs started up. She saw in a flash that her rosary had gone, and that she had no chance of catching the rider now galloping furiously away on a horse that moved like the wind.

She racked her brains in search of her most terrible curse. She found it.

'My curse upon thee!' she shrieked. 'If thou be man, be now woman! If thou be woman, be now man!'

In the twinkling of an eye the young girl turned into a young man.

Lulizar and her rider returned to the palace, where the young man gave the King his grandfather's long-lost rosary, and then went to greet his princess.

This time when the princess came to see her father, she was not angry.

'I find that my husband is a man after all,' she said. 'I would not change him for any other, so I beg you to stop sending him on perilous missions!'

The King gave the young couple a wealthy city to govern for themselves, and they all ate, drank, and made merry, and lived happy ever after.

Three apples dropped from Heaven: one for the story-teller, one for him who listens, and one for him who marks it well.

> *Tgha dardzogh akhchikë*, told in 1913 by the illiterate watermill-keeper Avetis Nazarian of Oshakan village, province of Ayrarat; *APT*, I, no. 12.

Kandek and the Werewolf

There was once a man and his wife, who had seven daughters. One day the husband went out into the fields, to till the soil.

Left alone, the wife said to herself:

'What shall I do with all these daughters? Oh bother, I'll light the oven, and put them all inside, and burn them up!'

So she stoked up the fire and pushed all her daughters into the red-hot oven—all, that is, except for her youngest daughter Kandek, who escaped by crawling behind the oven and hiding.

When all were burnt to a cinder, the wife was troubled.

'Oh dear,' she said, 'I have not kept a single one to take my husband his lunch!'

Kandek's voice floated from behind the oven.

'Mother dear,' she said, 'I shall take father his lunch.'

So Kandek's mother wrapped up her husband's lunch, gave it to her little daughter, and sent her to the fields with it. Kandek found the ploughmen, and gave her father his lunch.

'Go for a walk, my child,' said her father, 'but take care not to eat any apples from that apple-tree yonder!'

Kandek walked over to the edge of the field, but no sooner had her eyes fallen on the large, shiny red apples hanging on the tree than her wits abandoned her, and she picked one of the apples and ate it.

At that very moment an old woman came hobbling along.

'Give me an apple, my dear,' she said.

She was a werewolf, and blind, and she ate human flesh.

'Come nearer, and I'll throw you one,' said Kandek.

'I am blind and cannot see,' said the old woman. 'You come over here and put it in my mouth.'

The little girl picked an apple, and went over to the werewolf to put it in her mouth for her. The werewolf grabbed her, stuffed her in a sack, tied it securely at the top, slung it over her shoulder, and hobbled off homewards. On the way Kandek called out to her to let her out for a moment, to do her wee-wees. The old werewolf put the sack down on the ground and let Kandek out. The girl rapidly filled the sack with stones, and ran away. Since the werewolf was blind, she could not see what had happened, and when she slung the sack across her shoulders again, she muttered to herself:

'Kandek, my child, how heavy you have grown!'

When she got home and untied the sack, all she found in it was stones. She went back to look for Kandek, found her, grabbed her, and put her back in the sack, and again hobbled off homewards.

On the way Kandek called out to her to let her out to stretch her legs. The werewolf put the sack down on the ground and let Kandek out. The girl quickly filled the sack with snow, and ran away. The werewolf slung the sack across her shoulders, and walked on. The snow began to melt.

'Kandek, my child,' muttered the werewolf. 'You are wetting me!'

When she got home and emptied the sack, all she found was a heap of melting snow. She went back to look for Kandek, found her, grabbed her, put her back in the sack, and hobbled off again in the direction of home. On the way Kandek found another pretext to be let out of the sack for a moment, claiming that she was stifling and needed some air. She then filled the sack with brambles, and ran away. The blind werewolf slung the sack across her shoulders, and walked on. Soon the thorns began to prick her through the sack.

'Kandek, my child,' she muttered, 'you have a needle on you which is hurting my back!'

When she got home and emptied the sack, all she found was a bunch of brambles. She went back again to look for Kandek, found her, grabbed her, and put her back in the sack. This time when Kandek called to her to let her out, she took no notice, and walked straight to her house. Here she instructed her daughter to kill Kandek and heat the stove and boil her for supper. The werewolf's daughter heated the stove, prepared a cauldron of water, and was about to cut the little girl's throat, when Kandek snatched the knife from her hand and killed her instead. Kandek put the daughter's body into the cauldron, added a handful of rice, and climbed up into the rafters of the house to see what happened.

The werewolf returned in the evening, and finding the cauldron bubbling away on the stove, and everything prepared for supper, she chortled:

> *'Kandek's flesh is sweet, O!*
> *Kandek's flesh is sweet!'*

But then Kandek's voice floated down from the rafters:

> *'Daughter's flesh is sweet, O!*
> *Daughter's flesh is sweet!'*

The blind old werewolf was very surprised.

'Kandek, my child, how did you get up there?' she said.

'Pile up some sticks and climb up after me!' said the girl.

The werewolf piled wooden sticks up to the ceiling and started to

climb up towards Kandek, but since she could not see where she was going, she tumbled down again, and hurt her back.

'Kandek, my child, how did you get up there?' she said.

'Pile up some wool carders to the ceiling, and climb up after me!' said the girl.

The werewolf piled the metal combs to the ceiling, and began to climb, but the sharp teeth cut right into her feet, and she fell down again.

'Kandek, my child, how *did* you get up there?' she cried.

'Make a pile of the salt sacks, and climb up after me,' said the girl.

The werewolf made a pile of salt sacks, and began to climb, but the salt entered the many wounds in her feet, and she died in agony.

Kandek climbed down from the rafters and went and told the other werewolves that the old werewolf was dead, and they came and took away all her possessions.

Mardageli heqiathë, 'The tale of the werewolf', told in Vagharshapat *c.* 1876, the identity of the narrator being now unknown; printed for the first time in *APT*, III, no. 48.

Badikan and Khan Boghu

There was and there wasn't (and there was no one good but God), there was a King who had forty sons. As soon as each boy came of age he sent him off to a distant land to perform feats of valour and to find a suitably pleasing girl to marry. By the time this story begins, thirty-nine of his sons were already married, but the Lord knows what feats of valour they performed, or whether they performed any at all. In any case, it was now the turn of the youngest son, whose name was Badikan. His father, the King, gave him a sword and bow and arrows, money and servants, set him on his charger, and with a 'God prosper thy cause' sent him on his way.

Badikan travelled the length and breadth of many countries. He saw the Kingdom of Darkness, and the Kingdom of Light. Think of Agog-Magog, the demon Aznavor, man and beast—Badikan did battle with them all, overcame them, and passed on his way. But in the end not one of his retinue was left alive; his money was all spent, and he was all alone when he came at last to a magnificent palace. There was no building like it on this earth. It had been built in the distant unremembered past, of huge solid blocks of iron and stone, and the strength of the ramparts beggared description. Badikan walked round and round the walls, peered in at the gate and windows, but saw neither woman nor maid, man nor beast.

'Lord God, what sort of place is this that I have come to?' he said.

He waited around until it grew dark, when suddenly he saw someone coming. It was a huge giant. His armour was of steel, his casque and shoes of bronze, his bow and arrows of wrought iron, and whenever his foot trod the ground, the whole earth rumbled.

The giant stopped, sniffed the air, and said:

'A man! There is the smell of a human being! I spend all day hunting in the mountains, and the prey comes knocking at my door. Where are you? Who are you? Come forward, so that I can see you, or I'll crush you to dust between my hands!'

What could Badikan do? No arrow or sword would make an impression on that beast. He stepped forward into the presence of the giant.

'Who are you,' asked the giant, 'to dare to enter this terrain? Have you not heard the name of Khan Boghu?'

'I have heard of you,' replied Badikan, 'and that is why I came to see you. My name is Badikan, and I have travelled all over the world. I have fought and defeated demons and dragons, and now I have come to fight and defeat Khan Boghu.'

Khan Boghu looked Badikan in the face and snorted, and Badikan picked himself up a mile away.

'Come back, Badikan!' called the giant. 'You're a brave fellow! If you wish I'll keep you on. Bring your sword and bow and arrows and serve me; they won't do me any harm and may be useful for hunting.'

Badikan gave his assent, and began to dwell with the giant in his palace.

One day Khan Boghu said to Badikan:

'You will have observed that I cannot suffer pain or death, but nevertheless there is an ache in my heart. The King of the East has a daughter who has not her like on earth. Seven times I have tried to carry her off, but never have succeeded. If you fetch her here, say what you want and you shall have it. Here is a horse, money, and weapons. Take whatever you want and go.'

Badikan gave his promise to return, and off he went to the city where the girl lived. He dressed himself in the local garb, learned the local dialect, and finding employment with a gardener, began to work in the vicinity of the King's palace. One day the King's daughter was looking out of her window and saw that when Badikan was left alone he would put on the most magnificent robes and parade proudly up and down, obviously a much grander person than a common gardener.

Well, the princess lost her heart to Badikan, and began to dream of him. And Badikan fell in love with her.

The girl did not hesitate long, and soon sent one of her maids to declare her love to Badikan, who in turn told her that he was the son of a King, that he had performed many brave exploits, and that her fame had brought him thither. Having seen her, he had fallen in love with her and awaited her command.

Now the city was heavily fortified, and the inhabitants, both male and female, strong and warlike, since they daily expected an attack from Khan Boghu. Therefore the princess arranged to come outside the city to disport herself on the banks of the lake, whence Badikan, 'if he were a man, might carry her off'.

So the princess left the city with a retinue of forty handmaidens, Badikan swooped down on horseback, swift and light as a fairy, caught the princess up on to the saddle behind him, and soared away like an eagle. Those left behind just stared, open-mouthed, until they came to their senses and ran into the city to tell the news to the King. The King and all his citizens leapt on their horses and galloped after Badikan. By this time Badikan had hidden the princess behind a plane-tree, and went back on his tracks to meet his pursuers. When they arrived he slaughtered and massacred them all, until the battlefield was

covered with corpses, one on top of the other. Then he returned, swept
the girl on to his horse and spurred it forward. They came to the sea,
swam on the back of the horse to the other shore, and saw in the distance
the garden-house and seraglio where Khan Boghu dwelt.

'Badikan, may I die for your soul!' said the maiden. 'We have ridden
such a long way, and you have not spoken a word to show that you love
me. Tell me the truth, for the love of God. Was it for yourself that
you carried me away?'

'You have appealed to me in the name of God, so I must tell the
truth,' said Badikan. 'I carried you away for Khan Boghu. I gave him
my word.'

'However much Khan Boghu had tried,' cried the princess, 'he could
never have captured me, nor can you think that you would have
succeeded either by cunning or sword, had I not wished it so. May all
maidens walk in widow's black weeds, for they are the slaves of their
heart! I came to be your wife, and if I cannot be, then I shall drown
myself in the sea or dash myself against a rock, and become food for
fishes or birds.'

And many reproaches did she make to Badikan, and cursed men of
stony heart and deceiving speech, and made ready to cast herself into
the sea. Badikan's heart was touched, and he called upon God to witness
that they would find a way to liberate themselves from Khan Boghu
and marry.

Then Khan Boghu came to meet them, and expressed his gratitude
to Badikan. He was delighted to see his beloved princess, and commanded that she be carried to the garden-house, treating her very gently
lest she should be repelled by his appearance and do herself a fatal
injury.

'Are you quite well? Tell me your heart's desire, that I may fulfil it,'
he said to the princess.

'Thank you, I am very well, and you shall be everything to me,'
replied the maiden. 'But my father and mother made me promise not
to take a husband for seven years, otherwise they would curse me, and
cut me off from the fruits of my father's labour and my mother's milk.
Will you accept not to be my husband until the seven years are
up?'

'Gladly,' said Khan Boghu. 'Since you are in my hands, I should be
patient not for seven years, but for forty-seven.'

So they struck this bargain, and decided that Badikan should remain
with them and should hold the cross above their heads as best man
at their wedding.

For some time all abode by this arrangement, but the princess and
Badikan were not at ease. If they wanted to kill Khan Boghu, sword
and arrow would not touch him; if they fled he would overtake them,
and they would not escape his vengeance.

One day Khan Boghu rested his head on the princess's lap, and talked with her, and she with him.

'Why do you live all alone?' said the girl. 'And how do you manage to survive when so many arrows and sword strokes rain upon you? Where is your soul? If you will not tell me this, I know you do not love me; and if you do not love me, say so, and I have no reason to live on.'

She said many other things, and so cunningly, that Khan Boghu was persuaded to tell her his secret.

'Seven days' journey from my palace,' he said, 'there is a white mountain; in this mountain dwells a white ox, completely indomitable, for neither man nor beast can approach him. For seven days he goes without drinking, and on the seventh day he mounts to the summit of the white mountain. There, there is a spring of white water flowing through seven spouts of white marble. The white ox drinks from each of the seven white spouts, and then withdraws for seven days. In the belly of the white ox there dwells a white fox, and in the belly of the white fox there is a box of mother-of-pearl. In this box there are seven white sparrows. They are my soul, my seven secret powers. The white ox cannot be overcome, the white fox cannot be caught, the white box will not open, and the white sparrows no hand can seize. And therefore is it that I remain invulnerable, unconquerable and immortal: for if the ox is slaughtered, the fox runs off; if the fox is caught, the box will not open; if the box is opened, the sparrows fly away.'

It was not long before the princess related Khan Boghu's secret to Badikan, saying:

'If you are a man, do what you have to do. I have done my part.'

A few days later, Badikan asked Khan Boghu to let him have his horse of blue fire, that he might travel to distant places and then return. Khan Boghu gave his permission, and Badikan set off. He went straight to the dervishes and sorcerers, and asked them:

'How may an invulnerable man, whom fire and iron will not harm, be overcome; and how may an indomitable animal be tamed?'

The dervishes and sorcerers answered and said:

'A strong man is overcome by woman, a wild beast by wine.'

Badikan loaded a mule with seven barrels of seven-year-old wine, took them to the white mountain, and emptied them into the spring. The white ox came to the spring, smelt the wine, jumped higher than seven poplar-trees, bellowed, and galloped away. The second day he came again, parched with thirst. What could he do but drink the wine, get drunk, stagger back to his lair and fall asleep? Badikan followed him, drew his sword, and cut off his head.

At that moment Khan Boghu was out hunting; as the ox's head fell, his own head began to throb, and his whole body trembled.

'Akh!' he cried. 'The white ox is dead. The princess has told my

94

secret to Badikan, or to some other suitor. I am dying, but I shall kill her first. If I cannot have her, no one shall!'

He ran furiously into the palace.

By this time Badikan had cut open the ox's belly, and seized the fox by the tail before it had a chance to flee. He cut off the fox's head, and blood began to flow from Khan Boghu's nose. Badikan found the box of mother-of-pearl, and broke open the lock; Khan Boghu tasted blood in his mouth, but he hastened on to the garden-house. The princess was terror-stricken and ran up on to the roof, determined that the giant should not take her alive. She was prepared to throw herself down from the roof.

Badikan strangled two of the white sparrows, and Khan Boghu fell to his knees.

Badikan strangled two more white sparrows, and Khan Boghu's arms grew numb.

Badikan strangled yet two more sparrows, and Khan Boghu's heart and liver burst.

Badikan caught the seventh sparrow by the wing and squashed it under a stone. At the very same moment Khan Boghu fell forward and dashed his brains out against a boulder. A black smoke issued forth from the giant's mouth and nostrils, and he rolled over on the ground and lay finally still.

Badikan galloped back on the fiery horse, the princess came down from the roof of the garden-house, and they embraced and congratulated each other. And submitting to the will of God they married, and lived happily ever after.

Recorded in Turkish Armenia and first published in G. Sërvandztiantz, *Hamov-Hotov*; see *Acknowledgements*.

The Valiant Swineherd

There was, there was not, there was once upon a time a King. He was a very powerfully built man, and much devoted to hunting. One day, after he had wandered through the forest for hours on end, he suddenly came upon a bird, sitting on a branch, and pouring forth a melody to the sun in the sky most wonderful to hear.

The King whispered a command to his vezier:

'Find a way to catch it alive,' he said. 'It would be a great pity to kill it.'

So they set a snare, caught it, and bore it back to the palace.

'Build a glass cage for it,' ordered the King, 'and put it in it so that everyone may come and see it.'

So they built a room of glass for it, and put it inside, and the whole country came to see it. Everyone who saw it was amazed and delighted.

Now the King had an only son, and when he had reached the age of thirteen, he took his bow and arrows and went out hunting. One day he shot his arrow and it broke one of the panes of glass in the cage and fell at the feet of the bird.

The prince went up to the bird and asked it to give him his arrow back.

'Go and fetch the key your father keeps under his pillow,' said the bird. 'I'll give you your arrow back, and you will set me free. I am weary of captivity, and with your kind help may now end it.'

'My father will kill me,' said the boy.

'He will not kill you,' said the bird. 'You are his only son.'

So the prince went and fetched the key, and opened the door of the cage.

'If your father ill-treats you,' said the bird, 'come and find me. I shall be by the spring in the middle of the forest.'

And so saying, it flew away.

As soon as the King found out that his son had set the bird free, he was very angry.

'Cut off his head!' he roared.

But his counsellors and ministers restrained him.

'He is your only son!' they said. 'What is the sense of killing him for the sake of a bird? Banish him from your house, and let him go whither he will!'

The King summoned the son of his vezier, produced a handful of coins to cover the cost of travel, and said:

97

'Take this, and take my son with you. If you kill him, you will know how; if you let him live, you will know why. It is at your discretion. But he is never again to set foot in my land!'

The son of the vezier and the son of the King rose and went. They walked much; they walked little; they came to a forest.

'I shall kill you here,' said the son of the vezier.

The son of the King burst into tears, and pleaded with him not to kill him.

'If you give me your golden armband, I shall not kill you,' said the son of the vezier.

'Take my armband! I do not want it! You can have it!' cried the prince.

When the son of the vezier had taken the prince's armband, he said: 'From today forth I am the King's son, and you are my slave.'

'I am your slave! So be it!' said the prince. 'What can I do about it?'

The son of the vezier went and fell asleep beneath a tree. The son of the King went for a walk. He walked and walked until he came to a spring, and there he saw the bird, perched on a near-by branch. The prince burst into tears, and told the bird all that was on his mind.

'It is nothing,' said the bird. 'I shall make it possible for you to save yourself. Go and drink of the water of the spring.'

The prince went and drank.

'Strike this tree with your fist,' said the bird.

The prince struck the tree, and it came out by the roots.

'Go and drink some more water,' said the bird.

The prince drank again of the spring, and came back.

'Strike this larger tree with your fist,' said the bird.

The prince struck the larger tree, and it leapt out of the ground, roots and all.

'Is that degree of strength sufficient for you, or shall I give you more?' said the bird.

'A little more, and we'll see if that will be enough,' said the prince.

'Go and drink some more water,' said the bird.

He went and drank and came back. He punched at a tree the size of the other two put together, and it flew right up into the sky.

'Is that enough?' said the bird.

'It is enough, thank you,' said the prince.

The prince left and went back to the son of the vezier, and they went on their way. They walked much; they walked little; they came to a royal city.

The vezier's son sent word to the King, saying that he was the son of such and such a King, and had come to see him.

The King sent his men and welcomed him with full honours.

The King liked the two young men, and said to the vezier's son:

'I shall soon give you the hand of my youngest daughter, and you

98

shall be my son-in-law. You will be living in the palace, so what shall we give your servant to do?'

'You know best. Give him whatever task you think fit.'

'Will you go and look after our pigs for us?' the King asked the real prince.

'I will,' he replied.

So the prince went to the pigsty and led the pigs out to graze. When evening fell, he brought the pigs back, and saw that there was a huge wooden beam lying near his hut. The next morning he picked up the beam to use as a staff, let out the pigs, and led them off to pasture until dusk fell.

Early next morning he took his staff, went to the King's balcony, and thumped at it, *whoom! whoom!* with the huge wooden beam. Everyone woke up, rushed down, and shouted:

'What do you want?'

'Give me a penny, to buy some husks with!'

'You can have a pound!' said the King.

'I do not need a pound. Where would I change it? Give me a penny!' said the prince.

He took the penny, smashed down the door of a corn-chandler's with his beam of wood, took some husks, or carobs, to the value of one penny, and led off his pigs to graze.

When he returned in the evening, he went to the King.

'Have a good iron staff made for me,' he said.

'That's a fine lump of wood you've got in your hand. Isn't that good enough?' said the King

'No, it's a mere twig,' said the prince. 'Make me a rod about twenty-five hundredweight in weight.'

The King promised to have one made.

Morning came again, and *crash! crash!* the balcony shook to the blows of the huge beam.

When the court issued forth, the prince said:

'Give me a penny, to buy some husks with!'

They gave him the penny, and battering in the doors of five to ten shops, he took the husks, returned to his pigs and led them off. In the evening he came home, and went to bed.

In the morning he saw that his iron staff was ready. He picked it up, and weighed it in his hand.

'That's the staff I wanted!' he said, and placing it on his shoulder, he collected his pigs, and went off.

He led his herd of pigs up to the boundaries of the land of the Black Dev. Here he found himself confronted by an enormous gate.

'There must be some sort of mansion here,' he said to himself. 'Let us look.'

He went nearer and saw that the huge forbidding gate was shut.

Standing back a little, he gave it two blows with his iron staff. Some pieces flew to the east, and some pieces flew to the west! He led his pigs through, and found himself in a great garden, with melons and pumpkins and all good things in abundance. He let his pigs run loose, and lay down to sleep under a tree.

Lunch-time came round, and the Black Dev returned—returned to find his door smashed to pieces and pigs all over his garden, uprooting and devouring his melons and pumpkins.

'By the Lord God!' he cried. 'Who has had the temerity to enter here?'

He walked around the garden, and found the prince sleeping under a tree.

'Son of earth!' he roared. 'Son of earth!'

The youth heard his voice, but did not move.

'No bird on the wing or snake on its belly has ever dared to enter my garden!' roared the Dev. 'What are you, that you have so dared!'

'You surely will not be bold enough to compel me to get up from my resting-place?' said the prince. 'There'll be a fight!'

'Your ear will be the largest piece of you left when I have finished with you!' roared the Dev. 'Tell me who you are!'

The young man stirred, and rubbed his ears.

'Stand back a bit,' he said, 'and address me from there.'

He rose to his feet.

'Shall I have the first blow, or you?' said the Dev.

'You go first,' said the prince.

The Dev hurled his mace with such force that the young man disappeared entirely within a cloud of swirling dust.

'May my arm perish!' cried the Dev. 'Had I thrown with less force, there would at least be two large lumps of him left to gobble up!'

The dust cleared. The prince was unharmed.

'My turn now,' said the prince. 'You'll find that I'm not dead yet!'

The young man picked up his iron staff and gave the Dev such a mighty blow on the nape of the neck that his head flew right off. Up and away it went, and it's probably still flying through the air today!

The prince got up and made his way to the Dev's castle. In one of the chambers he found ten black horses, with ten fully armed men dressed in black mounted upon them, ready for battle.

'What manner of men are you?' asked the prince.

'We are mighty warriors, forcibly brought here by the Dev against our will,' they said. 'If you let us go, we shall rush to your aid whenever you call!'

The young man fetched the Black Dev's black horse, fastened a fine black suit of clothes to its saddle, and first plucking one hair from the tail of each horse, he permitted the black knights to depart. Then he rounded up his herd of swine, and returned to the King's palace. On

100

his arrival, he found all the court echoing to the merry sound of pipe and drum.

'What is the news?' he asked.

'We are celebrating the wedding of the King's eldest daughter!' they said.

The young man took his pigs and shut them up for the night, and then went to his room and sat down.

Before long the King's youngest daughter came along to see him.

'Greetings!' she said.

'Greetings!' he said. 'What do you want?'

'I have come to talk to you,' she said.

'I'm a swineherd. Why should you want to speak to me?' he said. 'Do you want to smell of pigs? Go away!'

'My heart forces me speak to you,' she replied.

'No! no! go away!' he said. 'I don't need you!'

The girl burst into tears and left, but all her thoughts turned to the young swineherd. She went and baked some bread, then came back and knocked, *tap! tap!*, at his door.

The young man got up, opened the door, and saw the princess standing there again.

'What is it now?' he growled.

'I've brought you some bread. Open the door and we'll eat it together.'

He snatched the bread from her hands, thrust her away, and slammed the door.

The girl fell down, then got up, and went away crying.

The next morning the young man arose, went to the palace balcony, and beat, *whoom! whoom!*, hard against the railings.

'What is it, man?' cried the courtiers.

'Give me a penny, I'm off to buy some husks for the pigs!'

They gave him the penny, and off he went. In the evening he returned, to find the whole town weeping and wailing.

'What has happened?' he asked.

'The devs have come and intend to take the King's eldest daughter off with them,' they answered. 'The King has assembled his army, and is preparing to do battle.'

The young man led his pigs back to the piggery, and saw the King's youngest daughter standing there, crying her eyes out.

'Why are you weeping?' he asked.

'I am broken-hearted,' she said. 'The devs are taking my eldest sister away.'

'But what are you doing here?'

'I have come to ask you to save my sister.'

'I am only a swineherd, and it is as much as I can do to look after my pigs!' he said. 'Why don't you ask your betrothed? He's the son of a King!'

'He is not suited for that sort of work. With that iron rod of yours you can do anything.'

The swineherd pushed her away.

'Go away, and don't bother me!' he said.

The girl burst into tears and went away.

The next morning he got up, put his staff over his shoulder, went to the palace balcony, and *whoom! whoom!! whoom!!!*

Those inside wailed and screamed:

'The devs are here! What shall we do?'

'Give me a penny, to buy the husks with, and hurry!' he said. 'The pigs are still in their sty.'

They gave him his penny, and off he went to buy his husks, gather his pigs together, and march out of town. He let his herd loose in a field, took from his breast-pocket the tail-hairs of the Black Dev's horses, and burned them. Behold! there stood the Dev's black horse with the ten black knights! He took the fine black clothes from the Dev's horse, put them on, mounted the horse, and they all rode off together.

The King had taken his army and marched out to face the devs. The eleven knights galloped up, swiftly took up position in the van-guard of the army, and advanced. They fell upon the hordes of the devs, laid about them, and massacred them where they stood. Only one dev survived, and him the young swineherd seized. He pulled out all his teeth, and then let him loose.

'Go back whence you came and tell your ruler of your prowess!' he said.

Then they all wheeled their horses round and galloped away.

'Stop them! stop them!' the King yelled. 'We must give them a reward!'

But the horsemen galloped off post-haste, and vanished from sight.

The young man dismounted, changed back into his old clothes, dismissed the knights, rounded up his pigs, and returned home. He found the whole town in festive mood: the pipes were piping and the drums were drumming for all they were worth. He went back to the piggery.

The youngest princess collected a generous trayful of the wedding cakes and sweetmeats and brought it to the swineherd.

He opened the door.

'Well, what do you want, girl?' he said, brusquely.

'I am seeing to your needs, and have brought you some food, to eat with you,' said the princess.

'It's not necessary. Go about your business!' said the young man. He took the tray from her hand, and pushing her out, shut the door.

The princess burst into tears and returned home.

In the morning the young man got up, fetched his penny, filled his haversack with husks, led out his pigs, and wandered off until he came to the boundaries of the land of the Red Dev. He found himself under a large wall.

'It seems there is another dev's castle here,' he said. 'I can take my pigs in and give them something good to eat.'

He went up to the gate, gave it two taps with his iron staff, and the pieces came to earth in Aleppo, and China, and some even farther afield.

He led his pigs through, and found himself in a large garden.

'This will be fine,' he said. 'Let them eat to their hearts' content.'

He went and lay down in the shade of a large tree and fell asleep.

At lunch-time the Red Dev returned home and found his gate all smashed to pieces. He seethed with rage. When he went in and saw that pigs had trampled all over his garden, he dashed angrily from one side of the garden to the other, until he came upon the youth asleep under the tree.

'Son of earth! Son of earth!' he cried. 'Get on your feet!'

The young man woke up to find the Red Dev by his pillow.

'Why are you standing there like a fool?' exclaimed the swineherd. 'Why won't you let me sleep in peace?'

'Your ear will be the largest piece of you left when I have finished with you!' bellowed the Dev. 'You have done all this damage and you still have the impudence to speak to me like that? No bird on the wing or snake on its belly has ever dared to enter my garden. How did you get here? My teeth are grinding already! I'll tear you to shreds!'

The young man picked up his iron staff and stood to his feet.

'You have first go,' he said to the Dev.

The Dev hurled his mace with such force that the young man disappeared entirely within a cloud of swirling dust.

'What a pity!' muttered the Dev. 'Not a single piece of him left to gobble up!'

But when the dust cleared . . .

'My turn now,' said the youth, and raising his iron staff he gave the Dev such a mighty blow on the nape of the neck that his head came right away and flew off in the direction of Mount Ararat, causing severe earthquakes the whole length of its trajectory.

The young man got up and made his way to the Dev's castle. In one of the chambers he found ten red knights, all ready for battle.

'What manner of men are you?' asked the prince.

'We are captives, brought here against our will by the Red Dev,' they said. 'If you let us go, we shall rush to your aid whenever you call!'

The young man fetched the Red Dev's red horse as well, and

fastening a fine scarlet suit of clothes to its saddle, plucked one hair from the tail of each horse, and then let them all loose. Then he went back, rounded up his pigs, and returned home.

The whole town was feasting and making merry.

He took his pigs back to their sty. The youngest princess came along.

'Come to my chamber,' she said. 'It's my middle sister's wedding day, and the whole town is eating and drinking. Why are you skulking about in here?'

'Go away!' said the young man. 'I am not worthy of you. I am only a swineherd.'

'I love you!' said the princess. 'In my eyes you are a king!'

'Go away! I am not coming,' said the young man. And pushing the princess away, he shut the door on her.

The girl went and prepared a generous trayful of wedding cake, and brought it to the swineherd. He opened the door, and she went in.

'I have brought something to eat,' she said. 'Get up, and we'll eat it together.'

The young man took the tray from her hand.

'This is no place for you!' he said, and pushed her out.

The next morning he got up, and *whoom! whoom!* . . .

'Give me my penny and I'll buy the husks!'

He bought the husks, and went on his way. When he returned in the evening, he found the whole town weeping and wailing again.

'What has happened now?' he said.

'Tomorrow the devs are coming to take away the King's middle daughter,' they said.

He led the pigs back to the piggery. Full of tears the King's youngest daughter came to see him.

'God is up there, and you are down here. It is to you, as his agent on earth, that I appeal!' she said. 'I know that it was you who rescued my eldest sister. Please rescue my middle sister.'

'Go away! Go to your King's son and your vezier's son and tell them to go and free her. I am a swineherd, what can I do?'

'No! no! they can't do anything. If you wish to, you can save her!'

The young man got up, took her by the arm, and led her to the door. The princess went away in tears.

The next morning he rose, took his pigs and led them to a field. He burned the horses' hairs, and the horse of the Red Dev and the twenty red knights appeared. He donned the scarlet suit of clothes, mounted his horse, and galloped off.

The King suddenly saw them approaching in a cloud of dust.

'Bless your eyes!' he cried. 'They're coming to save us!'

When they drew near, the King, beside himself with joy, could barely tell his ankle from his elbow.

'Advance, lads!' cried the King.

The horsemen passed through the enemy ranks like a consuming fire, fell upon the devs, smashed them to pieces, and ground them to dust.

All were slaughtered but for one, and him the prince seized. He cut off his ears, and said:

'Now go back whence you came, and tell them of this defeat!'

The horsemen then withdrew.

'Stop them! stop them!' yelled the King to his men. 'We must give them a reward.'

But the knights galloped away and disappeared.

'Alas! alack!' sighed the King. 'If we had managed to detain them, we might have seen what manner of men they are.'

When the youth returned in the evening, he found the whole town resounding to noisy and joyful celebrations. He returned to his pigsty, and sat down.

The youngest princess ran down to see him.

'Get up,' she said. 'Let us go to my chamber, and eat, drink, and be merry. You can see that the whole town is celebrating.'

'I am a swineherd,' said the young man. 'What have I to do in your chamber? Go away! Be off!'

'You are my heart's beloved!' cried the princess. 'Why are you sitting here in this filthy place? Get up! Let's go to my chamber!'

'No. I am a swineherd. I am not right for you.'

The princess went away, full of tears and regrets.

She prepared a goodly trayful of wedding cake and took it to the swineherd.

'If you won't come, you won't,' she said. 'Let us sit here together and eat these cakes.'

'Go away!' said the young man. 'You can't eat in this pigsty.'

'As long as I'm with you, I care nothing for that!' cried the princess.

The young man got up and took her by the arm.

'Just go away!' he said, and leading her to the door, he thrust her outside. The girl went away, weeping bitterly.

The next morning the swineherd got up, took his pigs and marched out of the town. He walked and walked, until he came to the borders of the land of the White Dev, where he spied another huge gate.

'This might be another dev's castle,' he said to himself.

He went up to the gate, and found it locked. One blow of his twenty-five hundredweight rod, and of gate and gate-posts not a trace remained. He led his pigs into the orchard, where he found melons and pumpkins and all manner of fruit in great abundance. He let his pigs run loose, washed himself in a fountain, lay under a tree and went to sleep. At lunch-time the White Dev came back home, to find his gate shattered to pieces. A great fit of trembling seized him, shaking him from the fibres of his heart to the marrow of his bones.

He went in, and found the pigs trampling all over his garden and

106

eating fit to burst. He went on and found a man lying under one of his trees. He was beside himself with rage.

'Son of earth! Son of earth!' he roared. 'Get up!'

He stamped his foot, and the whole world shook.

The young man awoke.

'What's wrong with you?' he asked. 'Can't you let a man sleep?'

'It's seven years now since I tasted human flesh!' roared the giant. 'My teeth have gone blunt. Stop talking, and get up! All that will be left of you when I have finished with you will be part of an ear!'

The youth grasped his iron rod, and got to his feet.

'It's your go,' he said.

The White Dev stood back and hurled his club with all his might. A cloud of dust rose into the air, and the young man disappeared.

'He's gone right through the ground!' exclaimed the Dev. 'There's not a morsel left of him to gobble up!'

But the dust cleared, and there stood the young man.

'You boast too soon,' he said. 'I am still in my place, and it's my go. Watch!'

So saying, he swung his iron rod and prepared to strike the giant in the nape of his neck.

'You can have two goes,' said the Dev.

'I was born in one go, and I shall kill at one go,' said the youth, and the giant's head leapt from his shoulders and hurtled away, and it is still going, that's for sure.

The young man entered the giant's castle and found ten white horsemen there.

'What manner of men are you?' he asked.

'We are captives of the White Dev, who brought us here against our will,' they replied. 'If you let us go, we shall rescue you from whatever danger may befall you.'

The youth went and found the White Dev's white horse. He tied a fine suit of white clothes to its saddle, plucked a hair from the tail of each of the horses, placed them in his breast-pocket, and then let them all go. Then he returned to the orchard, rounded up his pigs, and went home.

As soon as the young princess saw him returning, she ran up to greet him as usual.

'Let us go to my chamber,' she said.

'One says a thing once and keeps to one's word,' replied the young man. 'I am not coming. I am a swineherd, you are the King's daughter. What sort of couple do we make?'

'I would die for you, and so may my father and my mother also!' cried the princess. 'In my eyes you are the country's benefactor!'

'Go away! Don't bother me so!' said the young man, and taking her by the arm, he led her out of the hut and closed the door.

The girl burst into tears and went away.

She prepared a large trayful of sweets and cakes and went back.

'Let us sit here and eat them together,' she said.

'Are you here again?' said the youth. 'Go away!'

'You may kill me, but I shall not go!' cried the princess.

He got up, took the girl by the arm, and thrust her outside.

The next morning he took his pigs to the fields, and returned with them in the evening. When he got back to the town, all were weeping and wailing.

He went to the piggery. The young princess ran up in tears, burst through the door and fell at the young man's feet.

'As you saved my two sisters, now save me!' she cried. 'The devs have come to take me away!'

'If they're taking you, they're taking you!' said the young man. 'What can I do about it?'

'I implore you, save me as you saved my sisters!'

'Go about your business. I can do nothing. I am a swineherd. I only know about pigs,' said the youth. 'Be off. Your intended, the King's son, or the vezier's son, will save you!'

'Pah! I shovel earth on their heads!' cried the princess. 'What are they good for?'

The young man got up, took the princess by the arm, and told her to go. She stood up, and went away weeping. She prepared a tray of food, and brought it to the swineherd's hut.

'Are you back again?' he said. 'Have you no brains in your head at all?'

'I have brought some food. You must have something to eat. Sit down, and we'll eat together.'

The young man sat down. The princess began to eat, casting sidelong glances at the swineherd, her eyes full of tears.

'What are you crying for?' he asked.

'My heart is breaking. How should I not cry, seeing that the devs are coming to carry me off tomorrow?'

'What? As they carried off your sisters?'

'You saved my sisters, but you refuse to save me!'

'I shall save you, too,' said the young man. 'But do not breathe a word to anyone!'

The princess went back to the palace, and found her mother in her room.

The Queen noticed that her daughter was quite gay.

'What has happened?' she asked. 'The devs are coming to carry you off in the morning, and you are smiling!'

'Don't worry, mother! He who saved my sisters will save me too!'

'Are you sure you'll be as lucky this time?'

'He gave me his word.'

'Who gave you his word?'

'The man who saved my sisters.'

'Who was it? Tell me!'

'You will not tell anyone?'

'Of course not.'

'It's our swineherd!'

'What are you talking about?'

'As God is my witness, it's the swineherd!'

'Well, let's go and fetch him!'

'If he finds out that I have told you about him,' cried the princess, 'he'll kill me, and you too!'

The next morning the King assembled his army and marched out to face the enemy. But he was very afraid, and kept glancing up every minute to see whether the mysterious horsemen were coming from the hills or not. Then he saw a white knight approaching, followed by thirty others.

'Bravo, my lads!' he cried. 'Advance! Advance!'

The army moved forward, and the horsemen fell upon the devs. Slash! and slash again! Strike! and strike again! Slay! and slay again! They massacred them all, until only one remained.

The white knight seized him, cut off his ears, and his snout, and said:

'Now go back whence you came, and bear the news of this defeat with you!'

The white knights galloped back towards the main army.

'When they draw close, surround them, so that they cannot escape this time!' the King quietly instructed his men.

As the group of white knights drew near the King, the young man who had led them into battle said:

'Now make your escape! If I am captured, so be it!'

The horsemen galloped away. The prince drew his knife, made a small cut in his arm, and slowed his pace. The King's men came up and seized him, and brought him to the King.

The King ran to him, kissed the forehead of his horse, put his arm round the young man, and kissed him on the forehead also.

'My kingdom is yours!' he cried.

When he saw blood flowing from the young man's arm, he took his handkerchief out of his pocket and bound it round the wound. No sooner had he done this, however, than the youth leapt on to the back of his horse, gave it two touches on the flanks with his stirrups,[1] and flew off and away like the wind.

When a safe distance away, he released the white horse, changed his apparel, rounded up his pigs, and returned home. When he got back,

---

[1] Spurs are rare in Armenia. Cf. the reference by Captain R. Wilbraham, *Travels in the Transcaucasian provinces*, London, 1839, p. 297, to 'the large shovel stirrup, which serves in lieu of spur'.

he encountered the gay music of fife and drum, and the lights of brightly coloured lanterns. All over the city they were eating, drinking and making merry, to celebrate the great victory.

The youngest princess had prepared a large trayful of delicacies and brought them to the swineherd's hut. This time they sat down, and feasted together.

The King told the Queen how a white knight with thirty companions had come and destroyed the devs; how they had caught him; how he had been injured in the arm; how he, the King, had taken his own handkerchief and bound the wound; how he had wanted to bring him home; and how he had leapt on to his white horse, spurred it on, and escaped.

The Queen was wearing a happy smile.

'What are you smiling at?' asked the King.

'Well,' said the Queen. 'That knight you are talking about is our swineherd.'

'What are you talking about?' said the King.

'What I say is true,' said the Queen. 'Summon him in the morning, and see.'

The King sent for him that very instant, saw that his arm was bandaged, undid the bandage, and recognized his handkerchief.

'What does this mean?' he said.

'When the King's son becomes a swineherd, and the vezier's son becomes the son of a King,' replied the prince, 'it is obvious that the true King's son will act strangely. If you don't believe what I say, call your supposed King's son, and see if he is wearing my gold armband or not!'

The King summoned his intended son-in-law, learned that the armband he was wearing belonged to the supposed swineherd, and put his ideas upon this into effect.

'Executioner!' he cried.

The executioners came and chopped off the impostor's head.

The King returned the armband to the real prince.

'You shall have my youngest daughter as a reward,' he said.

Seven days and seven nights the wedding feast continued, and then the marriage crowns were held over their heads. Five days after he had wed his bride, the prince returned with her to his own country, found that his father had died in his absence, and he reigned in his stead.

And so they achieved their hearts' desire, and whatever any man here may wish for, may his wish come true.

Khozarats, told in 1913 by the illiterate verger Manuk Khachatrian, aged 55, in Vagharshapat, province of Ayrarat; *APT*, II, no. 6.

The Forty Thieves' Apprentice

Once upon a time there was a field-labourer called Ohan. He had one son, and on him the light of the countenance of the Lord failed to shine. He was completely good for nothing! When his father saw that he could not drive any sense into him, he conceived the idea of getting rid of him. He was, however, his only son.

'Wife,' he said, 'I am going to take the boy to learn a trade.'

'Take him anywhere you like!' said the mother.

So he took him, and went. His son, being very green, had no idea of what was afoot. Whether they went a long way or a little way, God alone knows, but they eventually came to some flat, arable land where a couple of houses stood.

'What luck!' said the son. 'We can stay the night here!'

The poor fellow did not know what sort of place it was.

Ohan and his son went into one of the houses. There in front of them sat forty thieves!

'What luck!' said the thieves. 'We have been scouring hill and valley for food, and our prey have come to us on their own little legs! Well, fellow,' they said to Ohan, 'what manner of man are you?'

'I have brought my son to you to learn your trade,' said Ohan.

The forty thieves burst out laughing.

'What sort of trade do you think we are engaged in, that you should want your son to learn it?' they said.

'What is that to me?' said Ohan. 'You make a living by it. Let him too make a living by it!'

'Very well, old man,' said the robbers. 'Stay here tonight, and leave in the morning. When your son has learned our trade, we shall bring him back to you.'

The next morning, after his father Ohan had left, the forty thieves handed the young man a pitcher.

'You will find a well near by,' they said. 'Go and fill this pitcher with water, and bring it back.'

The young man took the pitcher, went to the well, dipped the pitcher in and filled it with water. When he made to take it out again, however, it would not come. He gave it another tug, and this time it came partly out of the water. A pale white hand was clinging to the handle! The young man seized the pitcher with one hand, and the white hand with the other. The owner of the white hand gave a shriek, and quickly pushed a small goblet towards Ohan's son as the price of its liberty. The young man let go of the white hand, took his pitcher out of the spring, and examined the goblet. It was covered with dirt, but when he polished it, he found that it was made of solid gold. He tucked it under his shirt, and took it and the full pitcher back to the thieves' den. The forty thieves had not been expecting him to return, and when they saw him, they were astounded, and looked at him questioningly.

'Where did you get the water, son?' they asked.

For nobody ever returned from the well to which they had sent him to fetch water. Somehow they always tumbled in and drowned, and were never seen again.

'From the well near your house,' replied the youth. 'I dipped the pitcher into the water, and when I went to draw it out again, it would not come. I pulled harder, and saw a white hand clinging to the handle. It was as white as snow. I caught hold of it, but its owner, under the water, put his other hand to his breast-pocket and pulled out this goblet and pushed it towards me. I let go of the hand, and took the goblet. Look, here it is!'

And he took the golden goblet from under his shirt.

The thieves took the golden goblet, examined it, and went mad with excitement.

'This goblet is priceless!' they cried, and all forty thieves embraced their new apprentice. 'Well done!' they cried.

Then, turning to his companions, the robber-chief said:

'Robbery and the life of an outlaw is not for us from now on, lads! Let us sell the goblet for cash, and as long as we live, we shall want for nothing. Lead out my horses. I shall ride into town, sell the goblet, and come back and share the money equally between us. Everyone shall take his share, and return to his own house!'

The robber-chief mounted his horse and rode into town. He went to a money-changer, and asked him to change the goblet for cash.

'This is beyond me,' said the money-changer. 'The only one who can change this into cash is the Jewish money-changer.'

The robber-chief took the goblet to the Jewish money-changer. He took the goblet, examined it, walked up and down, thought, and finally said:

'Let us take this goblet to the King. He will value the goblet, and then I shall pay you the money.'

So they went to the King.

'Your Majesty,' said the Jew. 'That year when they robbed my shop and stole my rubies and jewels, this precious goblet was also stolen. Now the thief himself has brought it to me. I appeal to you to judge this matter. Return my property to me!'

'How did this goblet come into your possession?' the King asked the robber-chief.

'Long live the King!' said the robber. 'We have an apprentice. He found it in a well.'

'What is your trade, then, that you have an apprentice?' said the King. 'Speak plain, or I shall chop off your head!'

'To tell the truth, we are a band of forty thieves,' said the robber-chief. 'We have undertaken to train a new apprentice. It was he who brought the goblet to us.'

The King sent his men to fetch the other thirty-nine thieves and their apprentice.

The apprentice thought quickly.

He came, bowed seven times to the King, and said:

'Long live the King! I found the goblet. If I bring you eleven more like it, you will see that the Jewish money-changer is lying, and you will drive him from your city. If I do not bring you eleven more goblets like it, then you may hang me up by the neck, and my forty friends.'

'Very well,' said the King. 'Ho there! Seize the forty thieves, but permit the apprentice to go in search of the other eleven goblets!'

The youth mounted the robber-chief's horse, took the golden goblet, and rode, and rode, and rode. Whether he rode a long way or a little way, God alone knows, but eventually he arrived at a city which was the capital of a certain kingdom. He went up to one of the houses, and went in. He saw a very old woman sitting there. Her huge beetle brows were so closely knitted together that any flea that fell between them when first they frowned would now be crushed into a hundred pieces!

'Why are you frowning so, grandmother?' the youth asked.

'Uff, don't ask me such things!' said the old woman. 'Sit still, and eat!'

'For the love of God, grandmother,' said the young man, 'tell me why you are frowning so. Perhaps I may be able to find a way to rid you of your sorrow.'

'Alas, fortunate one,' said the old woman. 'Many young men such as you have gone forth and tried to find a cure for my sorrow, but not one has ever succeeded!'

'What is wrong, grandmother?' said the apprentice. 'Tell me!'

'Our King had once a handsome son, but he died, and they buried him. During the day he remains in his tomb, but in the night something digs him out again, and casts him on the surface of the earth, and in the morning he is found with his grave-clothes torn to shreds. We have to wrap him in a fresh winding-sheet, and bury him again.'

'Clear the table, grandmother,' said the apprentice, son of Ohan. 'I have had enough to eat.'

'Why do you not eat, my son?' said the old woman.

'I have had enough, grandmother,' he said. 'It sticks in my throat. Take me to the King. I shall guard his son's tomb, and see that no one removes his gravestone. If I do not succeed, may he hang me up by the neck!'

The old woman led the youth to the King, and told him what he had promised.

'Let him go and keep watch, then,' said the King.

The youth went and placed himself some distance away from the prince's tomb, and sat and watched. At midnight three doves flew up and alighted in front of the tomb. Then they discarded their feathers and turned into three beautiful maidens.

'Let us eat now,' said one to the others. 'Then we shall take the prince from his tomb, and eat again.'

'May your house fall in!' said another. 'Should such a handsome youth remain in the tomb while we eat? Will the food not stick in your throat?'

One of the nymphs took out a table-cloth, held a crimson wand in her hand, tapped the table-cloth with it, and said:

'Table-cloth, spread thyself!'

The table-cloth spread itself over the ground, and a whole meal assembled on top of it, meat, bread, plates, cups, knives, forks and spoons.

The nymphs stood up, went to the entrance of the tomb, and struck the front of it with the crimson wand.

'Stone, swing open!' they commanded.

The heavy stone door to the tomb swung open.

'Earth, gape open!' they commanded.

A gaping hole appeared in the damp earth of the grave. The nymphs lifted out the prince's corpse, laid it on the ground, and struck it with the crimson wand. It immediately came to life, and sat up. The nymphs dressed the dead prince in fine clothes, and placing him at the head of the table, sat in a row in front of him and began to eat.

The young apprentice saw that the three nymphs sat in a single row opposite the prince at the head of the table.

'If I shoot an arrow at the nymphs,' he thought, 'there will be no danger of hitting the prince.'

He loosed an arrow at the three nymphs, just missing them. They fell into great confusion, and had barely time to put on their feathers and fly away. The table-cloth and the crimson wand they left behind. The apprentice went up to the prince.

'Good evening, prince,' he said. 'I am your father's watchman. Let us eat together.'

They ate their meal.

'Now I must return you to your grave,' said the apprentice.

'But I have just been liberated!' protested the prince. 'Let us go to the palace.'

'No, you must stay tonight in your grave,' said the apprentice.

114

He tied the table-cloth round his waist, and picked up the crimson wand. Noticing a ring lying at the edge of the cloth, he picked that up too and put it on his finger.

'Lie down in your grave,' he said to the prince.

The prince did as he was told, the apprentice struck the tomb with the crimson wand, and everything returned to its proper place.

When day broke, the King's men came to find him, and saw that the door of the tomb was in place, and that there was no sign of the prince's desecrated corpse. The chamberlain went to tell the King.

'Your Majesty,' he said, 'light to your eyes! The tomb is just as we left it yesterday!'

The apprentice was brought to the King.

'How did you manage to guard the tomb so well?' asked the King.

'Bring the Queen, and I shall show you,' said the apprentice.

The King, the Queen, the chamberlain, and the apprentice went to the tomb.

'Your Majesty, you can see with your own eyes that the tomb is undisturbed,' said the apprentice. 'What will you give me if I restore your son safe and sound to you?'

'Make any wish, and I shall grant it!' said the King.

The young man took out the golden goblet.

'I want eleven goblets just like this one,' he said. 'Forty comrades of mine are imprisoned on account of it.'

'I have no goblet like that,' said the King. 'Ask for my daughter, she shall be yours! Ask for treasure, it shall be yours! Ask for a city, it shall be yours! But I cannot give you what I do not possess!'

'I have no need of anything else,' said the young man.

He struck the gate of the tomb with the crimson wand, commanded the stone door to open and the earth to render up the dead prince as he had observed the nymphs to do, touched the corpse with the wand, and restored the prince to the world of the living.

Then he sadly mounted his horse, and rode away.

He rode on and on, whether a long way or a short way God alone knows, and finally came to another great city, the capital of a kingdom. Here he entered a house, and found its owner sitting dejectedly inside, his eyebrows also knit together in one great frown.

'Welcome, be my guest, you come with a thousand blessings!' said he. 'But what can I do for you? I can offer you nothing to eat, for there is not a morsel of food in the whole city!'

'Do not worry, brother,' said the apprentice. 'I have food enough with me, whereof you too may eat!'

He took out the magic table-cloth, tapped it with the crimson wand, and the table was laid forthwith.

'Call your children, and let them come and eat their fill,' said the apprentice.

The children came, and they all sat down to eat.

'Tell me,' said the apprentice, when all had eaten, 'how does it happen that there is no bread in your city? Have you no land you can plough, and sow, and harvest?'

'We have no dry and arable land here, brother,' said the man.

'Where do you get your food from, then?' asked the apprentice.

'Our food comes by ship, and we collect it from the harbour.'

'Then why do you not collect it?' said the apprentice.

'Alas, whenever we go to the harbour to collect our wheat and flour from a ship, a hand comes up out of the water and pulls the ship under. We do not know what to do against the hand!'

'If I go and deal with the hand, and bring the ship safely to harbour, and fill your land with food, will your King grant me a wish?' asked the apprentice.

'What would he not give for that?' said the man. 'Anything your tongue can ask for, he will give!'

They rose and went to see the King.

'What will you give me, O King,' said the apprentice, 'if I bring a ship into harbour, and fill your land with food?'

'Make any wish, and I shall grant it!' said the King.

The young man entered a small boat, and rowed out to meet the fleet of merchant vessels. There were forty large ships approaching the shore, all fully laden with flour. As the apprentice rowed up to them, he saw a white hand, with a white bracelet round its wrist, rise out of the foaming sea. He grasped the bracelet firmly in his hand, and pulled hard; as he pulled, the bracelet slipped off the hand, and remained in his own. The hand disappeared swiftly into the depths of the sea. The ships hove to, and came safely to harbour. The city was filled with food to overflowing.

The apprentice went to the King.

'Grant me my wish, Your Majesty,' he said, 'and I shall leave.'

'Make your wish,' said the King.

The young man took out the golden goblet.

'I want eleven goblets identical with this one,' he said.

'Alas, my friend!' said the King. 'That goblet alone is worth my whole kingdom. How should I have eleven like it? Ask for my daughter, she shall be yours! Ask for this city, it shall be yours! Ask for my kingdom, it shall be yours! But I cannot give what I do not possess!'

'There is nothing else I need,' sighed the apprentice. 'My forty comrades languish in captivity, and I cannot sleep or rest, until I take back eleven goblets like this, and so free them.'

'If that is the case,' said the King, 'I shall have a word with my sea-captain, and let you know his answer in the morning.'

The King summoned the old sailor.

'Do you know the feeding-place of the daughters of the King of the Houris?' he asked.

'I do,' said the captain.

'Very good,' said the King. 'There is a youth here. I want you to show him where it is.'

He called the apprentice.

'The captain will show you the feeding-place of the daughters of the King of the Houris,' he said. 'That is where you will find the goblets.'

The young apprentice left his horse with the King, boarded the ship and sailed away. For seven days and seven nights he sailed the seas with the old captain, until they finally dropped anchor on a distant shore. Not far from the coast stood a mansion with a small iron gate.

'That is where you will find the daughters of the King of the Houris,' said the captain. 'When do you intend to return to the ship, so that I may come and fetch you?'

'Give me fifteen days,' said the apprentice.

He knocked on the gate, and went in. He saw a white-haired old man, with his sleeves tucked up to his elbows, preparing a stew.

'May you prosper, grandfather!' said the apprentice.

'All good comes from God! A thousand greetings, son of man!' replied the ancient.

The old man's face was so beautiful, that the young man, try as he might to keep his eyes fixed on it, had to avert them.

'No serpent on its belly, no bird on its wing has ever penetrated as far as this,' said the old man. 'How did you come here?'

'Love of you drew me here,' said the apprentice.

'That is pleasant to hear,' said the old man. 'Hide yourself under these sheets and blankets. The houris will soon be coming, and if they see you, they will do you harm, and then it will be all up with you.'

The apprentice concealed himself beneath the sheets and blankets as he was told, and remained silent.

It was not long before the daughters of the King of the Houris arrived.

'Aha!' they said. 'There is the odour of a human being here!'

'May your house prosper!' said the old man, preparing the stew. 'I am a man. It is me you can smell!'

'No,' they said. 'It is the smell of a stranger!'

'You can see there is no one here.'

'Well, if our meal is ready, let us eat.'

The old man laid the table, and the three sisters sat down. As they did so, the chamberlain of the King of the Houris arrived with a letter in his hand, and asked to come in.

'Be patient,' said the houris. 'Let us eat first, then we shall read the letter.'

During the meal the eldest houri poured out the wine and said:

'I shall drink a toast. I drink to the health of the youth who, though forty thieves for seven years could never drink the water of my well, came to fetch some in a pitcher. The rogue caught me by the wrist and tugged so hard, that I took out a goblet and threw it to him, and so escaped. Long live the apprentice!'

The second sister laughed.

'I must drink a toast, too,' she said.

'Drink!' said her sisters.

The three glasses were filled once more.

'I drink to the health of the youth who seized my table-cloth and my wand, and caused my dead mortal to rise from the grave. Long live the apprentice!' said the second sister.

The youngest sister laughed.

'I shall drink a toast, too,' she said.

'Drink!' said her sisters.

The three glasses were filled again.

'I drink to the health of the youth who seized me by the wrist, stole my bracelet, and robbed me of forty ships laden with flour. Long live the apprentice!' said the youngest sister.

The old man soon guessed who lay concealed under the bedclothes. 'Supposing the youth whom you have so taken to your hearts should appear here,' he said, 'what would you give him?'

'We should give him whatever he wished for!' all three replied together.

The apprentice slipped out from under the bedclothes and stood before them.

'Greetings, angelic nymphs!' he said.

The jaws of the houris dropped in amazement.

'Come, sit with us, and eat!' they cried, when they had recovered their wits.

They all sat down together, and ate.

When the meal was over, the chamberlain came in, bowed seven times, handed a letter to the eldest sister, crossed his hands over his chest, and waited.

The houri opened the letter, read it, and tears welled up in her eyes. The second sister took the letter and read it, and she too began to weep. The little sister took the letter and read it, and she wept more than the others.

'What is in the letter to make you cry so?' asked the youth.

'Shall we tell him?' the sisters asked each other.

'We shall tell him,' they decided.

The eldest sister went to the cupboard, opened it, took out a picture, and brought it to the apprentice.

'We have a brother,' she said. 'For seven years he has been held captive by the giant Azrail, and we have never been able to devise a

118

way of freeing him. If you devise a way, and succeed in freeing our brother, we shall grant you whatever you desire.'

'I shall go and get him,' said the young man.

'It is true that you succeed where no other man has ever succeeded before,' said the houri.

'But what of my own forty brothers who are in captivity?' said the young man. 'What of liberating them?'

'That is easy,' said the houri. 'We can take you to them any day between lunch and supper.'

'Seeing them is easy,' he said. 'But I need another eleven goblets to free them!'

'Oh, what is that to us? We shall give you twenty such!'

'Very well, then!' said the apprentice. 'Let us all visit your father, the King.'

So they all went to the King. The apprentice bowed his head seven times, folded his arms across his chest, and waited.

'What son of man is this that you have brought me, daughters?' said the King of the Houris.

'We have brought the one who shall free our brother from captivity.'

'What! This man can free my son?' said the King. And turning to the apprentice, he said:

'*Can* you free him?'

'With God's help,' said the young man.

'Very well,' said the King. 'Go and free him. Have you ever seen Azrail?'

'No, Your Majesty.'

'You must be well prepared. What do you need for the journey?'

'Let me go to your stables and choose any horse I want. Let me gird your own sword about me, and hang a bow and a quiver of arrows round my shoulder. Give me a mace in my hand, and I shall go and bring back your son.'

'They are all ready for you,' said the King. 'Do you need anything else?'

'I should like a guide to show me the mountain where the giant Azrail dwells,' said the apprentice.

'You shall have one,' said the King. 'God be with you. We are impatient to see what comes of it!'

The young man went to the stables and chose a very fine horse, one which had never beheld the face of the sun, but had danced with the stars. He girt the King's own sword about his loins, hung the bow and quiver of arrows round his shoulder, took the mace in his hand, returned to the King's court, and stood outside. His horse squealed and whinnied, and the King came out. When he beheld the young man fully armed and caparisoned, his soul trembled within him.

'Oho!' he said to himself. 'This son of a dog is sure to bring back our son!'

'Well,' said the youth. 'Tell the chamberlain to mount his horse, and we shall ride forth!'

The chamberlain mounted his horse and rode out in front. They rode and they rode, whether a long way or a little way, God alone knows, until they came to the foot of Mount Djandjavaz, where they halted.

'I had permission to come as far as this, but no farther,' said the chamberlain.

'Farewell, then!' said the apprentice, as he spurred his horse on.

He rode up the mountain-side, and came to a group of tall buildings. The faint sound of voices emerged from them.

'Whoever is the owner of these houses,' shouted the youth, 'let him come forth! I have come to claim blood-money!'

Two large negroes emerged.

'What manner of man are you?' they demanded.

'I have come to claim blood-money,' repeated the apprentice.

The two negroes came across the square and barred his path.

'What fellow is this, that we should disturb our master's sleep and bid him rise on his account?' they said.

The youth saw that the two negroes intended to bar his way, and drawing his sword, he struck off both their heads with a single blow. He dismounted, picked up the two heads and flung them up on to the balcony. The noise woke the giant Azrail. He came out on to the balcony, and saw a hot-blooded young fellow shouting his lungs out below. And how he shouted!

'Wait!' said Azrail. 'I am coming! I am going to chop you in little pieces and leave only your ears!'

He came down, saddled and harnessed his horse, and came out on to the square to confront the young man.

'Welcome! a thousand times welcome, young man!' said the giant. 'We shall fight by striking blow for blow in turn. Who shall go first?'

'You go first,' said the apprentice. 'I am only a guest. You have seven maces, seven arrows, and seven swords. Strike first! God shall decide between us!'

Azrail hurled his club at the youth. Mountains and valleys shook, but it passed over the head of the apprentice. The young man picked it up.

'There is no time for games!' he said. 'Take it back and throw it again, this time in earnest!'

The giant threw all his seven clubs, and all missed. He shot his seven arrows, and all flew past the apprentice. He hurled his seven swords, and all smashed against the rocks.

'Now it is your turn!' he said, and stood ready.

The young man spurred his horse. The horse galloped furiously towards the giant, and the sweat streamed from its forehead, half blinding it. The young apprentice sped to the edge of the square, stood up in the saddle, and flung his club. It caught Azrail on the side of the head, and smashed it right in. The giant fell down stone dead. The youth dismounted, and struck off his head with his sword. The gigantic head rolled off along the ground.

'Where is it rolling to?' wondered the young man, and raising his sword again, he gave it a tremendous slash, and cut it into two.

'One more blow!' pleaded the head.

'I cannot,' panted the youth. 'I was born with only one such blow in me!'

He tethered his horse to the gates of the mansion, and went in.

In one of the rooms he found the son of the King of the Houris trussed up in chains. He struck them off with his sword. 'Come, let us return to your father,' he said.

The prince rose, mounted his horse, and rode off with the apprentice. As they approached the city of the King, the prince said:

'Brave youth, when you bring me to my father, and he asks you what you want as a reward, tell him you want my little sister as your bride, and the ring on his finger.'

They entered the palace. Father, mother, and sisters all rushed to embrace the prince, and wept for joy.

'Make a wish,' said the King to the apprentice, 'and I shall grant it!'

'I wish for the health of your soul!' said the young man.

'Make a wish for yourself!' said the King.

'I desire your youngest daughter to be my bride, the ring from your finger, and the eleven golden goblets, O King of the Houris,' said the apprentice.

'They are yours,' said the King. 'Take them, and prosper!'

The wedding celebrations went on for seven days and seven nights. The houri princess and the young apprentice were married and lodged in a suite of rooms in the palace. On the wedding night the young husband drew his sword and placed it between his bride and himself.

'Do you not trust me, or my father,' said the princess, 'that you draw your sword and place it between us?'

'Before anything else,' said her husband, 'I must go and free my forty comrades, who languish in gaol!'

On the morrow the young man rose, took the eleven golden goblets, and prepared to travel back to his native land. He took his bride back to her father's part of the palace before he went, much to the King's amazement. Then he made his way back home, went to his own King's palace, and laid the eleven golden goblets before him. The first was placed among them, and the Jewish money-lender was summoned and confronted with the twelve golden goblets.

'Tell us which one of these goblets belongs to you,' said the King.

The money-lender picked them up, looked from one to the other, and could no longer recognize the one he had claimed to be his. The King saw that he had been basely deceived, and ordering the forty innocent thieves to be released, he called for his executioner, and made mincemeat of the treacherous money-lender.

Then the apprentice left the palace, and summoned his young bride to be at his side. It was not long before one of the courtiers told the King of the presence of the houri princess in his city.

'The young man brought a most beautiful maiden with him,' he said. 'Summon her to your presence and see for yourself.'

The King was very old, and had no heir to his throne. He summoned the houri princess, and when he saw her, his head reeled, and the earth seemed to shake under his feet.

'Whose daughter are you, good maiden?' he asked at last.

'I am the daughter of the King of the Houris.'

'Have you accepted this young man to be your husband?'

'I have.'

The King summoned his people.

'I declare my intention to give my kingdom, of my own free will, to this young man,' he cried. 'Do you agree?'

'We agree!' shouted the people.

The King took the ring from his finger and gave it to the young apprentice.

'As you give me your kingdom by token of this ring,' said the young man, 'so I give you this royal ring.' And he handed the King the ring given to him by the King of the Houris.

And so the young apprentice became King, and appointed his comrades, the forty thieves, to be veziers, chamberlains, ministers and officials in his kingdom.

And so they all achieved their hearts' desire, as may you also!

Three apples fell from Heaven: one for the story-teller, one for his listener, and one for him who lends an ear.

> *Ohan rénchpari tghi heqiathë*, literally, 'The tale of the son of the labourer Ohan', told in 1912 by the illiterate vine-dresser Gevorg Gevorgian, aged 60, in the village of Ashtarak, province of Ayrarat; *APT*, I, no. 8.

The Little Seamstress

Once upon a time there was a tailor and his wife, who had an only daughter, as dear to them as the apple of their eye.

One day the father took his daughter and placed her with an old woman to learn to sew.

Opposite the old woman's house stood the royal palace. The King had an only son, and from morn till eve the prince would walk up and down the balcony, wondering how to catch a glimpse of the girl's face, and how to get her to talk to him.

For whenever she passed by, the little seamstress would keep her eyes modestly fixed on the ground, and pay not the slightest attention to the prince.

One day the prince thought of a way to make her speak to him, and he called to her from the balcony as she passed:

'Hey there, tailor's daughter, little bitch! How many threads are there in a piece of cloth?'

The girl did not reply.

The prince repeated his question three times.

Then the little seamstress, still averting her head, said:

'Hey there, King's son, son of a dog! How many stars are there in the heavens?'

The little seamstress repeated her question three times. She still would not look up at the prince.

The next day the prince thought and thought, wondering how to play a trick on the girl, and get his revenge. He summoned the old woman who was teaching the girl to sew.

'Grandmother,' he said, 'I shall give you whatever you want, but you must bring me to your little apprentice, so that I may give her a kiss.'

'Very well, prince,' said the old woman. 'May I be a sacrifice to your head and your life! Your wish is my command.'

The following morning she got out a large wooden chest, and unbeknown to the little seamstress, summoned the prince and hid him inside, covering the outside with various dresses. She then gave her girl apprentice the following instructions:

'My child, when you go back to the house, put your needlework away in the large wooden chest you will find there.'

'Very well,' said the girl; and when she returned to the house, she lifted the lid of the chest to put her needlework in. Out popped the prince, who caught her round the waist and kissed her.

The little seamstress made no song and dance about it. She said nothing, and went home. Lying in bed and pretending to be ill, she did not return to the old woman's house for one or two days.

'What shall I do to get my revenge?' she kept asking herself.

Her mother and father saw that she was brooding.

'My child,' they said, 'what are you brooding about? Tell us what you want, and we shall do it for you, if we can!'

'Father,' said the little seamstress. 'Sew me a large white cloak, and make it so that only my eyes will be visible when I put it on. Stitch some feathers on the back to look like angels' wings, and cover it all over with little bells and baubles, so that there is not even room for the head of a needle to penetrate.'

Her father made the cloak as she instructed, and brought it to her.

'Try it on, my child,' he said. 'It has given me a lot of trouble. Walk about in it, so that I can see if it needs altering.'

She put it on, flounced about and flapped the wings, and was satisfied that she really did look like an angel in it. She took it off again.

'I am going to my sewing-mistress's house now,' she said. 'I shall not be back tonight.'

She went to the old woman's house.

'I am going to stay with you again tonight,' she said. 'My mother and father have had to go on a journey.'

'Very well, my child,' said the old woman. 'If you want to stay here, stay.'

That evening, after supper, the little seamstress secretly left the house and went to the palace. When everyone was asleep, she crept into the prince's antechamber, put on her new costume, and then tip-toed into the prince's bedroom. Here she hopped about and flapped her arms, and the sound of tiny bells filled the room.

The prince opened his eyes and saw the strange white figure standing over him. He was terrified!

'Eugh! What are you! What do you want of me?' he stammered.

'I am the angel Gabriel,' said the vision. 'I have come to take your soul!'

'I am an only son!' cried the prince. 'Take all my treasure! Take my hidden gold! But do not take my soul!'

'If it is like that,' said the apparition, 'I shall give you ten days' grace. But I shall have to take a token from your bedroom with me as surety!'

The prince was trembling and shaking hand and foot.

'I leave it to you!' he chattered. 'Take whatever you can find!'

The angel picked up the golden wash-basin.

'Prepare yourself!' she said. 'In ten days' time I shall come for your soul!'

Then she left.

The little seamstress took off her disguise, went back home, wrapped the golden wash-basin in some old clothes, and put it in a chest. Dawn broke. The little seamstress sat down to her work.

The prince was completely shattered by his experience with the Angel of Death. He got up half paralysed, then crawled out, very slowly, on to the balcony.

'Before I do die,' he said, 'I shall make that girl talk to me!'

And when she passed by, he called out:

'Hey there, tailor's daughter, little bitch! How many kisses are there in a wooden chest?'

He repeated his question three times.

The little seamstress raised her head.

'Hey there, King's son, son of a dog!' she replied, 'how many angel Gabriels are there? King's son, son of a dog! How many golden wash-basins are there? King's son, son of a dog! How many ten days' grace are there?'

The prince pondered deeply on these words.

'That girl is an astrologer!' he said to himself. 'She has read the stars and learned of my coming death!'

He went in and threw himself on his bed.

'Woe is me! woe is me!' he wept. 'I am going to die!'

As he lay there, he began to think.

'That girl knows all about my coming death, about the number of stars in the sky, about the angel Gabriel. I must marry her!'

And he devised a way to get the little seamstress to be his wife. He sent his valet to his father, the King, to tell him that he was dying, and needed a priest.

His father and mother hurried to his bedside.

'What does our kingdom lack, that you should lie there and cry "Woe is me! woe is me!", son?' they cried. 'We shall send a man from one town to another to find you a good doctor!'

'I want the tailor's daughter!' said the prince. 'Ask for her hand for me.'

'Very well,' said the King. 'If she will come voluntarily, well and good; but we'll fetch her by force if need be, so long as you get better!'

He summoned his chamberlains and ministers, and sent them to the tailor's house to ask for his daughter's hand in marriage for the prince. When his daughter came home, her father said:

'They have come from the court to ask for your hand, daughter. Do you want to marry the King's son?'

'If you are willing to give me away, father,' she said, 'then I am willing to marry him.'

126

So the parents took the little seamstress to the palace, and she was married to the prince.

The girl had taken her angel's robe with her, together with her dowry and trousseau.

But after the wedding, her husband refused to get out of bed, and lay there crying, 'Woe is me! woe is me! I am going to die!', all day long. He paid not the slightest attention to his new bride.

'King's son,' she said, 'if you do not like me, why did you marry me?'

'Alas, tailor's daughter!' sighed the prince. 'What can I do? In six days' time I am going to die!'

'If you have only six days left,' said his wife, 'I am leaving you!'

She rose and dressed, went out into the antechamber, and donned her angel's robe.

'My wife has left me!' wept the prince. 'And I am going to die!'

Just as he said that, the girl came into his bedroom dressed in her angel's robe with the feathery wings and little bells, and flapped and fluttered about.

'Alas!' lamented the prince. 'The angel Gabriel has come while it is still day!'

The apparition spoke.

'Now that you are married,' it said, 'I may as well take your soul straight away!'

The prince could not utter a word, and his knees knocked.

When his wife saw this, she relented, lest the prince should fall really ill, and she nudged him with her elbow.

'You silly fool!' she laughed. 'I am not the angel Gabriel! I am your wife!'

This the prince could not believe.

'If you are my wife,' said the prince, 'show me my golden wash-basin!'

The little seamstress went to the chest of drawers, took out the golden wash-basin, and placed it in front of the prince. He was still incredulous.

'If you are my wife,' insisted the prince, 'take off that robe, and let me see!'

The little seamstress took off her disguise.

'Wife, you must be a witch!' said the prince. 'Tell me straight, are you on familiar terms with angels? Can you see the future?'

'I foresee that you will have a long life, and never die, and will one day be king of this land!' replied the little seamstress.

'How many stars *are* there in the heavens, then?' asked the prince.

'Since you asked me, you must know!'

'Then tell me how many threads there are in a piece of cloth,' replied his wife, 'for that is just the number of the stars in the heavens!'

Her husband saw how he had been outwitted, and he laughed. He

127

rose from his bed, and the wedding festivities continued for seven days and seven nights.

And as they achieved their hearts' desire, so may you also.

Derdziki aghdjik, 'The tailor's daughter', told in the 19th century by a certain Ephrem Vasakian, of whom nothing but his name is known: *APT*, III, no. 12.

The Rose Garden of Shah Abbas

Once upon a time there was a poor woodcutter living in Isfahan, which was the capital of the Persian King, Shah-oghlu[1] Shah Abbas. However much he longed for an heir to the throne, the King had no son, and finally, in desperation, he vowed never again to set foot in his beloved Rose Garden, Gulshan, until God should grant him one.

One day the poor woodcutter and his wife were talking together.

'Husband,' said the wife. 'From now on, of every two loads of kindling you gather, we shall sell one to buy food with, and keep the other for a time of need, for when we are ill, or too old and weak to gather any.'

'You are right, wife,' said her husband. 'Wake me very early in the morning, and I shall go and fetch two loads of brushwood. One load we shall sell for food, and the other I shall give you to keep for a rainy day.'

The cock chanced to crow while it was still night, and the wife woke her husband.

'Get up, husband,' she said. 'It is time for you to go to the forest.'

Her husband got up, washed his face, crossed himself, and went out.

'I am off now, wife,' he said. 'Bolt the door after me.'

It was still dark. He walked towards the sea-shore, and there he saw three men sitting by the sea. They were writing something in a large book.

'When did you start out then, to get here before me?' asked the poor man, in some amazement. 'I suppose you will have gathered all the brushwood worth having. What shall *I* do?'

'We are not woodcutters,' they said.

'What are you, then?' the poor man asked.

'We distribute Light and Darkness among men,' they said.

'May I die at your feet!' cried the poor man. 'Can you not do something for me? This going back and forth to gather firewood has worn me out, and I have no son to help me.'

'God has prepared great things for you,' said the three men.

'What are they?'

'God has granted you twin sons. One shall rule the Kingdom of the East, the other shall rule the Kingdom of the West,' said the three men. 'And since you have been so fervent in your prayers, old man, we

[1] i.e. 'son of a Shah'.

shall give you an egg which will shine in the dark, and which you must keep hidden under a pot during the day. Say nothing about this to anyone. Every evening take the egg and place it before you, make forty genuflexions in front of it, recite the evening prayer, and then go about your business.'

The woodcutter took the proffered egg, put it in his breast-pocket, gathered two loads of brushwood, put them on his back, and went to the bazaar. Here he sold both loads, took the money, and went home.

'Light to your eyes, wife!' he said.

'Husband, what has happened?' said his wife. 'Where is the brushwood?'

'Wife, take care not to tell anyone what God has given us!'

'What has he given us?'

'He has given us an egg.'

'But the house is full of *eggs*, at least!' cried his wife. 'What is special about that?'

'Wife, this is an egg that shines in the dark! We shall never need to spend any more on candles.'

'Let me see!'

They went to a dark part of the house, solemnly laid out their worn old carpet, and placed the egg in front of them. It shone like fire, and illumined the whole room!

'That is surely from God,' said the wife.

The poor man and his wife recited the evening prayer, and made forty genuflexions. Then they went about their ordinary tasks. This they repeated every evening.

Now it happened that Shah Abbas had commanded his herald to proclaim a curfew throughout the city of Isfahan, forbidding anyone to keep a light burning after dark. For his capital had become a prey to great disorder, and it was his intention to walk through its streets at night, to try to find the cause of the mischief.

'Bring me two dervish's robes,' he commanded his vezier, 'and we shall put them on and walk through the streets of the capital in disguise.'

The Shah and his vezier put on the robes, and set out at nightfall to walk abroad through the streets of Isfahan.

'Find a high place and climb to the top of it, vezier,' ordered the Shah, 'and see if you can see a light burning anywhere in the city.'

The vezier did as he was bidden. He climbed on top of a high mound, and looked about him.

'There is no light anywhere, Your Majesty,' he said, 'except for a small ray of light which is shining on the extreme edge of the city.'

'Let us go and find it!' said the Shah. 'That is where the brigands will be, for sure!'

The King and his minister made for the edge of the city, and came to the poor woodcutter's house.

'Did you perpetrate any misdeeds in your youth, vezier?' asked the Shah.

'I am not a criminal, Your Majesty!' protested his chief minister.

'Then you had better not go in there,' said the Shah. 'They will see straight away that you are not one of them! Climb on to the roof and see what they are doing.'

The vezier climbed on to the roof, looked through the skylight, and saw a man and a woman asleep in bed, with a bright light burning in a bowl beside them.

The vezier climbed down from the roof.

'You would not understand if I told you, Your Majesty,' he said. 'Climb up and see for yourself.'

The Shah climbed up on to the roof, looked through the skylight, and saw what his vezier had seen. The woodcutter and his wife lay asleep, dead to the world. The Shah realized what it was that emitted the bright light in the bowl, and started.

'Vezier!' he exclaimed. 'That must be a jewel they have stolen from my counting-house! What luck to have found it again!'

He climbed down.

'We shall put a mark on the door. In the morning we shall summon the man to the palace, and send him to the gallows!'

Dawn came, and the woodcutter and his wife got up.

'Give me my rope, wife,' said the husband, 'and I shall go and gather the brushwood.'

As the wife got up and handed her husband his rope, there was a loud hammering on the door.

'Who is there?' said the woodcutter.

'Open the door! The Shah has summoned you to the palace!'

'What have I done?' protested the poor woodcutter. He clasped his hands to his head, not knowing what to say. He opened the door, and was led away.

They brought the poor woodcutter to Shah Abbas. He bowed seven times, crossed his hands on his chest seven times, and waited.

'Well, fellow!' said the Shah. 'Who gave you the stone?'

'Long live the Shah!' cried the woodcutter. 'Three men sitting writing on the sea-shore and distributing Light and Darkness among men gave me it.'

'Do not lie to me, or I shall chop off your head!' thundered the Shah.

He called for his executioners, one, the *milchi*, skilled in putting out eyes with a red hot bodkin, and another in chopping off heads, and they ran in and stood before him.

'Do not kill me, Sire!' said the poor woodcutter. 'I have told you the truth! Three men distributing Light and Darkness among men gave me the egg!'

132

'If that is true, go and fetch it and give it to me,' said the Shah. 'I shall pay you what it is worth.'

'Give me seven days' grace, Your Majesty,' pleaded the poor man, 'and I shall give you the stone. You know that I will not run away!'

'Very well,' said Shah Abbas. 'I shall give you seven days' grace.'

The woodcutter returned home.

'Alas, wife!' he cried. 'The Lord giveth and the Lord taketh away!'

'What has happened?' said his wife. 'Tell me what has happened!'

'We must give the magic stone to the Shah,' replied her husband. 'But what if we give half to him, and keep half for ourselves? He has given us seven days' grace. We shall fast for those seven days, lament and call upon God, and perhaps the stone will divide into two, so that we may give one half to the Shah, and keep the other for ourselves.'

For seven whole days the poor man and his wife fasted, lamented, and prayed to God, and in the end the stone broke into two. The woodcutter took one half and gave it to the Shah, and they kept the other for themselves.

One night the woodcutter's wife gave birth to twins, two boys. They were graced with such beauty that they might well have bidden the sun to cease to rise in the heavens, and to leave the work of lighting the world to them!

The poor woodcutter went out to find someone who would be willing to act as their godfather and spiritual guardian. Search as he might, he could find no one.

'If that is how it is, wife,' he said, when he returned home, 'I shall have to find the three men who granted us these children, so that they may come and consecrate their gift. Wrap me up two loaves of bread, and I'll be on my way.'

His wife wrapped him two loaves, and the woodcutter set out to search high and low for the three mysterious scribes. When he came to the Northern Range, he saw the three beings sitting at the edge of a lake, writing in their book.

'Greetings, O Givers of the Priceless Jewel!' he said. 'Come and consecrate the children you have granted us, for I can find no one to be their godfather and guardian.'

'Return home, woodcutter,' said one of the men. 'Tomorrow I shall stay as a guest at the royal court. I shall take one of the children, and give the other to Shah Abbas. Return in peace to your house, and wash and clean it thoroughly, so that when the Shah and I arrive, everything shall be spotless.'

The woodcutter, reassured, returned home and did as they commanded.

One of the Fates was a young, handsome man, and it was he who went to the court of Shah Abbas to be his guest. When he arrived, the Shah was much impressed, and took him to be a king like himself.

'Why do you disregard the poor, O King?' said the visitor.

'What do you mean, brother?' said Shah Abbas.

'If you care to look, brother, you will find many sinless men among the poor. Free them from their poverty! If you have a door that is shut, open it. If you have a door that is open, shut it. I have heard that you keep the gate to your famous Rose Garden, Gulshan, closed. Open it. Spread carpets all the way from your palace to the poor woodcutter's cottage. Place lighted candles all along the route, with guards at every one to ensure that none go out, and we shall go together to the wood-cutter's dwelling. I shall be godfather to one of his twin boys, and you shall be godfather to the other.'

The Shah willingly agreed. They rose and made their way to the poor woodcutter's house. One took one boy, and one the other, and brought them to the church, where they were baptized, and hugged to their godmothers' bosoms.[1]

'Brother King,' said the Distributor of Light and Darkness. 'When our godchildren grow up, will you undertake to have them taught to read and write?'

'I shall,' replied Shah Abbas. 'And I shall adopt the one who does best to be my son, for I have no son of my own to inherit my throne.'

The poor woodcutter continued his lowly occupation. The children grew quickly, and by the time they were eight or ten years old, they were sturdy young boys.

'Dear, what cares the children bring us!' exclaimed the woodcutter's wife. 'But the King has acted as godfather to one of them, and it is time to ask him to have them taught to read and write.'

The woodcutter got up, and hurried off to the King.

'Long live the King!' he said. 'The time has come to educate the children.'

'Return to your dwelling,' said the Shah, 'and tomorrow morning the Queen and I shall visit you.'

And to the Queen he said:

'Light to your eyes, Queen! We who were childless shall now be the parents of a son!'

Then he summoned the gardener.

'Water all the flowers in my Rose Garden, Gulshan, that they may flourish as they did once before when I first saw them in the company

[1] It is not, of course, possible for a Muslim to act as godfather to a Christian child. But Shah Abbas, who settled the Armenians in New Julfa by Isfahan in A.D. 1604 to encourage trade in his kingdom, is in fact known to have attended important Christian festivals in the Armenian cathedral. The fictional procession from the palace to the woodcutter's house described above may even reflect an actual occasion such as that of 6th January 1619 when the Epiphany procession, with crosses, silver bells and lighted candles, to the banks of the Zanderood river, was joined by Shah Abbas and two of his (own) sons along roads especially cleared for his passage (see J. Carswell, *New Julfa*, Oxford University Press, 1968, p. 6).

of my father, the late Shah!' he said. 'As for those that do not appear to flourish, cut off their heads!'

Shah Abbas took with him two fine suits of clothes and two royal ribbons, so that those who saw what the boys wore would understand that they were close in succession to the throne, and he accompanied the Queen to the woodcutter's hut.

'Greetings, gossip,' said the King. 'Where are the children? Call them for us.'

The woodcutter fetched his sons.

'These are my two sons, may they serve you well, Your Majesty,' he said.

To the music of twelve minstrels, who had come to accompany the joyous occasion, the Shah dressed the two boys in the rich clothes he had brought, and tied the royal ribbons to their arms.

'Now let us proceed to the Rose Garden,' said the Shah, and he bade the woodcutter and his wife farewell.

Shah Abbas took one boy on his arm, his Queen the other boy on her arm, and to the accompaniment of lutes and singing voices, they all made their way in procession towards the royal Rose Garden.

Everything was already well prepared in the Rose Garden when they entered. They sat down to a banquet, and ate and drank merrily. Two nightingales flew down on the two boys, and settled on their heads. They began to sing.

'It would be pleasant to know what the nightingales are saying, King,' said the Queen.

'Your Majesty, if you will permit me, I shall tell you,' said the younger of the twins.

'You have our permission, my son,' said the Shah. 'Tell us!'

'The nightingales are saying, "What a pity it is that the Shah should make such a wasted effort on the twins' behalf, for one boy will eventually acquire the Kingdom of the East, and the other the Kingdom of the West!"'

'Would God grant that to people of humble birth?' exclaimed the Shah, in amazement. 'Surely such things do not happen to commoners?'

'Your Majesty will surely not believe that nonsense,' said the elder twin.

'No,' said the Shah. 'In any case, it is said to be for the future. I have been very generous to you so far, and there is no reason why I should not continue to favour you.'

He took the children back to his palace with him, and entrusted them to the care of a tutor.

'How many years will it take to educate these children properly, schoolmaster?' he said.

'Seven years, Sire,' replied the tutor.

'Then take them away and do what is necessary,' said the Shah.

The tutor took the children and led them away to his school. When seven years had passed, the Shah summoned the Queen and his twelve veziers and they all went to visit the school. Knocking on the door, he called upon the schoolmaster to assemble all his three hundred pupils.

Outside the two nightingales who had perched on the boys' heads in the Rose Garden seven years previously flew down and perched on the window-sill, twittering excitedly.

'Open the windows and let the birds in!' said the Shah.

When the windows were opened, the two nightingales flew in and settled on the boys' heads as before. They began to talk, and it was clear that they had much to say to each other. The Shah commanded that if anyone among the three hundred pupils in the school understood what they were saying, he should speak.

The younger godson raised his hand.

'Shall I tell you, Your Majesty?' he said.

'Tell me, my son,' said the Shah.

'The nightingales are saying, "What a pity it is that the Shah of Persia should bear the expense of educating the twins, for one of them shall rule the Kingdom of the East, and the other shall rule the Kingdom of the West." '

The Shah paid the schoolmaster his due.

This time he took notice of the nightingales' prophecy, and decided that it would be better for the two young men to depart from his kingdom, and seek the fortune said to be in store for them.

'You must go out into the world and see what awaits you there,' he told them.

The twins returned to their mother and father, said good-bye, and set off to seek their fortune. Whether they went a long way or a little way, God alone knows, but they finally arrived at a fork in the road.

'Well, brother,' said the elder of the twins, 'this is my way, and that is your way. I am going to the East, and you to the West.'

The elder brother walked on until he found himself in the middle of a large forest. He came to a well, and since it was growing dark, he decided to pass the night in its proximity.

'If I sleep on the ground,' he said to himself, 'I could easily be attacked. I shall climb up a tree, spend the night in its branches, and continue my way tomorrow.'

He climbed up the tree over the well.

Now although he was not aware of it, he had in fact already arrived in the Kingdom of the East. The King's son chanced to have spent the day hunting game, and now, in the evening, he led his horse to the well to allow it to quench its thirst. But the horse suddenly caught sight of the reflection of the young man in the tree on the surface of the water, and it shied away. The prince glanced up, and saw a handsome youth resting in the branches of the tree.

'Ho there!' he cried. 'You have frightened my horse! Are you a man, or some fiery sprite?'

'I am a man like you, brother,' replied the youth.

'Come down, and tell me who you are, and whose son you are.'

'I am the elder son of Shah Abbas.'

'Where are you going?' asked the prince.

'I am looking for a beautiful bride,' said the young man.

'You will find one at my house!' said the prince. 'Come down and hold my horse, and I shall go and tell my father the King to invite you to the palace with full honours.'

The young man came down and held the prince's horse, while the prince went back to his father's palace.

'Light to your eyes, Your Majesty,' he said.

'What is it, my boy?' said his father.

'A young man has come to ask for the hand of my sister in marriage.'

'Who is he, my boy?'

'The son of Shah Abbas.'

'Why are you on foot? Why have you left your horse in the forest?'

'I have come to fetch some men to accompany the prince hither in fitting style.'

The King flared up.

'You have been tricked, my son!' he cried. 'He will have stolen your horse by now! It is useless to go back!'

'There is no danger of that, Your Majesty!' replied his son. 'He is clearly not that sort of man. Give me some men, and I shall go and fetch him.'

At this moment the Queen came in.

'What is the matter?' she asked.

'The son of Shah Abbas has come to ask for the hand of our daughter,' said the King.

'In that case, our daughter shall prepare for the young prince's visit,' said the Queen.

The prince took ten good men to the forest, and they accompanied the young man back to the palace in great style.

The King gave him a very friendly reception.

'What do you want, my boy?' he asked. 'Make a wish, and I shall grant it.'

'I wish only for your good health, Your Majesty,' said the young man. 'Nothing else.'

He withdrew to his bedchamber to sleep. In the morning, he came down and went to wash his face in the marble fountain. The King's daughter brought a towel and put it in the young man's hand. He wiped his face, returned the towel to the princess, and went away without saying a word.

The girl went back to her mother.

'Mother!' she said. 'If I live, may it be at the side of that young man! If I die, may it be at the side of that young man! But why will he not speak to me?'

The Queen told the King of the young prince's strange behaviour.

'Ask that young man why he has come here, King,' she said. 'Perhaps he is too shy to ask for the princess's hand.'

The King approached the young man.

'My son,' he said, 'why do you say nothing? I have asked you to make a wish, which I shall grant. Do not be shy! Ask for something.'

'What I want, O King,' said the youth, 'is your daughter's hand in marriage. That is my reason for coming here.'

'If that is so, I give you my daughter and my kingdom, for when I am dead, the kingdom shall be yours.'

The wedding festivities continued for seven days and seven nights, and they married the young man to the princess. And after a few months the young man acquired the kingdom also, for his father-in-law was very old and his son very stupid, doing nothing but ride in and out of the forest to hunt for game. The affairs of the city were in a state of chaos when he came to the throne, but he put them in such order, that in the whole world no city was ever so well organized as his. Whenever a merchant came there, he was required to pay tribute to the King in exchange for the privilege of selling his wares in the city, which guaranteed the prosperity of the realm.

Let us then leave the woodcutter's elder son ruling over his Kingdom of the East, and return to his younger brother.

The younger brother rode on until he came to a small group of dwellings nestling in the midst of a range of mountains.

'What good fortune!' he said. 'I shall spend the night here and depart in the morning.'

He entered one of the houses, and found forty thieves sitting in front of him.

'Greetings, brother robbers!' he said.

'A thousand welcomes, prince,' they replied.

Now it was the custom of the robber-chief to cut the throat of every traveller who came there.

'Who are you, and whose son are you?' he now asked.

'I am the son of Shah Abbas,' replied the young man. 'My father is most tyrannical, and I have left home to travel to the West.'

'Whoever comes to our house,' said the robber-chief, 'usually has his throat cut. But you have an easy and pleasant manner about you, and I shall adopt you as my son.'

'Why?' said the young man.

'Well, you must know that the daughter of our King of the West is a formidable female warrior. Any man that goes to woo her must do battle with her, and if he loses, his head is chopped off. Fifty young men have lost their heads for her already. A pity about your own head, for you are about to try your luck yourself. But I shall teach you a stratagem by which you may overcome the princess. When you become king, you shall make me your vezier. I am tired of being an outlaw.'

The robber-chief gave the young man a horse, a bow and arrows, and a mace.

'Tomorrow morning,' he said, 'I and my men shall ride to the jousting-ground with you to test your valour. I have already witnessed what the princess can do.'

At daybreak the following day they all sallied forth to the jousting-ground. The forty thieves formed up on one side of the square, and the young man stood alone on the other.

'You throw your mace first,' said the robber-chief.

The young man spurred on his horse.

'Robber-chief,' he cried, 'your horse is about to perish, but I shall not harm you!'

And he hurled his heavy club straight at the head of the robber's horse. The animal staggered at the impact, and fell down stone dead.

'Well done!' cried the robber-chief. 'I did not expect such prowess. You clearly have all the accomplishments of a nobleman. Go and marry the princess. I shall give you money for the journey, so that you may stay at the inn like a gentleman. At daybreak tomorrow you shall go to the jousting-ground and do battle with the princess.'

He took out a fat purseful of coins, handed them to the young man, and kissed him on the forehead.

'Go, and God be with you!' he said. 'Bring me word of what happens.'

The young man mounted his horse and set off for the city. He put up at the inn, stabled his horse, and went to his room.

'Greetings, young man!' said the innkeeper. 'Where are you from?'

'I am the son of Shah Abbas, and I have come to ask for the hand of the daughter of your King,' he replied.

'Alas! your journey is in vain, my son!' said the innkeeper.

'Why so?'

'So long as no one is capable of prevailing over her in combat, so long will her suitors' heads continue to roll,' said the innkeeper. 'It would be a pity to waste your young life. Go back where you came from.'

'Tomorrow, dead or alive, I shall be at the jousting-ground,' said the youth.

The innkeeper sent one of his servants to inform the princess that a young man had come to ask for her hand, and that she should come and see him for herself.

The princess, whose name chanced to be Gulshan, or 'Garden of Roses', like that of Shah Abbas's favourite pleasure-garden, put on her clean clothes, and accompanied by forty handmaidens, made her way, singing softly, to the inn where the young man was staying. She went in, and as soon as her eyes fell upon her new suitor, she felt as though the ground had been knocked from under her feet!

'Tomorrow this youth will vanquish me and win me as his bride, that is certain!' she said to herself. 'The hand is the servant of the head, and my hand will not have the power to throw a mace at him. For where should I find another like him to be my husband?'

She returned to the palace.

'Your Majesty,' she said to her father. 'A young man has come to sue for my hand who is more handsome than all the angels in Heaven! When I beheld him, my senses reeled! How shall I be able to throw a mace at him?'

'My child,' said the King. 'If you are sure you will not have the power to vanquish him in single combat, let me send a messenger and summon him to the palace, and give him your hand without more ado.'

'Father,' said the princess. 'I do not know whether I am alive or dead! Let me have him for my husband without the usual combat. Let us accept him right away!'

The King sent a messenger to the young man, summoning him to the palace. But the young man would not go.

'Until the princess and I have met on the jousting-ground,' he said, 'I shall not go to the palace.'

The good light of day broke upon them, and the Shah's adopted son rose, washed his face, ate his breakfast, harnessed his horse, led it from the stable, mounted, and rode out to station himself at the head of the jousting-ground.

The King was informed. His daughter dressed herself in black Arab robes, mounted her horse, and rode to the other end of the square to confront her adversary.

The King ordered all shops to shut so that everybody could come to the square to watch, and see that justice was done in deciding who had won the contest. All the people assembled in a great multitude. The King and Queen sat in their seats, the people in theirs.

The young man bowed low before the King, and asked for his permission to do battle with the princess.

The battle commenced.

'You are at the head of the square, good youth,' said the princess, 'and I at the foot. It is your turn to throw your mace.'

Her adversary wheeled his horse round three times, and the princess observed that he was an exceptionally well-built young man.

'The son of a dog is a powerful brute,' thought the princess. 'He is sure to get the better of me!'

The young man rode in front of the King and Queen, and bowed low before them seven times.

'The fate of our daughter is out of our hands,' said the King to the

Queen. 'What a strong fellow that is! We must pray that his mace hits the horse, and not our daughter!'

The woodcutter's son took his place on the jousting-ground, and stood up in his saddle.

'This is for your horse's head!' he cried, and hurled his heavy mace. It struck the princess's horse between the eyes, and it fell dead on the spot. The young man dismounted, and drew his sword. Placing it between his teeth, he rushed at the princess, and threw her to the ground with his bare hands. He placed his knee on her heart, seized her by her sixty golden ringlets, and thrust her head back hard, baring her throat. He took his sword in his hand, and made as if to strike off her head!

The King and the Queen ran quickly up.

'Stop, brave youth!' they cried. 'We grant you our daughter's hand in marriage, and will give you our kingdom too!'

The young man sheathed his sword, and taking the princess by the arm, helped her to her feet.

The people were jubilant.

'Hurra!' they shouted. 'You truly deserve our fair princess!'

The young man took the princess again by the arm, and led her back to the palace. There he took his ring from his finger and gave it to the princess, while she took hers and put it on his finger.

The people came to the court.

'Your Majesty,' they said, 'the young man is truly worthy to be our king.'

The wedding festivities continued for seven days and seven nights. The young man was married to the princess, and when the wedding was over, the King spoke to the bridegroom.

'I am very old now,' he said. 'From this day forth, you are King of the West.'

The capital city was in a state of great disorder when the woodcutter's son came to the throne, but he re-established order, mainly by forbidding any man to wander abroad at night.

He had not been long on the throne, however, when one day a letter arrived from the King of the East, announcing that from that day forth they were in a state of war. Since he did not know what had happened to his brother, he could not know that he was the King who threatened him.

He sent back his answer straight away.

'Give me a little time to prepare,' he wrote, 'and if you wish to fight, then we shall fight!'

For in those days rival kings fought one another in single combat, not with armies.

At the same time the new King of the West wrote a letter to the robber-chief, appointing him vezier.

'Men,' said the robber-chief to the other thirty-nine thieves. 'We have had enough of our former life. Let each man return to his own home. My wealth is there to share among you.'

Then he went to the palace, and became vezier.

'Vezier,' said the young King. 'I have received a letter from the King of the East. Read it, and tell me what I should do.'

'Your Majesty,' replied the robber-chief, when he had read the letter. 'There is a remedy for everything, but if we devise no remedy against the wiles of the King of the East, we shall all be made captive!'

'How is that?' asked the King of the West.

'He will attempt to catch you with his lariat of tanned Isfahan leather,' said the vezier. 'You must make sure he misses!'

The following morning early they marched to the battlefield, and saw the huge enemy army ranged against them. The stars in the heavens have their number, but none could count the ranks of that enemy force! The two armies held back and waited, while the two rival Kings met. They did not recognize each other, being in full armour.

'Brave King of the West,' said the King of the East, 'are you prepared to meet me in single combat, or will you surrender your city to me now?'

'As long as I am alive and well,' said the King of the West, 'you shall not possess a single stone of it!'

'Very well,' replied the King of the East. 'You shall have the privilege of throwing first.'

'Keep your eyes well open, Your Majesty,' warned the vezier, 'or he will catch you in his lariat.'

The King of the East suddenly stood up and cast his lariat at the King of the West. The noose fell around the neck of the King of the West, and the King of the East tugged, and tugged, and tugged, but the neck of the King of the West held firm. But the King of the East darted forward and tied his adversary's hands together with a swift twist of the lariat, rendering him quite helpless. Then he threw him over his horse, and marched upon the city followed by his army.

The news of her husband's capture reached the Queen. She immediately donned her black Arab robes, and sparks of fire flashed in her eyes. She rode out to meet the enemy army, who took her to be a man.

'Wait, King of the East!' she said. 'I, too, am a king. Let us fight!'

The maiden gave a terrible war cry, and when he heard it, tears welled up in the eyes of the captive King of the West.

'Alas!' he said. 'I marched out in vain, and now my wife will fall into the same trap!'

The battle raged for seven days and seven nights, until the Queen's horse caught its hoof in a hole in the ground, and stumbled. The King of the East then cast his lariat, and it fell around the Queen's neck. He secured her hands also, and threw her over the neck of his horse.

The city was taken, and the King of the East rode back to his own capital with his two captives. He determined to put out the eyes of the one on one day, and the eyes of the other on the following day—for the custom is that a blind man cannot rule, and so they would prove no threat to his own throne—and in the meantime he cast them into the dungeons, but in separate cells.

The next day he summoned his *milchi*, the official putter-out of eyes. 'When I give the word, "Put out their eyes!", put them out that very instant,' he instructed.

Then he summoned the King of the West, who came, bowed, and stood before him.

'Recount to me the story of your life, from your early childhood,' commanded the King of the East, 'or I shall have your eyes put out right away!'

His own Queen sat on her throne beside him, and all his veziers and ministers were seated round him.

News reached the people of the Kingdom of the East that they were going to put out the eyes of a young foreign king, and everyone, man, woman and child, thronged round the throne to watch.

The King of the West began to relate in detail all that had befallen him since his earliest childhood.

The King of the East soon realized that the man he had captured was his own twin brother, and he began to weep, and fell upon his brother's neck.

'The other warrior with whom you fought for seven days and seven nights and whom you take to be a man is in fact my wife,' said the King of the West. 'Set her free! It is cruel to keep her locked up in your dungeons!'

The King of the East went to the dungeons immediately and released his brother's wife. He kissed her tenderly on the forehead.

'You held out against me for seven days!' he said. 'You are indeed a worthy wife for my brother!'

The King and Queen of the West remained a few days longer with the King and Queen of the East. Finally the King of the East said to his brother:

'Take your wife and your army, and return to your country. When you get back, order a woman's robe to be made of priceless silks. Then return here with it, and together we shall go and visit our parents, and redeem the debt we owe to Shah Abbas for his good deeds towards us.'

The King of the West took his wife and returned to his own kingdom. He ordered the robe to be made, put it in his saddle-bag, entrusted the kingdom to the care of the Queen, and marching at the head of his army, returned to rejoin his elder brother.

His brother in the meantime had made his own preparations, choosing priceless gifts for his mother and the wife of Shah Abbas. The two brothers set out together, and rode at the head of their armies until they came to the outskirts of Shah Abbas's capital city of Isfahan. At midnight the King of the East shot an arrow into the city so that its sound should announce their arrival to Shah Abbas.

When the Shah heard the noise of the arrow, he looked out and saw that his city was surrounded on all four sides by burning torches. His hands trembled, and his knees knocked.

'Alas! Alack!' he cried. 'My kingdom is to be taken from me!'

He burst into tears, and sent a horseman to discover what manner of men had arrived on the borders of his city.

'We are friends,' they said. 'We have come to visit Shah Abbas as his guests.'

In the morning Shah Abbas, greatly frightened, took his army and marched out to meet them.

'What manner of gifts shall I give them,' he thought to himself, 'that they may be well disposed towards me?'

He went to the royal tent, extended an invitation to the two Kings, led a royal parade in their honour, and returned to his own palace.

That night the two Kings remained outside the city.

'What could they have come for?' Shah Abbas asked his wife. 'If we creep out during the night and chop off their heads, it would be a pity, since they are so young. But if we do not chop their heads off, what can we offer them, that they may leave us in peace?'

'Why do you worry so?' said the Queen. 'Give them the woodcutter's magic egg. That will suffice. They will be very pleased to receive it.'

The good light of day rose and shone upon all, and Shah Abbas went to visit the two Kings, and greeted them civilly. They returned his greeting.

'Do you know what, O King?' said the two brothers.

'Tell me! I am ready!' said Shah Abbas, prepared to hear the worst.

'We would like to take our two saddle-bags and walk through the streets.'

'Very well. Let us go together,' said the Shah, puzzled, but relieved.

The two brothers took their saddle-bags, and walked through the streets with the Shah. They walked out of the city limits and came to their old home.

Shah Abbas watched them as they went, and saw that the eyes of the two Kings were strangely bright.

The elder brother ordered one of his men to take the two saddle-bags to the poor woodcutter's house, and tell the man and his wife to dress themselves in the clothes they would find inside, ready to receive the visit of the Shah.

The servant entered the poor hut, and saw the old woodcutter and his wife squatting, half-naked, in front of an empty stove.

'Old man!' said the servant. 'Prepare yourselves, the Shah is coming to visit you!'

'What do we possess, my son,' said the old man, 'that the Shah should come and visit us?'

'Do not waste time in talk,' said the servant. 'Put on these clothes which the Shah has sent you!'

'God has sent us clothes!' cried the old woman to her husband. 'Let us render thanks to him and put them on!'

The old woodcutter and his wife dressed themselves in the fine robes. Shah Abbas observed that tears were now streaming from the brothers' eyes. He began to half suspect that the two young men were his godsons.

They entered the hut.

'Greetings, gossip!' said the Shah.

'All good things are from God! A thousand welcomes!' said the old couple.

The two brothers embraced their father and mother and burst into tears.

'We are your two sons!' they cried. 'Do you not remember us?'

When their mother heard this, she fainted right away. They gave her some water to sip, and she slowly regained consciousness. She embraced her long-lost sons, and wept for joy.

They remained a while longer in the hut. Then Shah Abbas proposed that they all went to his Rose Garden to celebrate the brothers' home-coming and reunion with their parents.

When they were in the garden and were taking their ease, the two nightingales once again flew down and settled on the young men's heads, and began to chatter away.

'Your Majesty,' said one of the young men. 'Do you remember when I told you how the nightingales were saying that one of us would rule the Kingdom of the East, and the other the Kingdom of the West? The nightingales' prophecy has come abundantly true!'

And so they ate, drank, and were merry. Then they all rose, and went into the palace. The two godsons asked Shah Abbas and his Queen to accept the two saddle-bags full of fine clothes they had brought them, and to put them on. When the Shah saw the clothes, he found that they were supremely beautiful, far beyond any price. In return, he fetched the magic egg their father had given him, and presented it to them as a gift.

That night they all remained at the palace. In the morning, the Shah ordered two fine horses to be brought from the stables, and on one he set his godsons' father, and on the other he set their mother.

'Take your father and mother back with you to your kingdoms,' he said, 'that they may be compensated and consoled for having lost you for so long. Let the father stay with the elder son, and the mother with the younger!'

145

The two Kings rode back together until they came to the parting of their ways. There they embraced each other, the elder son took his father, and the younger son his mother, and they returned to their own countries, to the Kingdom of the East and the Kingdom of the West.

And as they achieved their hearts' desire, so may you also.

Three apples fell from Heaven, one for the story-teller, and two for his listeners.

Gyulshani heqiathë, told in 1912 by the illiterate vine-dresser Gevorg Gevorgian, aged 60, in the village of Ashtarak, province of Ayrarat; *APT*, I, no. 33.

Zangi and Zarangi, or Blackie and Goldie

Once upon a time there was a poor labourer who lived in a village. He and his wife had one young son, and a baby daughter three months old.

One day the labourer's wife lit the oven, kneaded three loaves of bread, placed the dough in the oven to bake, and went out to fetch some water. The boy was sitting beside the oven, while his baby sister lay in her cradle.

Suddenly the young boy saw his sister climb from her cradle, take the three loaves from the oven, gobble them up in a trice, and then crawl back to her cradle. Then she fell asleep.

The boy was greatly surprised, and when his mother came back, he told her what had happened.

'Mother!' he said. 'My sister climbed out of her cradle and gobbled up the bread in the oven!'

His mother would not believe a word of this, however, and smacked him hard.

'You are sitting right on top of the oven!' she cried. 'You ate it! How could that poor little mite eat three large loaves of bread?'

The boy wept a little, and his mother went out. She returned with a chicken, which she put in the oven to roast, and then went out again. The boy watched as his baby sister climbed out of her cradle again, took the chicken from the oven, gobbled it up, and crawled back to her cradle, to fall asleep.

She was clearly a monster of some sort!

When his mother came back into the house, the boy told her what had happened. But again his mother would not believe him, and she scolded her son, and beat him.

'How could that poor little pet do such a thing?' she cried. 'May the earth close over your head!'

Well, the boy saw that whatever he said was said in vain, and he decided to run away.

Whether he went a long way or a little way, God alone knows, but he walked on until he came to a city. It was a very large city, but look as he might, he could not find any inhabitants there at all. However, he walked this way, and he walked that way, and finally spied some smoke rising up into the air.

'Let us go to where the smoke is coming from,' he said to himself. 'There must be people dwelling there.'

He made his way to the source of the smoke, and saw before him a tumbledown old house. He went through the doorway, and beheld two people, an old man and his wife, sitting inside. Their eye-sockets were completely empty!

'Greetings, grandfather and grandmother!' said the boy.

The couple were astounded to hear his voice.

'What does this mean?' they said. 'Does anyone dare come here, undeterred by the dragons, the *vishaps*?'

The old man turned his blind face to the young man.

'Are you giant or genie,' he said, 'that you should venture here? Have you not heard of the dragons that infest this region?'

'I have not!' replied the young man. 'I am a stranger here. My mother beat me, and has driven me from home. I walked away and came here. If you like, adopt me as your son, and we shall live together.'

'Very well,' said the old man. 'I am willing. We have no way of making our living as we are. Three dragons dwell here. They have gathered all the inhabitants of the city and the villages together and assembled them in a large enclosure so as to eat them up one by one. They have kept us, my wife and myself, to milk two goats and two sheep, so that they may eat and drink their produce. But first they plucked out our eyes and took them away and hid them.'

'Very well, if that is the case,' said the young man, 'I shall take the sheep and the goats to pasture, and bring them back to be milked.'

The blind old couple agreed, and adopted the young man as their son. His name, by the way, was Suren.

'When you take the sheep and goats to pasture, Suren,' they said, 'take care the *vishaps* do not find you. Lead them to a safe and well-protected place.'

The young man took the sheep and goats to pasture one day, two days, three days. On the fourth day he had led them to pasture and was about to sit in the shade of a tree, when he saw a lion approaching his little flock. Suren picked up his club and prepared to protect his sheep and goats.

The lion halted, and spoke in a human voice.

'Do not be afraid of me!' said the lion. 'I can see that you are a brave youth. I have come to give you a pair of good dogs to guard your sheep and goats.'

And straightway the lioness, for such it was, gave birth to two cubs, which she gave to Suren. Then she went away again.

Now these were fairy-tale 'dogs', which grow in one day as much as ordinary dogs in a month. Within fifteen days the two cubs had become two enormous lions.

Suren grew very fond of his two 'dogs'. He called one Zangi or 'Blackie' and the other Zarangi or 'Goldie'. Henceforth, he returned every evening with his sheep and his goats and his dogs, and set out again with them every morning.

One day he was sitting playing with his dogs, when they suddenly jumped up, and ran off barking loudly. The young man leapt to his feet, and saw a gigantic female *vishap* creeping and crawling, slithering and sliding, towards him, a voluminous mane streaming behind her.

Seeing the dogs about to leap at her, the dragon spoke:

'My humble greetings, brave youth!' she said. 'Call off your dogs and let me pass. I have something to say to you.'

From the moment he caught sight of the dragon, Suren knew that it was one of those that were devouring the whole population of the city and villages, but with Zangi and Zarangi to protect him, he was not afraid. He called his dogs off, and they returned to sit beside him under the tree.

Now the dragon dearly longed to pounce on the young man and gobble him up, but with the two huge dogs sitting at their master's side and eyeing her closely, her courage failed her. Furthermore, her teeth had grown a little blunt, and needed sharpening. So, with great cunning, she said:

'Good youth, could you pick the nits out of my hair for me?'

Suren immediately sensed a trick.

'Very well,' he replied. 'Come under the tree, and I shall look for your nits.'

The young man placed the dragon's head on his knees, glanced behind him, and secretly tied the long hair of the dragon's mane to the trunk of the tree. The dragon remained unaware that she was thus secured and proceeded to file away at her teeth to make them sharp enough to gobble the boy up.

'What are you doing there?' asked Suren, pointing to the file.

'Nothing. I've got some pips in my teeth,' said the dragon.

The young man got up.

'Oh!' he said. 'Wait there a minute. One of my goats has got away. I must go and bring it back!'

'It's all right,' said the dragon. 'Nothing will happen to it.'

'No, I must go and get it,' said Suren. 'I'll come straight back and see to your hair.'

The young man got up and walked away. The dragon made to dart at him from behind and gobble him up. To her surprise, however, she found that she was tied by her hair to the tree and could not move.

Suren caught hold of the goat he had used as a pretext to get away, and came back and stood at a little distance from the dragon.

'Why have you tied my hair to the tree, good youth?' said the dragon. 'What harm have I done you?'

'You are the dragon who terrorizes the city,' replied the young man. 'That much I know! You are the one who plucked out the eyes of my

149

father and mother! Tell me where you have hidden them, and give me the key!'

'My elder sister has the key,' said the dragon. 'Let me go, and I shall fetch it to you.'

'Zangi, Zarangi!' cried the youth, when he heard this. 'Devour this dragon, and make sure that not a drop of her blood falls to the ground!'

Zangi and Zarangi leapt at the dragon, tore her to pieces, and there remained not one drop of blood to be seen anywhere.

Five days, ten days passed, and the young man suddenly saw another dragon approaching him. And what a dragon she was! Far huger and more frightening than the first one!

The dogs leapt at her straight away, and the dragon called out to their master:

'Call off your dogs and let me pass,' she said. 'I have something to tell you.'

Suren guessed that this was the first dragon's elder sister. He called his dogs off, and bade them sit beside him under the tree. The dragon would dearly have loved to pounce on the young man and gobble him up, but she was too scared of the dogs. They were as good as dragons themselves, anyway. So she asked the young man, as her sister had done, if he would look through her hair for her.

'Very well,' he said. 'Come over here and I shall look for your nits.'

The *vishap* went and laid her head on the young man's knees, and he secretly tied her hair to the tree, as he had done for the first. Then he got up.

'Oh!' he said. 'One of my goats has wandered off. I must go and fetch it back.'

'Nothing will happen to it. It's nothing to worry about,' said the dragon. 'Stay here a little longer and then go and fetch it.'

'No, I must go. The goat will get lost. I shall be back,' said Suren.

As the young man got up to walk away, the dragon struck at him from behind, intending to gobble him up. To her surprise, however, she found that she was tied to the tree by her hair and could not move.

'Alas, why have you tied my hair to the tree, good youth?' she wailed. 'What harm have I ever done you?'

'You have done more than enough!' said Suren. 'Where have you hidden the eyes of my father and mother? Give me the key, and I shall untie your hair.'

'My little sister's got it,' said the dragon.

'May the earth rest heavy on your head!' cried the young man. 'I have already slain your little sister! Are you trying to trick me, too?'

'If that is the case,' said the dragon, 'my *big* sister's got the key!'

'Zangi, Zarangi!' cried the youth. 'Devour this dragon so that not a single drop of her blood falls to the ground!'

Zangi and Zarangi, who had been sitting there as docile as pet

Persian lap-dogs, now sprang up and leapt at the dragon, and tore her to pieces. They ate every piece of her, and not one drop of blood fell to the ground.

And so she went the way of the other. A month passed, then two, until one day, when the young man was busy chopping wood, his dogs began to bark. He lifted his head, and what did he see! A gigantic dragon was approaching, so huge that the hills and valleys trembled beneath her weight.

'It will not be easy to kill that cursed brute!' Suren thought to himself. He called his dogs. Now you must know that such dogs can speak.

'Zangi, Zarangi!' he said. 'Do not fret. Drink enough milk to give you the strength to overcome that dragon, otherwise our efforts will be useless, and she will kill the three of us!'

'Very well!' said Zangi and Zarangi. 'But do not worry!'

The dogs withdrew to one side, and the dragon came up and said:

'Greetings, brave youth! Where have you come from, and what are you doing here?'

'Nothing,' said Suren. 'I am the son of a blind old couple.'

'Very good!' said the dragon. 'I have family connexions with them.'

The dragon came up and sat beside the young man, and would dearly have loved to gobble him up there and then. But she, too, was scared of the dogs.

So she too asked the young man to look through her hair for her.

The young man placed her head on his knees and secretly tied her hair to the tree.

'Oh!' he said, standing up. 'One of my goats has got away. Stay there a minute while I go and bring it back.'

As Suren got up, the *vishap* made to attack him from behind, intending to gobble him up. But to her surprise also, she found she was tied to the tree by her hair and could not move.

'Alas, good youth!' she cried. 'What harm have I ever done you, that you have wound my hair about the trunk of this tree? Come and undo it, and I shall reward you greatly.'

'I need no reward from you,' said the young man. 'Just give me the key to the place where you have hidden the eyes of my father and mother, and then I shall untie your hair!'

'My little sister has the key,' said the dragon.

'I have already slain your little sister!' said Suren.

'My other sister has the key, then,' said the dragon.

'I have slain your other sister too,' said Suren.

'So that is why I have not seen them lately!' exclaimed the dragon.

She realized that there was very little to be done. She bade the young man approach on the pretext of handing him the key, but really so that she could seize him in her fangs and tear him to shreds. Suren, however, would not go near her.

'Throw me the key!' he said.

The dragon took two keys from her bosom, and threw them to the young man.

'These are the keys to the place in which you have hidden my mother and father's eyes,' said Suren. 'Now give me the key to where you have shut up all the inhabitants of the city and villages.'

The dragon took another large key from her bosom and threw it to the young man.

'Zangi, Zarangi!' cried the youth. 'Devour this dragon so that not a single drop of blood falls to the ground!'

Zangi and Zarangi leapt at the dragon and tore her to pieces and ate her up, and not a single drop of her blood stained the ground.

Suren called to his dogs, and they all proceeded to the edge of the city. Here he beheld a large mansion.

'By Allah!' he exclaimed. 'It must be there that all the inhabitants have been imprisoned!'

Next to the large mansion stood a well-built hall. Do not say anything, but this had been the dragons' dwelling-place! Suren pushed open the door. . . . There was no one inside. But he found a little casket lying there, and when he opened it with the keys the eldest dragon had given him, there before him lay the eyes of his father and mother! He picked them up, put them in his pocket, and then proceeded to the large mansion, and unlocked the door. A loud wail rose from the people huddled up inside.

'They've come back!' they screamed. 'Which of us will they now devour?'

The young man pushed open the door and walked in. The people inside were struck dumb with amazement.

'Where have you come from, brave youth?' they said. 'Did the dragons not see you?'

'Have no more fears on that score,' replied Suren. 'I have slain the three dragons.'

He let the people out of their prison, and townsman and villager, all hastened back home and took possession of their property again.

Now the city itself had been ruled by a king, but the dragons had long ago eaten the king and his sons. The citizens therefore wished to make Suren king, and begged him to rule over them.

'There is still something I have to do,' he replied. 'I shall go and do it, and then I shall come back to you.'

'May it be done according to your wishes!' said the people.

The young man returned to his adopted father and mother, gave them back their stolen eyes and restored their sight. Then he decided to return to his real father's village, to see what had become of his monstrous sister, to find out whether she was alive or dead. He said farewell to his adoptive parents, took one hair from Zangi and one from Zarangi, and set out for home.

He walked on until he came to a road beside which he saw two men seated at their meal.

'Where are you from, brother,' they called to him, 'and where are you going?'

'I am from such and such a village,' he replied, 'and I am going to visit my father and mother.'

The two men looked at each other with a pitying expression.

'A monster has taken possession of the village you mention, brother!' they said. 'It has gobbled up the town, the villages, everything. Don't go there, or it will eat you, too. We also are from that village, and are lucky to have escaped the monster's clutches.'

'I have got the better of many such,' he said, 'and I shall get the better of this one!'

'We, for our part, are staying well away,' said the two men.

Suren bade them farewell, and went on his way. He walked on until he came to a small village. Now do not say anything, but this was the village he had left long ago, and the monster was his little sister!

He went into the village, and saw that it was completely deserted. But he remembered where he was, made his way back to his old house, put his horse in the stable, and went indoors. His sister was just at that moment lighting the oven, crouching in front of it. She had grown into a *ghovt*,[1] a terrifying she-devil!

When the young man entered the room, his sister straightened up.

'Greetings, dear brother!' she said. 'Where are you going to? Where have you come from? Are you on horseback, dear brother?'

'Yes,' said her brother.[2]

The monster bade him sit by the oven.

'I shall go and feed your horse,' she said.

'Do so,' said her brother.

His sister went to the stable, bit off one of the horse's legs, and ate it. Then she returned to the house.

'Brother, is your horse one with only three legs?' she asked.

'Yes,' said Suren.

They sat and chatted for a while, then the she-monster went back to the stable, and bit off the horse's three remaining legs, and ate them. Then she returned to the house.

'Brother, is your horse one without any legs at all?' she asked.

---

[1] Arabic (and Persian and Turkish) *quwwat* 'power, force'. The monster is known in Turkish tales as the cauldron-headed, axe-toothed sister.

[2] Suren answers all his sister's questions not with a forthright *ayo* 'yes', but with the less assertive *ha*!, which the missionary Dr. Joseph Wolff mistrusted as 'an expression signifying "yes" in this country, but used when the party means to tell a falsehood' (*Journal*, vol. II, 1828, p. 269). Cf. the 'yes' amounting to a 'no' below, p. 158.

'That's the one!' said her brother.

The monster again rose and went to the stable, and this time she gobbled the horse up entirely. She returned to the house.

'Brother dear,' she said, 'could it be that you have really come on foot?'

'That could be!' said her brother.

They sat and talked for a while.

'She's eaten my horse,' thought the young man, 'and now it will be my turn. But perhaps I'll find a way to get the better of her!'

He got up.

He went out through the door, and went up on to the roof, where he began to pace up and down.[1]

'Whatever am I to do?' he asked himself.

He removed his trousers, tied the bottom of each leg together so that nothing could fall out, then scooped up handfuls of ashes and stuffed his trousers full of them. Then he dangled them down through the skylight.

In the meantime—do not say anything!—the monster was busy sharpening her teeth, the better to eat her brother with.

When Suren had left the house, he had locked the door behind him, and when the monster tried to open the door and follow her brother up on to the roof to gobble him up, she found the door shut fast. She swiftly flew up to the skylight to get out on to the roof that way, and so caught sight of a pair of legs hanging through the skylight into the room. She thought they belonged to her brother, and snapped at them with her huge fangs, intending to gobble him up then and there. But the trousers burst open, and the ashes flew into her eyes and temporarily blinded her. She let out a mighty roar, fell down into the room, and started to break down the door. As soon as she got out, she would gobble him up for sure, thought her brother, and remembering his two dogs, Zangi and Zarangi, he took the two hairs from their coats from his pocket, and lo and behold! his dogs stood there beside him.

'Well, master?' they barked. 'Have we come to save the world, or to destroy it?'

'To save it!' said Suren. 'When the monster comes out, devour her, but this time leave one single drop of her blood on the ground!'

---

[1] Some typical houses in Armenia and the mountainous regions of Anatolia and the Caucasus generally are built out of the hillside in clusters, step-wise one above the other. To get to one's roof, which is flat and may serve as the forecourt of the house above, and as a promenade for one's own family, one has only to walk up the hill beside the house, which is usually lit by a window or skylight set into the roof. See James Morier, *The Adventures of Hajji Baba of Ispahan*, 1824, chapter XXXVII: '. . . the villages in Georgia, and in our part of Armenia, are built partly under ground, and thus a stranger finds himself walking on the roof of a house when he thinks that he is on plain ground, the greatest part of them being lighted by apertures at the top' (World's Classics, Oxford University Press, 1923, p. 211).

When the monster came through the door, Zangi and Zarangi leapt at her, and gobbled her up so quickly that in no time at all all that remained of her was a single drop of blood which lay glistening on the ground.

This one drop of blood the young man gathered up and wrapped in his handkerchief. Then he called his dogs and left the house. Not a living soul was left in the village. His sister had eaten them all up, his mother and father as well.

He made his way back towards the city where the inhabitants desired to crown him king. On the way he came across a group of thirty or forty people gathered round a log of wood. The log was filled with gold, and anyone who was able to guess the name of the tree the wood came from, they said, would be able to remove the gold from it and keep it. Suren stood by the log, and tried to guess the name of the tree. Having tried a few names without success, he eventually took out his handkerchief to blow his nose. As soon as he saw the spot of blood on the handkerchief, he remembered his sister.

Now his sister's name was Koknas, and that, or more exactly *Köknar*, in Turkish, is the name of the yellow fir-tree.

Do not say anything, but that was the name of the tree the wood came from.

'Poor Koknas!' sighed the young man.[1]

The people immediately took an axe, cut open the log, and gave the gold hidden inside to Suren.

The young man continued on his journey, striding across hill and valley, always on foot, and by the time he arrived at the city he had nothing left in his body to sustain him other than the mother's milk he had drunk when a child.

But when he finally arrived at the city, all the inhabitants rushed out to meet him, and escorting him to the royal palace, they crowned him their king. They chose a maiden as fair as a ray of sunlight to be his bride, and they crowned her queen beside him. And the wedding festivities went on for forty days and forty nights, and they were married.

And as they achieved their hearts' desire, may you also achieve yours.

Three apples fell from Heaven, one for the story-teller, one for his listener, and one for him who pays good attention.

Zangi-Zrangi, told in 1915 by Sargis Mikayelian, aged 27, cook, partly literate, in Alexandropol (now Leninakan), province of Shirak; printed for the first time in *APT*, IV, no. 5.

[1] The text actually reads: ' "The name of the tree is Köknas!" he said.' But the narrator has surely missed the point of the episode.

Habermani[1]

Once upon a time there was a poor, white-haired old man. He possessed nothing in the whole wide world. There was only his aged wife and himself. Every day the old man would go to the forest, gather brushwood and brambles, take it to town the next day, sell what he could of it, and take the rest back home to burn in the stove. That was how they made their living.

One day the old man went to the forest as usual, gathered as much brushwood and bramble as he could, took it home and placed it in a corner ready to be taken to town on the morrow and sold. All of a sudden he saw a king snake emerge from the pile of twigs, coil itself round the foot of the stove, and settle calmly and majestically down.

'Man of God, what is that snake doing here?' exclaimed his old wife. 'Have we got so much bread for ourselves that we can afford to feed that as well?'

'I did not bring it in with me on purpose, woman!' retorted the old man. 'It must have crept into the bundle of wood of its own accord. It does not matter. It is causing us no harm. The Lord will provide.'

And so the snake was accepted into the family as though it was their own son.

They went to bed, and got up the next morning. The old man swung his bundle of brushwood on his back, went into town, sold it, and returned in the evening. The snake sat down to eat with them, and suddenly spoke in a human voice.

'Do you know what you have to do?' he said. 'Tomorrow you must go to the King and sue for his daughter's hand on my behalf.'

'Are you mad, snake?' exclaimed the old man. 'Who am I? Just think what the King is! Do you want him to chop my head off? You are a snake! What do you want with his daughter?'

'I am not a snake, but the time has not come for you to know what I am. Go and ask the King on my behalf for the hand of his daughter. What does it matter to you? If he will not give it, I shall know what to do!'

The old man got up the next morning as day was breaking, and crawled to the King's palace, a picture of misery.

'Clear off, you scurvy old man!' shouted the King's officials, bearing down on him from all sides.

[1] Pronounced Hăbĕrmānī.

157

'For the love of God, brothers,' implored the old woodcutter. 'I have a request to make of the King. Bring me into his presence. I am full of aches and pains and worries.'

Well, they took the old man to the King. He bowed low seven times, blessed the King, and stood up in front of him.

'What is your request, old man?' said the King.

'Long live the King!' said the old man. 'How shall I put it? I have a son, and I have come to ask you for your daughter's hand in marriage on his behalf.'

'The man's gone mad!' thought the King to himself. Aloud he said:

'Very well, I shall give my daughter to your son, only you must first build in the course of this coming night a palace that will be quite the equal of my own. If the palace is ready by the morning, I shall give you my daughter. If not, I shall chop off your head!'

The old man returned home, feeling very sorry for himself.

'Well, what did the King say?' said the snake.

'What would he say?' replied the old man. 'He said something that amounts to nothing; a "yes" amounting to a "no". "Build a palace in the course of this night that will be the equal of my own," he said, "then I shall give you my daughter; if not, I shall chop off your head!" '

'Do not worry, old man,' said the snake. 'Do you remember the place where you gathered the brushwood the day I appeared?'

'I remember,' said the old man.

'Go back there,' said the snake, 'and you will see a hole in the ground. Stand by it, and call down in a loud voice, "Big Lady, Little Lady, Habermani desires a large palace!" '

The old woodcutter went to the forest, looked about, and found the snake's hole.

'Big Lady, Little Lady!' he shouted. 'Habermani desires a large palace!'

Then he turned about, and made for home.

But what did he see when he got back? On the spot where his old hut had stood a huge palace towered into the air! It quite put the King's own palace in the shade!

At daybreak the following morning, the snake said to the old man:

'Go to the King again and ask for the hand of his daughter.'

Well, the old man summoned up his courage and went to the King's palace.

'The old man who came yesterday is here again,' announced the officials.

'Bring him in and let us see what he wants,' said the King.

The old woodcutter came in, bowed low seven times, uttered a blessing, and stood up.

'Well, have you come to have your head chopped off?' said the King.

158

'Long life to Your Majesty!' said the old man. 'The palace you asked for is ready.'

The King went over to the window and looked out, and what did he see? A huge palace towering up into the sky where the old man's hut had stood, and putting his own palace quite in the shade!

'This white-haired old dog has found a way to do what I asked him to do!' the King thought to himself. 'I shall have to give him my daughter. Well, there is plenty of time for that! I shall ask him to perform another task, and *then* I'll give her to him!'

And aloud to the old man he said:

'All right, you have built a palace. Now you must go and lay out in front of it a fine pleasure-garden like my own. Have you ever seen my private pleasure-garden? It has marble fountains, Hazaran nightingales,[1] and it is for my daughter to walk in. Well, go and build one like it!'

The old man returned home, deeply downcast.

'Well, what happened?' said the snake. 'Why are you hanging your head? Did the King give you his daughter to be my wife?'

'My son, the King now insists that we build a garden like his before he will give you his daughter!' replied the old man.

'Very well, we shall do just that!' said the snake. 'Return to the hole in the forest, and shout down it, "Big Lady, Little Lady, Habermani desires a fine pleasure-garden!"'

The old man went to the forest, shouted down the hole in accordance with Habermani's instructions, and made his way back. When he arrived, he saw that a large pleasure-garden had been laid out in front of the palace, with marble fountains, Hazaran nightingales, and all, and far grander than that of the King!

He slept easily that night, and in the morning he rose, and went to the King.

'Long life to the King!' he said. 'I have made the garden. Now give me your daughter.'

The King went over to see the garden with his own eyes, and, of course, he could not but see that there really was a garden in front of the woodcutter's new palace, and that it was far grander than his own.

'Very good!' said the King. 'Now you must go and find a carpet, all in one piece, to stretch from the gate of my palace to that of your own, so that along it my daughter may walk all the way to your palace.'

The old woodcutter went home, and told Habermani what the King had said.

'Go back to the hole in the forest,' said Habermani, 'and shout down it, "Big Lady, Little Lady, Habermani desires a large carpet!"'

The old man did as the snake instructed him, and returned to find a carpet laid all the way from his own door to that of the King's palace.

The next day he again went to the King.

[1] See footnote on page 46.

'Long live the King!' he said. 'The carpet is laid. Have you come to the end of your requests, or not?'

'There is only one more thing to be done,' said the King. 'Do it, and then take my daughter. By tomorrow morning I want to see seven pairs of minstrels with pipe and drum assembled in front of my door, playing away for all to hear, but invisible to every eye!'

The old man returned, again empty-handed, to Habermani.

'So, old man,' said the snake. 'The King still has not given you his daughter, then? Now what does he want?'

The old man told him.

'There is nothing to worry about,' said the snake. 'Go back to the hole in the forest, and call down it, "Big Lady, Little Lady, Habermani desires seven pairs of invisible minstrels with pipe and drum!"'

The old man went and called down the hole in the forest in accordance with the instructions Habermani had given him, and returned home.

The next morning the King rose, went out, and perceived that the whole city rang to the sound of pipes and drums, but that there was not a single minstrel to be seen.

'The old man has got my daughter now!' thought the King.

The old man got up that morning, and taking the snake with him, went to the royal palace.

'Long live the King!' he said. 'Give me your daughter, and I shall take her with me.'

'Very well,' said the King. 'Where is your son?'

'This snake is my son,' said the old man, taking Habermani from under his robe. 'I have no other.'

Well, what could the poor King do, once he had given his word to bestow his daughter on the woodcutter's son?

'Very well!' he said. 'I can do no more. Take her with you. Everyone must bow to his destiny.'

Brother! for seven days and seven nights they played on the pipes and beat on the drums at that wedding, when the King gave his daughter to be the wife of the snake!

When all the wedding guests had departed and the couple were left alone, our snake suddenly threw off his scales, and turned into such a handsome young man that the princess swooned away in ecstasy.

'You now know that I am not really a snake, wife,' he said. 'I am the son of a king, and I have deliberately assumed the outward form of a snake. In the daytime I shall change into a snake, but at night, when we are alone, I shall throw off my snake-skin shirt, and become a man again. But beware of breathing a word about this to anyone! Others, your sisters for example, will have plenty to say. "Look!" they will say, "we have nice young men for our husbands, but you have married a snake! Your husband is a snake!" But you must not try to

160

contradict them. For the moment you say something like, "My husband is not a snake, he is the handsome son of a king, he is a thousand times better than your husbands!", my magic power will be broken, and this palace and everything else will be lost to me!'

'Very well,' said the princess. 'I shall not say anything.'

The time passed. One day a jousting tournament was arranged in the city. All the nobles took part in it, including the King's two sons-in-law. Habermani himself secretly took off his snake's skin, dressed himself in clothes fit for a king, mounted a blue horse and rode to the jousting-ground.

The King and his three daughters were sitting on the balcony watching the games. The contest began, and it was clear that the Blue Knight was far more skilled than all the others. Nobody, of course, knew who he was, and the King was greatly puzzled, for he knew that there was no one like him among his nobles. Only Habermani's wife knew that the Blue Knight was her husband.

'Look at that, girl!' exclaimed the two elder sisters to the youngest. 'See how good our husbands are! And where is yours? Your husband is a snake which cannot venture out of doors and mingle with real people. One would think that the world were empty of men, to see you go and marry that snake!'

These words deeply wounded Habermani's wife, and she could restrain herself no longer.

'May earth be heaped on your head!' she exclaimed. 'You think you are clever to have husbands to boast about! You think my husband is a snake, don't you? Well, if that bold Blue Knight is not my husband, who do you think he is, then?'

No sooner had she said that, than the Blue Knight was struck a heavy blow with a lance and thrown from his horse. Habermani lost consciousness, and was carried back to his palace. When he regained consciousness, he thus addressed his wife.

'Girl,' he said, 'I have nothing to say to you, other than that you must bind iron sandals to your feet, take a steel staff in your hand, and walk abroad in the world for seven years. You will pass by seven castles, and your iron sandals will be quite worn out, and your steel staff will be no more than a span long. Only then will you find me again!'

The palace disappeared, the garden vanished, and only the former tumbledown hut remained. Habermani went outside and walked away, and his wife was left to rue her rash action. She wept, how bitterly she wept, poor girl! Finally she stood up, bound iron sandals to her feet, grasped a steel staff in her hand, and set out on her long journey.

Where was Habermani, that she should ever be able to find him?

Habermani had walked on, and whether he went a long way or a little way only God knows, until he fell into the clutches of an old witch. The witch had an only daughter and she wanted to marry her to

161

Habermani. But such was Habermani's love for his real wife, the princess, that he fell into a fever in which his soul burned as though in Hell. The witch's daughter would fetch pitchers of water from morn till eve to pour down Habermani's throat, and their efforts to quench his thirst nearly killed both mother and daughter. But nothing helped.

'I am burning! burning! burning!' shouted Habermani, in his fever.

Let us leave him there for the time being, and return to his wife. She went on her weary way from mountain to mountain, from valley to valley, and when she had wandered about for a whole year, she finally came to a walled city built of clay. She saw a young girl hastening to the well with an earthenware pitcher in her hand.

'Greetings, fair maid!' said the princess. 'Fair maid, have you seen Habermani?'

'No, I have not,' replied the girl. 'Habermani is not here. Try the Crystal City.'

She ran to the well to fill her pitcher, and the princess continued her way across mountains and valleys without number, until at the end of another year she arrived at another walled fortress perched on a hill. It was completely made of crystal. The princess saw a young girl hastening to the well with a glass pitcher in her hand.

'Greetings, fair maid,' said the princess. 'Fair maid, have you seen Habermani?'

'I have not,' replied the girl. 'Habermani is not here. Try the Copper City.'

The princess walked on across hill and dale. She passed by the Copper City, the Iron City, the Steel City, one a year, and at every one of them she met a maiden fetching water from the well who told her that Habermani was not there.

She came to another walled fortress perched on a hill, in which everything, walls, houses, streets, paving stones, were made of silver. She met a girl hurrying to the well with a silver vessel in her hand.

'Greetings, fair maid,' said the princess. 'Fair maid, have you seen Habermani?'

'No, no,' replied the girl. 'Habermani is not here. Go to the Golden City.'

The princess kept on walking for yet another year, until she finally arrived at a walled city, on a hill, built entirely of gold. It glittered and sparkled like Paradise under the rays of the sun. It was the Golden City. The princess looked at her feet. Habermani had spoken the truth. Her iron sandals were completely worn out after her seven long years of travel, and of the steel staff in her hand, only a hand's span of metal remained.

'If God wills, I shall find Habermani in this fortress,' she said to herself.

She sank to the ground beside a well, and saw another girl, this time with a golden pitcher in her hand, hurrying towards her. It was the witch's daughter.

'Greetings, fair maid,' said the princess. 'Fair maid, have you seen Habermani?'

'Yes,' replied the girl. 'He is in our Golden City. It is our good luck, and your fair fortune. But Habermani is afflicted with a fever. He is all afire. He is burning away. I am killing myself fetching water from the well to pour down his throat, but nothing will cool him down!'

'Fair maid,' said the princess, 'I have some magic arts, and I know of a remedy for Habermani's sufferings. Let me drink from your pitcher, then take it and give the water to Habermani, and he will be cured immediately.'

The girl gave the pitcher to the princess, and the princess put her lips to it. As she did so, she secretly slipped from her finger the wedding ring Habermani had given her and dropped it into the golden vessel. The girl took the pitcher and innocently carried it back to the fortress, where she poured the water down Habermani's throat. With the last drop of water, the golden ring fell out of the pitcher and dropped on to Habermani's chest. He seized the ring, examined it, and recognizing it to be his wife's, he shouted for joy.

'My fever has passed!' he cried. 'I am cool at last! I need no more water to quench my thirst!'

Then turning to the witch's daughter, he said:

'Fair maid, tell me the truth! Did anyone else drink out of this pitcher?'

'There was a poor woman sitting at the side of the well,' replied the girl. 'She said she had some magic arts, and asked me to let her drink out of the pitcher. She said that if I brought it then to you, and you drank of it, you would be immediately cured. So I let her drink from it.'

'Go and bring the woman to me!' cried Habermani.

But the old witch, the girl's mother, had guessed the meaning of all this.

'Habermani's wife has finally found him,' she said to herself. 'But let her come! There is no harm done. I shall grind her head to pulp!'

So the witch sent her daughter to fetch the princess.

When his wife arrived, Habermani noticed that, as he had predicted, her iron sandals were worn out, and her steel staff had diminished to a mere span in length.

'You have found me at last,' he said. 'But now we must look for a way of escaping from the clutches of the old witch!'

When night fell, and it was just about time to go to bed, the old witch said to Habermani's wife:

'I am going to lie down now. Come and massage my poor feet until I fall asleep. Then lie down and sleep under my feet.'

163

But Habermani found an opportunity to whisper to his wife as follows:

'When you massage the old witch's feet and see that she has fallen asleep, do not lie down to sleep under her feet as she says. Put a large log of wood under her feet and come back to me. During the night the old witch intends to give a mighty kick to break you into seven pieces and imbed you deep into the ground!'

The princess did as her husband instructed her.

She went and massaged the witch's feet until the old woman fell asleep. The princess rose quietly, placed a large log of wood under the witch's feet and returned to her husband. In the middle of the night the old witch jumped up, gathered all her strength, and with a strangled 'Heu-eu-eugh!' gave the log such a mighty kick that it broke into seven pieces and imbedded itself deep into the ground.

But when the old witch rose the next morning, she found the princess walking about the house safe and sound!

'May he who warned you what to do fall and break his neck!' she muttered.

A few days passed.

'Girl,' said the old witch to the princess, 'today I must sew a counterpane for my daughter's dowry, and I need a lot of feathers to stuff it with. You must go and fetch me five sacks of feathers.'

The poor princess did not know what to do, and went and told her husband what the old witch had said.

'Where shall I get five sacks of feathers from?' she cried.

'Don't worry about it,' said Habermani. 'Go to the top of yonder mountain opposite, and cry out, "Birds, birds! Habermani is dead!" Then all the birds that fly above the face of the earth will come and drop a feather on the mountain, and then fly away. Gather them up, fill the sacks with them, and come back here.'

His wife took the five sacks and went to the top of the mountain.

'Birds, birds!' she shouted. 'Habermani is dead!'

All the birds that flew above the face of the earth came in their hundreds and thousands and each dropped a feather on the mountain-top, and then flew away again.

The princess joyfully filled her five sacks with the feathers, went back to the Golden City, and gave them to the old witch.

'Here you are,' she said. 'Here are the five sacks of feathers you wanted.'

'May he who warned you what to do fall and break his neck!' said the old witch to herself. 'Did Habermani tell you what to do by any chance?' she wondered.

A few more days passed, and the old witch again went up to the princess.

'You must go and find me twelve dresses such as no princess has ever worn before!'

164

Habermani's wife ran and told her husband what the old witch had asked her to do.

'This cannot go on!' he said. 'One of these days one of the godless old witch's ruses will succeed, and you will be destroyed. We must escape from her clutches right away!'

So Habermani and his wife stole quietly away from the old witch's house. When they had gone a fair distance, Habermani said:

'Look behind you, wife, and see whether anyone is following us.'

'There is something that looks like a cloud of dust and fog coming after us,' said the princess.

'That will be the old witch's daughter, I know,' said Habermani.

He immediately turned his wife into a windmill, and himself into the semblance of a miller. He dusted his face and hair with flour, and stood at the door of the mill.

The old witch's daughter rushed up, swift as the wind.

'Brother miller!' she said. 'Have you seen a man and a woman pass this way?'

'I can fit you in,' said Habermani, pretending to be deaf. 'What do you want me to grind for you?'

'What are you talking about?' said the witch's daughter. 'I asked you whether you have seen a man and a woman pass this way!'

'Wheat or barley, bring whatever you like,' said the 'miller'. 'I can grind either.'

'What sort of a fool are you?' snorted the witch's daughter. 'Have you quite taken leave of your senses?'

Frustrated and annoyed, the girl returned home, and told her mother what had happened.

'What!' cried the old witch. 'That miller was Habermani himself! May you fall and break your neck! Go back after them, seize them and bring them here!'

Her daughter rushed off in pursuit of Habermani and his wife.

As soon as the witch's daughter had left them, Habermani had changed the windmill back into his wife again, and they continued their journey.

When they had gone a fair way, Habermani again said to his wife:

'Look behind you and see if anyone is following us.'

The princess looked behind her.

'Who is it?' she said. 'There is something like a cloud of dust and fog coming after us!'

'Don't worry,' said her husband. 'It is the witch's daughter again.'

He immediately turned his wife into an orchard, and himself into the semblance of a gardener.

The old witch's daughter came rushing up again.

'Brother gardener!' she panted. 'Have you seen a man dressed as a miller pass by here with a woman?'

165

'How many carrots do you need?' asked the supposed gardener.

'What are you talking about?' cried the girl. 'What sort of answer to my question is that? I asked you whether you have seen a man dressed as a miller pass by here with a woman?'

'Weather's just right this year for the crops,' said the gardener. 'The garden's doing fine. Ask for your heart's desire. Whatever you fancy you can have.'

'Are you mad, deaf, or what?' cried the girl, and she stormed off home, and told her mother all that had happened.

'What!' cried the old witch. 'The gardener was Habermani himself, and he had turned that bitch into a garden! May you fall and break your neck! Why did you not seize them?'

The old witch tore her hair in fury. This time it was she who rushed off in pursuit of Habermani and his wife.

As soon as the witch's daughter had left them, Habermani had changed the orchard back into his wife again, and they continued their journey.

When they had gone a fair way, Habermani again said to his wife:

'Look behind you and see if anyone is following us.'

The princess looked behind her.

'What is that?' she cried. 'There is another cloud of dust and fog coming after us, but all Heaven and Earth seem to be mixed up in it!'

Habermani looked behind him, and saw that this time the cloud of dust and mist was different from the others, being far huger and more terrifying.

'It is the old witch herself,' he said. 'We must be very careful now. It will be very difficult indeed to escape from her accursed clutches!'

As the dark cloud approached, Habermani had just time to cry out to his wife, 'Throw your comb to the ground', and the old witch was almost upon them.

As soon as the princess's comb touched the ground, the hills and valleys around them became covered with a thick forest, hiding them from the witch. Habermani turned his wife into a tender shoot and himself into a small snake. He wound himself round and round the plant so that his head rested on top of it, and nothing remained to be seen of his wife.

With a terrible roar, the old witch descended like a fury into the depths of the forest.

'Aha, my tricky young fellow!' she cried. 'Do you take me for my daughter, that you think to fool me? You have conjured up this forest. You have changed that bitch into a tender shoot, and yourself into a small snake wound around it. Did you think I should not know?'

When he heard these words, Habermani flicked out his tongue, and said:

166

'Old woman, your god will be your judge! Do not bar my path! I know my heart's desire! Let me go and achieve it!'

'Aha!' cried the old woman, triumphantly. 'So you admit defeat, and beg me to spare you! Well, I cared for you for seven long years and hoped to make you my son-in-law. I shall spare your life. Put your tongue to my lips so that I may kiss you, and then go in peace, my son!'

The snake put his tongue to the old woman's lips, and she kissed him. Then the old witch turned, and went back to her Golden City.

Habermani changed himself back into a man, and the tender plant back into his wife, and they continued their journey together. Finally they arrived back in their own city, and went to the tumbledown hut on the spot which had been their home. The old woodcutter and his wife were long dead. Habermani changed the hut into the magnificent palace it had once been, with its pleasure-garden and everything in its proper place, just as it was before. The people who saw it happen went to inform the King.

'Long live the King!' they cried. 'Light unto your eyes! Your son-in-law and your daughter, his wife, have returned! Their palace, and pleasure-gardens, and things, they have established as they were before, and have taken up residence in them.'

The King rose to his feet and went to see for himself. Indeed, everything *was* as it was before! He went into the palace, and saw his daughter and her husband. He saw that his son-in-law had changed from a snake into an incomparably handsome youth, and that in his whole kingdom there was no other to be found as handsome as he.

The King ordered the wedding to be celebrated again. For seven days and for seven nights the festivities continued, and the King married his daughter to Habermani, this time as to a man, not a snake.

And as they achieved their hearts' desire, may you achieve yours also.

> *Habĕrmani*, told *c.* 1880 in the region of Alex-
> andropol (Leninakan), province of Shirak, no
> details of the identity of the narrator being pre-
> served; *APT*, IV, no. 1.

Tapagöz

There was and there was not, once upon a time there was a peasant who lived in a village.

This peasant possessed nothing apart from an only son.

This son was fifteen years of age, and his name was Samson.

One day Samson saw a girl in a dream and, it being God's will, he fell madly in love with her. This girl was the daughter of a king, and —but say nothing of this to Samson!—she had seen him in a dream, too, and had fallen madly in love with him. But let us leave her where she is for the time being, and return to Samson.

Samson suddenly awoke from his slumber, opened his eyes, and saw that there was no girl there, or anything else. The lad could not get to sleep again, and what remained of that night seemed to him to last a whole year. In the morning the good light broke and shone upon all men (God have mercy on your father!), and the young man got up, but from that day forth had neither peace nor quiet, slumber nor sleep, so constantly did the maiden occupy his thoughts and cause him to sigh for her.

So did a whole month go by, and very painfully!

One day a heavy drowsiness came over the young man, and he lost consciousness, and fell asleep. Suddenly he awoke, and found that he was covered in sweat. 'God has given me great power,' he said to himself. 'I have become a strong man. I shall go and seek my fortune!'

The young man needed to try out his strength, and going to the outskirts of the village, he saw the herdsmen of the village struggling with an ox. He went up, grasped the beast by the horns with one hand, and with the other gave it a blow that knocked it clean off its feet and sent it flying. When the herdsmen saw that, they were all greatly frightened, and they took to their heels and fled. In this way the young man was assured of the fact that God had given him great power.

He went and ordered a sword weighing thirty stones,[1] girt it round his loins and set off on his travels. He went a long way, or he went a short way—God alone knows the longness or shortness of a journey

---

[1] Literally, thirty litres. In Armenia, the *litr* is a measure of weight varying as a popular measure from region to region ('in Armenia 1 litre is 12 pounds, in Tiflis 9 pounds, in Akhaltzikhe and Akhalkalaki 20 pounds', *cit*. Malkhasiantz's *Dictionary*, vol. II, p. 200). The narrator of this tale from Leninakan adds an aside to the effect that 'one *litr* is 20 pounds'.

—and in the place he finally arrived at, he met a man. Do not say a word, but the man was in reality an angel, sent by God. The young man did not know that, however, and thought that he was a traveller.

'Where are you going, brother?' said the angel.

Without demur, the young man replied:

'Brother, if I kept it from you, could I keep it from God? I am going to Anatolia. In such and such a wilderness dwells my beloved. I am going to find her and bring her back with me.'

'Very good,' said the angel. 'You could walk on foot for ten years, and you would still not arrive. I shall give you some good advice. Yonder, by the sea-shore, a fountain stands beneath a tree. Take a bridle with you and keep watch under that tree. A fiery horse dwells in the depths of the sea, and he comes out to drink at the fountain, and then returns. When he is drinking, you will be able to slip the bit into his mouth and mount him.'

'Very well,' said the young man. 'I shall do that.'

He thanked the angel and walked on. Eventually he came to a tree as the man had told him, and under the tree stood a fine fountain. He bought a bridle, and went and kept watch under the tree. Suddenly, what did he see? As he looked, the waves of the near-by sea parted, and out of them flew a horse which seemed to be made of pure flame. The horse alighted by the fountain, and began to drink. The young man jumped up, slipped the bit into the horse's mouth, and leapt on its back.

'Dismount from my back, brave youth!' said the horse. 'Or I shall fly into the sky with you, cast you down to the ground, and smash you into a thousand pieces!'

'If you go up into the sky, I shall slip under your belly,' said the young man.

'Then I shall dash you against the ground, and break you into seven pieces!' said the horse.

'By that time I shall have climbed on to your back again,' said the youth.

The fiery horse saw that the young man was a most resourceful rider. 'I shall never find a better master than this,' he thought to himself. And aloud he said:

'Since it is thus, Samson, tell me what you desire, and I shall grant it.'

'It is my desire that you take me as quickly as possible whither I wish to go,' said the youth.

Well, the fiery horse leapt up into the sky, and flew off with its rider. It flew, and flew, and suddenly, what did it see? Tchk! two mountains lay in front of them, blocking their way!

The horse halted for a while, and said:

'If you will strike me in the belly with the stirrups so hard that the

169

milk my mother gave me comes into my mouth, I shall fly high, and we shall sail across the mountains!'

'Very well,' said the youth.

As they came up to the mountains, Samson spurred the horse on as it had instructed him, and it sailed over the mountain-tops, losing only a few hairs of its tail.

So they crossed the mountains, and went on their way.

They went a long way, they went a little way, and came to a park. The youth led his horse to graze there, and sat down to eat his bread. Do not say anything, but those gardens belonged to the King of the Devs. The park-keeper came up.

'Fellow!' he cried, 'do you not know that this place belongs to the devs, and that no mere man is allowed to come inside? *And* you have brought your horse in to graze! Go away, for if the devs learn that you are here, they will come and tear you to pieces, so that nothing remains of you but a pair of ears!'

'Go and bring your devs to me,' said the youth.

'Are you mad?' exclaimed the park-keeper. 'Go away! Clear off! Or you will get a taste of my stick round your head!'

The youth gave the keeper a push such as he had never experienced before in his whole life. When he was able to pick himself up, he hobbled off to complain to the King of the Devs.

'A human has entered your private park,' he said. 'I asked him to leave, but he laughed at me, and gave me a terrible blow!'

When the King of the Devs heard this, he flared up, called for his army, and marching out in front of his troops, prepared to wage war on the young man who had entered his pleasure-gardens.

The young man had eaten his meal and made all his preparations for departure, when he saw an army advancing towards him! The stars in the heavens may be counted, but those troops were quite without number!

Brother, that lad was a lad no longer: he was a ball of fire! He leapt on to his horse, drew his thirty-stone sword, and fell like a fury on the centre of the enemy horde. He struck out on one side, his horse lashed out on the other. This head was smashed in, that head was chopped off! Then he made for the King of the Devs, and slew him and many other devs. Then he continued his journey.

He went on and on, whether a long way or a little way God alone knows, until he came to a cave. A huge slab of stone blocked the entrance to the cave. A hundred men might have burst their hearts in the attempt, but they would never have shifted it.

You must know that whoever beheld the inside of that cave would inherit the earth!

The young man got down from his horse, took off his sword, went up to the stone, pulled it aside, and went in. Inside he saw a maiden, as fair as a fragment of pure light, seated on a carpet. 'Ah! I have found the one I have been seeking for!' he exclaimed, as soon as his eye fell upon her, and he fainted right away.

The girl also knew, as soon as she saw the young man, that it was her beloved, and she ran over to him, took some water, and sprinkled it over his face. He regained consciousness. And so the couple, who had been in love for so many years and whose hearts were almost burned up and consumed with frustrated desire, embraced each other so tightly it seemed they would never let go. In the evening the girl said to the young man:

'Samson, beloved, I was carried away against my will by a Tapagöz! My father and twelve other kings waged war against him, but could not overcome him, and in the end he carried me off and brought me here. He has gone out hunting, but wherever he may have gone, he will come back. I must hide you, so that he shall not eat you up!'

'What manner of thing is a Tapagöz,' said the youth, 'that twelve kings could not overcome him?'

'This Tapagöz is a man of iron. His soul is solid stone. He has one eye in the middle of his forehead. If he is struck in the eye, he will die. Otherwise no sword can touch him.'

'How do you know that, fair maid?' said the young man.

'It is true,' said the girl. 'I did not know, but one day when we were engaged in conversation, I wanted to know if there was anything that could do him harm, and he said, "If anyone rams a red-hot spit into my one eye, that will do me harm, but otherwise there is nothing in the world which can hurt me." I wanted to try it, while he was asleep, but I was afraid, and anyway I did not know how to reach a place of safety afterwards. Where should I go?'

The name of the maiden was Gulinaz.[1]

'What shall we do, then,' said the young man, 'to make the Tapagöz go to sleep?'

'Let us first bring your horse inside,' said the girl. 'I shall lead you to a safe place. But first take the slab of stone which you have pushed aside, and put it back in its place, so that the Tapagöz shall suspect nothing.'

Samson led his horse in, tethered him to a post in a dark corner of the stable, hoisted the slab of stone back into the doorway, and picking up his sword, crawled under the divan.

When it became dark, there was a loud rumbling sound, the hills and valleys shook, and Gulinaz saw the Tapagöz returning, driving a mixed flock of four bison, ten sheep, and a few cows and oxen in front of him. An uprooted tree served him as a staff.

He came to the entrance to the cave, lifted aside the heavy slab of

[1] Persian, denoting a young and tender rose.

stone, and drove his flock into the stable. Then he seized three of the sheep, cut their throats, skinned them, and threw their fleeces to one side. He made a fire, thrust all three sheep on to a wooden spit, and roasted them. Then, making three large sandwiches of them, he swallowed them one by one, whole. Then he sat down to rest a while. He looked this way, and he looked that way, and when the girl returned, he said:

'Girl, I smell the smell of a human being!'

'What are you saying?' said Gulinaz. 'Who would dare to come here and defy you? I am a human being. It is me you can smell.'

The Tapagöz was convinced by what Gulinaz said, got up, drank a huge tun of water, fetched one of the bison, roasted it, broke it into two pieces, swallowed them, and lay down to sleep.

As soon as the giant had fallen asleep, the girl stoked up the fire to produce a fine blaze, and thrust the heavy spit into it to make it red-hot. Then she went to fetch the young man. Samson, who had never yet set eyes upon a Tapagöz, was greatly amazed.

'Goodness!' he exclaimed. 'So that is a Tapagöz! His head weighs about fifty poods,[1] his nose fifteen poods, and each one of his teeth alone must weigh from four to five poods!'

Samson saw that the spit was now red-hot, and he picked it up and thrust it firmly into the one eye of the Tapagöz. As the spit went in, the giant screamed so loud that the walls of the cave trembled. He thrashed about for a while, and then expired.

The mighty youth picked the giant up and threw him into the valley, and then returned to celebrate his union with his beloved for five or six days. Eventually he said:

'Dear Gulinaz, let us leave this wilderness. It is not a hospitable place!'

So they got up, Samson fetched his horse from the stable, sat Gulinaz on the saddle behind him, and they set off.

The young man rode up to the gate to the King's private park, drew his sword, smashed the gate in, and went inside. There he set his horse to graze, spread out his felt cloak, erected a covering over their heads, and they sat down to eat.

A park-keeper came along, saw that the gate had been broken down, and that someone had gone inside, and was now letting his horse crop the grass, while he himself sat eating a meal with a young woman.

The keeper approached them.

'Who are you, young man,' he said, 'that you dare to enter the King's private park?'

'I am one who will put out your eye *and* that of your King!' replied Samson.

[1] A Russian measure, one pood being equal to 40 Russian pounds, or about 36 English pounds.

172

The park-keeper was taken aback, and he went to tell the King what the young man had said.

The King summoned his lala.[1]

'Can it be that the young man is hungry?' he said. 'Perhaps that is what has made him angry. Take him some bread, and let him eat it and be off!'

The lala took the bread, and went and gave it to the young man.

'Here you are!' he said. 'The King has sent you some bread, so that you can eat it, and be off.'

'I do not need any bread,' said Samson.

He took a piece of paper, drew a picture of fifteen camels fully laden with gold, and gave it to the tutor to take back to the King.

The man took the paper to the King, who understood that the young man demanded fifteen camel-loads of gold before he would go away.

The King picked up two eggs, and handed them to his lala.

'Take these to the insolent fellow,' he said, 'to show him that if he does not go away, I shall make his eyes as white as these eggs!'

The tutor took the eggs and gave them to the young man. Samson understood immediately what the King meant, that he would burn out the pupils of his eyes, and picking up two walnuts, he sent them to the King.

'Tell the King to break his teeth on these,' he said. 'He shall find I am as tough a nut to crack!'

The King sent back a handful of wheat, to indicate the army he would send would be as numerous as the grains of wheat.

The young man sent the King a chicken, saying 'Such an army as yours this chicken could gobble up', meaning that a single man would dispose of any army the King could send.

The King saw that there was nothing for it, and mobilizing his army, he marched out to do battle with the young man.

When he saw the enemy army approaching, Samson leapt on to his horse, took his thirty-stone sword in his hand, and galloped into the midst of the fray. This head fell to the ground, that head soared into the sky, and the blood flowed in torrents!

Brother, all the King's efforts were in vain! As many armies as he sent, so many did Samson crush!

The King had three devs at his command. He now sent these in against the youth.

Samson lopped off the heads of the three devs.

The King did not know where to turn. He summoned the members of his privy council, to advise him how they might escape the clutches of his youthful adversary.

One counsellor stood up.

[1] Turkish, a tutor or servant having charge of a young prince or gentleman.

'Long live the King!' he said. 'Let us summon a wizard, one skilled in bibliomancy, and let us see what the passages of Holy Writ instruct us to do!'

So they summoned a wizard, and he opened the Bible at random, and so interpreted the passage his eye lit upon:

'Long live the King,' he said. 'Twenty years ago a Tapagöz carried away the daughter of King Aslan. Do you remember?'

'I remember,' said the King.

'The young man who now faces your armies has gone to the giant's lair and slain the Tapagöz, rescued the princess, and brought her here. You and the rest of the twelve kings were never able to defeat the giant, and he has overcome him single-handed! What chance have you against him?'

As soon as the King heard these words, his heart grew light.

'If that is the case,' he said, 'do not send him fifteen camel-loads of gold, but thirty! The princess is the daughter of my friend!'

The King sent Samson thirty camel-loads of gold, and informed King Aslan of what had happened.

'Light unto your eyes!' he said. 'Your daughter, who was captured by the Tapagöz, has returned, and is now in my land!'

As soon as King Aslan heard this news, he rose up and came to his friend's kingdom, looked at his daughter, looked at the young man, and knew that the giant was really dead. He was overjoyed, and taking his daughter and Samson with him, returned to his own kingdom.

He told the young man's father what had happened, and summoned him to court. Then he took his daughter and gave her to the old peasant's son, and made him his son-in-law.

The wedding festivities continued for seven days and seven nights, and then the crowns of marriage were held above them, and they were wed. The King appointed Samson's father to be his Treasurer-in-chief, and abdicated his throne in favour of his son-in-law.

And as they achieved their hearts' desire, so may you achieve yours also.

Out of the sky three apples fell: one for the story-teller, one for his listener, and one for him who gives good ear.

Thapa-gyozi heqiathë, told in 1915 by Sargis Mikayelian, aged 27, cook, partly literate, in Alexandropol (Leninakan), province of Shirak, and printed for the first time in *APT*, IV, no. 6.

The Wolf, the Fox, and the Eagle

Once upon a time there was a poor man. Now this man had a mother, but naught else in the whole world. One day they set out together for a wild and deserted place, and the poor man built a hut in the middle of a forest, and they settled there. He was a good hunter, and every day he would go out into the forest, trap and kill some game, and bring it back for his mother to cook. They would eat it, and so survive.

One day the hunter trapped a beautiful bird, an eagle, and taking it home, he told his mother not to kill it, but to keep it safe.

On another day he trapped a fox, and taking it home, he told his mother not to kill it either, but to keep it safe.

On yet another day he trapped a wolf, and taking it home, he told his mother not to kill it either, but to keep it safe, also.

The time passed, and one evening he returned home, to find the Eagle, the Fox and the Wolf all sitting there with most sorrowful expressions on their faces. He went and scolded his mother.

'What does this mean?' he cried. 'Did you not give them anything to eat today?'

'What are you saying?' said his mother. 'I give them a great deal to eat every day!'

The young man returned to the animals.

'My Eagle, my Fox and my Wolf,' he said, 'why is it that you, who have hitherto been happy here, now have such mournful expressions on your faces?'

'God knows, and Man knows, that we have no sorrow or grief on our own account,' said the Fox. 'We sorrow and grieve only for you. We have been eating your bread and salt for a long time now, and we, in our way, are only human. We should like to go and capture the King's intended bride, and bring her to you, so that she can look after us. One day your mother will die, and who will look after us then?'

'Very well,' said the hunter. 'You shall do as you wish.'

So he let the Eagle, the Fox and the Wolf out of their cages, and set them free.

'Go wherever you will,' he said.

The three animals set off on their journey. The Fox, being a devil incarnate, thought up a plan on the way.

'The King is celebrating his wedding,' he said. 'We shall go to the feast. I shall lead the dance, while you, Wolf, shall bring up the rear of the file of dancers. You, Eagle, shall perch on the canopy over the bride, and when I reach the door, flap your wings hard! All the torches and lamps will be blown out by the draught. Snatch up the bride, and fly out through the skylight with her. The Wolf and I will follow and catch you up.'

And so they went to the mansion where the royal wedding was taking place. The Eagle flew up and perched on the curtain, the Fox led the dance, and the Wolf brought up the rear. When they had danced around for a while, the Fox winked at the Eagle, the Eagle flapped his wings hard, and all the lights went out. The guests were plunged into great confusion, and the Eagle flew down and grasped the bride, and flew off with her out of the skylight window. The Fox escaped through the door, but the Wolf got caught up in the crowd, and was beaten mercilessly. They took him out to be hanged, but somehow he managed to escape, and run away. But he was very, very angry! May God save him from worse!

The Eagle carried the bride to the top of a mountain and there set her down, and the Fox went and joined them. They sat down and waited for the Wolf to arrive. Covered in blood and groaning pitiably, the Wolf finally arrived. The Fox realized that the Wolf was very angry, and he ran out to meet him.

'May your house prosper!' he said. 'Why do you look so downcast? You shall be the bride's father-in-law. Then you will not have to put up with all the trouble that we have to put up with. The bride will wash your hands and massage your feet, while we stand and gape, and have to fend for ourselves.'

When the Fox said this, the Wolf swelled with pride, and his anger vanished. They all rose, seated the bride on the back of the Wolf, and set off.

Suddenly the Fox turned to look behind him, and what did he see! A whole army of men was pursuing them, and though the stars have their number, there was no counting *them*!

'Quick, let us hide under this cliff!' said the Fox. 'When the soldiers arrive, we shall suddenly rush out at them. Their horses will rear up, and their riders will fall off. You, Eagle, will peck at their eyes with your beak. You, Wolf, will rend their bellies with your fangs. And I shall gnaw at their faces with my teeth. If we fail to do this, they will kill us, and take the princess back with them.'

They saw the army approaching, and hid under the cliff. When the army drew level, they leapt from their hiding-place and hurled themselves at the enemy. The horses reared up on their hind legs, and their riders fell from their saddles. The Wolf rent open any belly he could get to, the Eagle pecked at their eyes and blinded them, while the Fox cunningly slunk about and gnawed at their faces.

And so they destroyed the pursuing army. But the Wolf was dropping from exhaustion, and could not move an inch. They sat down to rest for a while. Then the Fox said:

'Brother Wolf, put the princess on your back, and let us be off!'

'What are you asking, Fox?' exclaimed the Wolf. 'I can hardly carry myself, let alone the girl as well!'

The Fox winked at the Eagle.

'What can we do about it?' he said. 'You are the bride's father-in-law. If you like, let us leave her here, and return home without her!'

Well, the Wolf, being a bit of an ass, was easily swayed by the Fox. He gave in, placed the bride on his back, and they moved on. They walked and walked, and came to their master's house.

When the young hunter returned in the evening, he looked—and what did he see! A bright droplet of pure light illumined every corner of his humble hut!

Some time passed, and the King summoned an old witch.

'What will you ask to go and find my bride and bring her back to me?' he said.

'A pound of gold,' said the old witch.

'Bring her to me, and you shall have it,' promised the King.

The old witch jumped on her butter-churn, whipped her dragon, and flew up and away. She flew straight to the hut where the princess was living. Now the old witch had a tongue that could charm a snake out of the sea. She went up to the royal bride, and begged her to help her.

'What shall I do?' she said. 'I am a stranger in these parts. Give me shelter for the night.'

The princess was sorry for her, and invited her to be her guest.

One day, then two days passed, and the old witch said to the girl:

'Go outside and see what sort of a steed I have, my dear!'

The princess went outside and saw the enormous butter-churn.

'Granny,' she said, 'is that your steed?'

'Yes,' said the old witch. 'Now look inside, and see what pretty coloured things there are in it.'

As the princess bent down to look, the old witch gave her a push from behind and tumbled her into the butter-churn. Then she leapt in herself, whipped up the dragon, and flew off, and was back at the King's court in a flash.

The King took the bride, gave the old witch her pound of gold, resumed the wedding festivities, married the princess, and was happy again.

So let them remain, while we return to the Wolf, the Fox, and the Eagle.

When the three realized that the stolen bride had been stolen from them, the Fox said:

'Would it not be shameful, lads, if we did not go and fetch her back

178

again? You, Brother Wolf,' he said, 'are her father-in-law, and now you have lost her. Let us go and bring her back!'

They went to the city of the King, and hid themselves in a convenient place. One day they saw the royal bride come out of the palace to go for a walk, and they pounced on her. The Eagle flew up into the air with her, and the Fox ran off. The Wolf, however, was caught again, given a good hiding, and only just managed to escape with his life. He was furious, and caught up with the others vowing to tear the Fox to shreds and tatters.

The Fox guessed that the Wolf might be angry.

'Brother Wolf,' he said, 'why are you so angry?'

'Was it a manly thing to do,' cried the Wolf, 'to run away and leave me on my own?'

'May your house prosper!' said the Fox. 'Do you not understand that the Eagle was all by himself? I was afraid that someone might take the girl from him, so I made haste to join him, especially as I was sure that you would easily deal with our pursuers. What match are they for you?'

So did the Fox butter up the Wolf, as it were plastering his head with a sweet-smelling pomade, which effectively cut short any protest on his part. They took the princess and placed her again on the Wolf's back, and made their way back to their master's house. There they discovered that the young man had lost all desire to go out in the forest to hunt, or to occupy himself in any way, except to sit and mope. But as soon as he spied the Wolf, the Fox and the Eagle, and saw that they had brought back the princess, he jumped for joy, and embraced his bride.

And so a new marriage was arranged.

The Wolf, the Fox and the Eagle went to the wedding and congratulated their young master, and then took their leave, and went their separate ways.

Gel, aghves u artsiv, told in 1915 by Sargis Mikayelian (see *Zangi and Zarangi, or Blackie and Goldie*, p. 147) in Alexandropol, province of Shirak, and printed for the first time in *APT*, IV, no. 17.

The Hobgoblin's Bonnet

Once upon a time there was a young man who set out from home and wandered about in order to see the world. He walked on and on until he came to a certain place, and when he looked, he saw an old man sitting at a crossroads sunk in thought, telling his beads. The young man went up to him, greeted him courteously, and asked:

'Grandfather, where do these roads lead to?'

'The right-hand road leads to Good Fortune, the left-hand road leads to Misfortune,' replied the old man.

The young man thought and thought, and said to himself:

'Am I so blind as to walk willingly into Misfortune? I shall take the road that leads to Good Fortune.'

The old man remained where he was, and the young man set off along the right-hand road. He walked and walked, on and on, until he finally arrived at a deep valley, and there in the valley he saw two men thumping, tugging, and grappling among themselves.

'My good fellows, why are you fighting?' he asked.

'Good stranger,' replied one of the men, 'my younger brother and I are always squabbling, because we can never agree on what is a fair division of property. The inheritance left by our father must be shared equally between us, but whenever I lay claim to anything, my brother says it is his. Tell us, if you will, what would be the sensible thing to do.'

'What does your inheritance comprise?'

'Well, dear man,' said the other, 'it comprises one hobgoblin's bonnet, and one magic wand. If you put the hobgoblin's bonnet on your head, you become invisible, and if you wave the magic wand and say where you want to go, it will take you there. That is what our father left us.'

'Brothers,' said the young man. 'I can see only one way to reconcile you, and that is to take the bonnet and the wand myself. Then there will be no more words between you, and no more fights.'

'Why, brother, the Lord have mercy on your old father, you are right!' said the elder brother. 'Take these causes of many a headache away with you, and good luck to you.'

The young man took the hobgoblin's bonnet and the magic wand. He placed the bonnet on his head, and waved the wand.

'Come, O wand,' he said. 'Take me to the palace and pavilion of a king with a beautiful daughter!'

He immediately faded out of sight, and flew away.

The two stupid brothers made their way home, full of gratitude to the young man who had made such a judicious decision for them and had thus freed them for ever from their continual scuffling and squabbling.

The young man landed in a pleasant pavilion within a royal seraglio. He went inside, took off his bonnet, and put his magic wand on one side. The King's eye fell upon him.

'How did you get into my palace and pavilion?' he said.

'Long live the King!' said the young man. 'I have come to ask you to entrust me with a task. Appoint me magistrate or manual labourer, I shall not fail you!'

'Very well,' said the King. 'I have many tasks to be performed, and shall give you one. But it is very difficult!'

'Just tell me what it is, and never mind its difficulty!'

'Well,' said the King. 'Go to my daughter's pavilion and station yourself at the door. There make sure that no man or man-like creature, no wolf or wild beast, no animal or such-like being gets in to her. If you can do that, then do it. If not, I'll chop off your head!'

'I'll stake my eyes on success!' said the young man.

'God be with you then,' said the King. 'Go.'

So the young man set off, and whether he went a long way or a short way, only God knows, but he finally arrived on a mountain-side where the pavilion of the King's daughter stood. He stationed himself at the door, but when he had stood there for a long time, he could control his patience no longer, and he went into the princess's room. There in the room sat a damsel as fair as a young gazelle, playing with her long, dark hair. Her fingers rippled through her thick tresses as though through dark molten wax, and her black hair shone as though drops of milk or flakes of snow were sprinkled among it. The princess did not observe the young man, and finally tiring of her sport, she lay down to sleep. At midnight the maiden opened her eyes, and rose and went to open her casement window. As she looked out, she saw a gigantic demon, his mouth belching flames and fire, striding towards her. The apparition came to a halt beneath her window.

'Daughter of the King!' it cried.

'What is it?' replied the princess.

'I have come to carry you away.'

'Where to?'

'Back to my house, to be my wife!'

As it spoke, it came into the house, and the young man watched as it caught up the princess in its arms, and hugged and kissed her.

Finally it marched off with her back to its house, and showed her a great pile of golden treasure.

'Wand,' said the young man, left behind in the princess's pavilion, 'carry me to the giant's house!'

He placed the hobgoblin's bonnet on his head, and in the twinkling of an eye he stood in the giant's house, invisible, and listened.

'King's daughter,' the giant was saying, 'I shall give you all this golden treasure, if you will be my wife.'

'Very well,' said the princess, 'but give me until tomorrow to think it over.'

'Very well!' said the giant. 'You shall have till tomorrow to think it over. I shall go for a walk. But let me tell you what to do. Standing by the door of my room there is a long shaft of bone. Pick it up when you come, and give three loud knocks on my door with it. Then I shall know that you will be my wife, and I your husband. But if you give three soft knocks, that will mean that you do not accept me. Then I shall revert to my old, satanical ways, and shall come and settle my account with you!'

'So be it!' said the princess.

The giant skipped joyfully away, and left the princess to herself. Suddenly she saw the young man standing in front of her. He had removed the hobgoblin's bonnet.

'Oh!' she exclaimed. 'Who are you?'

'I am a servant of your father, the King,' replied the youth, 'and I have come to offer you care and protection.'

The princess's heart went out to the young man.

'Flee while you still have time,' she said, 'or the giant will kill you. There is, alas! nothing you can do.'

'Don't be afraid,' said the young man. 'The giant cannot touch me. Hurry, let us take the giant's golden treasure and escape with it. Wand, take us to the golden treasure, and then bear it and us back to the palace of the King!'

No sooner said than done! The princess and the young man flew back through the air with the golden treasure and alighted in the King's palace. The King was overjoyed to see his daughter again, and turning to the young man, he said:

'Young man, whoever up to now stood guard at my daughter's pavilion was never able to defend himself against the giant. How did you manage to save your skin, and bring my daughter back with you?'

The youth revealed his secret to the King, and then said:

'Long live Your Majesty! I have returned your daughter to you. But on our way here, we plighted our troth, and wish to marry. What is your pleasure in that matter?'

'I am well pleased, my son,' replied the King. 'So be it!'

'Then there is only one thing,' said the youth. 'There must be no wedding until the giant is slain.'

'I agree,' said the King. 'May the Lord grant you his aid!'

184

The young man set off and came to the giant's stronghold. The monster was hopping up and down with rage, foaming at the mouth, with huge flames coming out of his eyes and mouth, while his howls of wrath shook the countryside all around: there was no man or man-like thing, no wolf or wild beast, no animal or such-like creature, no rock or shrub, no earth or water that did not tremble and shake to hear him. The invisible youth drew his sword and struck off his head. Then he returned to the palace. The King commanded his men to see to the preparations for the wedding. For seven days and seven nights the wedding feast went on, and as they met their hearts' desire, so may you also.

Khipilki qoloz, told in 1908 by the illiterate land-worker Hakob Hadloyan, aged *c.* 40, in the village of Koph, province of Taron, and printed for the first time in *APT*, X, no. 2.

Haro and Baro

Haro and Baro became friends, and set out on the road together. On the way Haro became blind, and the stick in his hand had to take the place of eyes.

'However shall I manage to lead you about all the time?' complained Baro, who remained hale and hearty, at every opportunity.

They walked on and on until they came to a forest on the slopes of Mount Amarven, just as darkness was falling. They camped under a tree. Baro was very frightened, and was trembling with fear before anything had happened at all. When it was time to go to bed, Baro quickly climbed up the tree.

'If anything comes to gobble us up,' he said, 'it is better it should eat you. You are blind, and would be no great loss to the world.'

'Baro,' said Haro, 'why do you always throw my disability in my face? It is not very kind of you.'

Baro said nothing.

No sooner had the sun set, than a pack of wolves began to howl in the distance, and their howls grew louder and louder as they came nearer and nearer. When he heard this, Baro trembled so much up in the tree that he lost his grip, and slipped, and fell to the ground with a loud thud, biting his tongue and almost breaking his back. He crawled up to his companion.

'Don't be afraid,' said Haro. 'I shall arrange things so that when the wolves see us, they will think there are more than two of us here.'

And indeed, when the wolves arrived, their eyes shining in the darkness like candles, they halted some distance away from the tree. They huddled together and looked. Haro and Baro were walking nonchalantly about under the tree, seemingly unafraid.

'There must be quite a crowd of them over there,' said the largest among them. 'We should get the worst of it, so let us go about our business!'

So they left Haro and Baro, and went on their way.

'Do you see how I fooled the wolves?' said Haro. 'If they had seen you hiding in the tree, as you were doing before you fell down, they would have known that you were afraid, and they would have come and eaten you, and me with you!'

'They couldn't have eaten me!' said Baro.

'Why couldn't they?' said Haro.

'Wolves cannot climb trees,' said Baro.

'They would not have had to,' said Haro, 'since you would have tumbled out of the tree in sheer terror!'

Baro said nothing. They lay down and fell asleep. At daybreak they got up and resumed their journey. They walked on and on, but there seemed to be no end to the dark and terrifying forest. They grew tired, and lay down to rest under another tree. Baro clambered hastily to the top, while Haro remained underneath.

As soon as the sun set, the roaring of a pack of bears began to rumble through the forest. Bears? Every *one* was as big as an ox! No sooner had Baro heard them coming, than *thrump!* down he tumbled to the ground, biting his tongue and almost breaking his back! He crawled up to his companion.

'Don't be afraid,' said Haro. 'I shall deceive the bears as I deceived the wolves!'

And indeed, the bears came nearer and nearer, but they halted at some distance from the tree, not daring to venture any farther, for they also took the carefree behaviour of the two men to indicate the presence of many others.

'There must be quite a crowd of men over there,' said the biggest of the bears. 'If we try anything, we shall get the worst of it, so let us rather go about our business!'

So they left Haro and Baro, and went on their way.

'Do you see?' said Haro. 'If the bears had seen you hiding in the tree, they would have known that you were afraid, and they would have come and eaten you, and me with you!'

'They couldn't have eaten me!' said Baro.

'Why couldn't they?' said Haro.

'Bears cannot climb trees,' said Baro.

'It is true that bears cannot climb trees, but they would not have had to,' said Haro, 'since you always tumble out of the tree in sheer terror!'

Baro said nothing. They got up the next morning and continued their journey. They walked on and on, and still there seemed to be no end to the forest. They grew weary, and lay down to rest under another tree. Baro made immediately for the top of the tree, while Haro remained underneath, undid his bed-roll, and laid out a meal of bread, onions, and sour cheese.

'Baro,' he said, 'come and eat.'

'I am not eating,' said Baro, sulking.

'Why not?' said Haro. 'Are you not hungry?'

'I am hungry, but I do not want to eat anything.'

'Come on down,' said Haro, 'I cannot eat all by myself. I just could not swallow properly.'

So Baro came down from the tree, and they devoured the bread, onions and sour cheese with great relish. Then Haro grew thirsty.

'Baro,' he said, 'lead me to the spring.'

'Not I!' exclaimed Baro. 'I am not moving from here, by Allah! You go by yourself!'

So Haro picked up his stick, guided himself to the spring by the sound of its running waters, scooped up a handful of water, and drank it. Just at that moment a bird alighted in a tree, opened its beak and spoke.

'If you sprinkle your face with the water in that spring,' it said, 'your eyes will see again.'

Haro sprinkled his face with water from the spring, and immediately recovered his sight. Completely cured, he returned to his friend, and found him sitting up in the tree again. When Baro saw that Haro could see again, he marvelled greatly.

'What restored the sight to your eyes?' he asked.

'I could suddenly see again, just like that!' said Haro. 'Glory be to God, a bird told me what to do, saying that if I sprinkled my face with water from the spring, my eyes would see again.'

'Well!' said Baro. 'Let us go to the spring together, and I shall sprinkle my face with the water. Then I shall see even better.'

'Very well, let us go,' said Haro.

They went to the spring. Baro sprinkled his face with the water, but all went dark before his eyes, and he could not see at all.

'Haro!' he cried. 'You have betrayed me! I have gone blind!'

'How is that possible?' exclaimed Haro.

'There is no doubt about it, by Allah!' said Baro. 'I cannot see anything at all!'

Haro called up to the bird.

'Bird, bird, I beseech you, listen to me! I have got well, but my friend has gone blind. Show me how he is to be cured,' he said. 'It is very wrong. He is my friend!'

But the bird did not reply, and flying out of the tree, was immediately lost to view.

'What am I to do now?' said Baro.

'God is merciful,' replied Haro. 'Take my stick, and let us go on our way.'

Haro took his friend's arm, and they continued their journey. They walked on and on, and finally came to a place where they stopped to rest. It was right in the middle of the forest. The trees pressed thickly upon them. The light of the sun could not penetrate the dense foliage, and darkness reigned all around.

'Haro, I am very thirsty!' said Baro.

'Then let us go to the spring,' said Haro, and they went to the spring together.

Haro helped Baro kneel down, and scooping up a handful of water Baro drank it, and then sprinkled his face with the water hoping that

188

it would restore his sight. But it was no use: he remained as blind as before! They went back, intending to continue their journey, when they suddenly heard the whinnying of a horse, and the sound of men's voices. The voices came closer and closer.

'They are robbers!' said Baro. 'They will certainly kill us!'

'Do not be afraid,' said Haro. 'We have escaped from the wolves and bears. Why should we be frightened of men?'

No sooner had he said this, than a huntsman on a white horse, who was in fact the King of that country, came to a halt in front of them.

'Who are you? Where are you going?' he said.

'Long live the King! We are two travellers,' replied Haro. 'I am Haro, and this is my younger brother Baro.'

'What are you doing in this forest?'

'It lay on our path,' replied Haro.

The King turned to his men.

'These seem to me to be a treacherous couple!' he said. 'Seize them, tie up their hands, and take them back with us! We shall throw them into the dungeons, and see who they really are!'

The King's men tied their hands together, and pushing them in the back, drove them back to the King's capital, where they cast them into a dark, damp and freezing dungeon where not even a dog would survive for long.

'Haro,' said Baro.

'What is it, Baro?' said Haro.

'Where are we?'

'We are in a dungeon.'

'Can we ever get out of this predicament?'

'God is merciful,' replied Haro. 'He will open the door for us.'

A few days later they were brought before the King. At the side of the King sat his only daughter. Once you had set your eyes on her, you could eat and drink no longer! She was a queen of the maidens of Paradise. Her eyes were large and lustrous, her countenance like the full moon, her body whiter than linen. As soon as she saw Haro, her senses swam, and she fell deeply in love with him.

'You came to my country to spy and collect information for my enemy, did you not?' said the King.

'God bless the King!' said Haro. 'We know nothing of such things! We are two poor, unfortunate youths who are seeking employment and a way to make our living.'

'I do not believe you,' said the King.

'Then do not believe us,' said Haro. 'We are not deceiving you, but if you wish to, hang us, or burn us alive!'

The King clapped his hands, and half a dozen of his men armed with lances ran up.

'Take them away and hang them!' commanded the King.

At this, however, the princess turned to her father, the King.

'Father,' she said, 'why are you having these men hanged? They seem innocent enough to me. Do not harm them. Keep them with us, and let us interrogate them. If they prove to be false, let us hang them, and throw them into the fire. But unless you test a man, you cannot know his worth.'

The King did not wish to reject his only daughter's suggestion, and declared that it was his pleasure that each of the two companions should give an account of himself, separately, to the princess, that she might decide whether or not they were telling the truth.

So the two friends told their story to the princess separately, whereupon she went to see her father, the King.

'Your Majesty, father,' she said. 'Their story is such and such. He who can now see, was blind; and he who could once see, has become blind. Command the physician Loqman the Wise to restore the sight of him who is blind.'

And so the famous Loqman[1] went to the dungeon and restored Baro's sight. Baro fell at the princess's feet.

'O wise princess,' he cried. 'You do not yet know the whole of our story! You have saved us temporarily from hanging. You have restored my sight, so that I now see better than ever before, and yet do not know how to look my friend in the eye! I beseech you, hang me, but do not touch my dear companion Haro!'

'Indeed it is true!' said Haro. 'Unless you test a man, you cannot know his worth!'

Haro took one arm, and the princess the other, and they lifted Baro to his feet. The maiden went back to her father the King, explained to him her intentions, namely to marry Haro, which the King welcomed gladly. And so Haro became the husband of the fair princess, and Baro was their best man.

Three apples fell from Heaven: one for Haro, one for Baro, and one for the fair princess.

Haron u Baron, told between 1900 and 1914 by Hakob Hadloyan (see *The Hobgoblin's Bonnet*, p. 181) in the village of Koph, province of Taron, and printed for the first time in *APT*, X, no. 3.

---

[1] See p. 77, note 1.

FABLES

The Price of Reputation

It is related in the chronicles that a poor man once went to the Emperor Alexander the Great, who was exceedingly rich and known to be the soul of generosity, and asked him for charity. Alexander gave him a whole city and its revenues.

'Why did you do that?' asked his ministers, in amazement. 'He does not deserve a whole city!'

'That may be,' replied the Emperor. 'But he who is known as the soul of generosity must give memorable gifts!'

VARDAN[1]

The Smith, the Carpenter, and the Gardener

Once, when building a new palace, the Emperor Alexander rewarded the blacksmith more generously than the carpenter and the gardener. The carpenter and the gardener were envious of the smith, and complained to the Emperor: the carpenter, they said, had constructed

---

[1] Vardan of Aygek monastery near Antioch (now Antakya in Turkey), born near Aleppo (Syria), c. 1160, studied at Drazark Monastery near Sis (now Kozan in Turkey), died c. 1230.

practically the whole of the building, and the gardener had supplied food for the whole household.

The Emperor summoned his wise men, and asked them to decide upon the respective merits of the three artisans.

'It is true,' said the chief vezier, 'that Adam was a gardener and tilled the soil. But before he could do this, he had to invent the craft of the blacksmith, who makes tools for himself, the carpenter, and the gardener, so that the carpenter needs the blacksmith, and the gardener needs them both. The blacksmith, therefore, must have pride of place.'

The carpenter and the gardener were persuaded by this reasoning, and envied the blacksmith no more.

MEKHITHAR[1]

The Prince and the Flea

There was once a prince who was tormented by a flea. He finally caught it under his shirt.

'Do not kill me!' said the flea. 'The harm I have done you is very small!'

'All the harm that was in your power to do, you did!' replied the prince, and squashed him to death.

VARDAN

Divide and Rule

When engaged in forming the creatures of the world God became afraid that they might turn against him, and accordingly he mixed the heavy with the light, and the weak with the strong, so that if they should turn against anyone, it should be against each other, and not against him.

This fable teaches kings so to arrange the high and low estates of the kingdom that they may wage war against each other, but not against the king.

MEKHITHAR

The Revolt of the Stars

Once upon a time the stars all gathered together, and the eldest among them said:

'We are many. How is it then that we do not illumine the sky like the sun and the moon, who are but two?'

[1] Mekhithar Gosh, jurist and monk of Getik and New Getik monasteries, born at Gandzak (now Kirovabad in U.S.S.R.) c. 1140, died 1213.

One star said: 'Because we are not united.'

They swallowed their pride for the sake of unity, but when they assembled all together in the evening to out-shine the sun on the morrow, they were all turned pale by the rising of the moon.

'Since we are so eclipsed by the moon,' they said, 'what can we hope to do when the sun comes up?' And so, regretfully, they admitted defeat.

The moral is that although a group may be composed of great numbers, if they are all weak they will still not be able to overcome the strong.

MEKHITHAR

The King of the Trees

The trees once had an argument about who should rule over them as king, and some said it should be the palm-tree, since it was so tall, and bore sweet fruit.

But the vine objected, saying, 'I gladden the hearts of men, so I should be king!'

And the fig-tree said, 'I am sweet to the taste, so it should be I.'

The buck-thorn said, 'I am severe and can inflict punishment, so I am fit to rule.'

Thus these three trees praised themselves excessively, unaware of any faults. The palm-tree realized that they would not agree to accept the rule of another, not wishing to share their special powers with anyone else.

'Am I not richly fitted to be king!' he protested.

The three trees gave their opinion.

'You are indeed very tall, and give good fruit, but you have two faults: one, you take more than a lifetime to produce any fruit; two, you are not suitable for cultivation. Moreover, because of your great height, your fruits are beyond the reach of many.'

'Very well,' said the palm-tree. 'To counteract these faults, I shall make you princes in my kingdom, and so rule over you, and my sons after me.'

And so he made the vine, which gladdens the hearts of men, the royal butler; the fig, oozing sweetness, prime minister; and the buck-thorn, prickly and painful, chief executioner. And he allotted fitting tasks to the other trees, placing the cedars in charge of building, brushwood in charge of heating, and brambles in charge of the prisons.

This fable shows that no one can wield authority without the help of the less glorious, or rise high without the co-operation of the lowly; and again, that with ready gifts in their hands, the many may be discouraged by their masters from harbouring higher hopes.

MEKHITHAR

Be Wary

Mother Crow gathered her fledgelings about her to teach them the ways of the world.

'My children, be not over-confident,' she said. 'Beware of Man, especially when he stoops to pick up a stone.'

'And what should we do, mother,' said the little crows, 'if he has a stone in his hand already?'

'Good children,' replied Mother Crow. 'Your question shows that you are already too wary to come to much harm.'

VARDAN

Priests and Princes

The little vultures once asked their parents:

'Why do you bring us only dead animals' bones to eat, whereas the eagles and the hawks take their children live prey?'

'Children,' they replied, 'God granted us a long life, ordaining that we kill nothing and content ourselves with the dead, like the priests, and prey not on the living, like the princes.'

MEKHITHAR

Doctor Toad

A Toad hung a mortar and pestle round his neck, took a jar of ointment in his hand, and wandered abroad.

'I am a doctor,' he announced. 'I know the cure for every ill!'

All the animals flocked to him to be healed of their afflictions.

Then the Fox came by, and seeing the doctor, said:

'You are nothing but warts and pimples from head to toe, and you claim to cure others?'

Such is many a man, who forgets his own defects and gives advice to others.

VARDAN

Everyone to his Trade

A wolf passed by a sheepfold, and spying a handsome lamb inside, seized her and ran off with her. When he made to eat her up, the lamb fell imploringly at his feet.

'God has given me into your hands,' she said. 'But before you eat me up, grant me the favour of listening to your wonderful trumpet call, for my parents always told me that the race of wolves were magnificent trumpeters!'

The wolf was flattered, and squatting on his haunches, he threw open his mouth and began to hoot away at the top of his voice. The noise awakened the watchdogs, who darted up and fell upon him, biting him severely.

He escaped, however, and went to the top of a hill to lick his wounds, full of self-reproach.

'That I deserve!' he moaned. 'I have always been a butcher, and the son of a butcher before me. Who, in God's name, made me a trumpeter?'

VARDAN

Lions and Foxes

A lioness gave birth to a lion cub, and all the other animals gathered around to congratulate her and join in the happy event. During the celebrations, a vixen came by, and standing in the midst of the assembled crowd, she loudly rebuked the lioness.

'Is that the best you can do, one cub?' she exclaimed. 'I produce several at a time!'

'It is true that I give birth to one cub at a time,' replied the lioness. 'But it *is* a lion, and not a litter of little foxes!'

VARDAN

It takes Time to grow Big

A camel, a wolf and a fox became friends and were travelling abroad together when they found a loaf of bread dropped by other travellers.

'What are we to do?' they said. 'There is clearly not enough for all of us?'

'There is indeed only enough for one of us,' said the fox. 'Let the oldest among us have it all to himself.'

They agreed.

'Well, I am the oldest,' said the wolf. 'I am the male wolf that Noah sheltered in his Ark at the time of the Flood.'

'Then you are the same age as my grandson,' said the fox, 'for I am the fox that God placed before Adam when he named the beasts of the field.'

The camel had already stretched out his long neck, lifted the loaf aloft, and was chewing it contentedly.

'You have a lot to say, for little creatures!' he said. 'Do you imagine that I, who have grown legs like this, was born yesterday?'

And he swallowed the bread.

The wolf and the fox circled round him, but seeing that they could do nothing to harm him, they left him and went their own way.

VARDAN

197

Fair Shares

A lion, a wolf and a fox formed a team, and in the course of a hunting expedition captured a ram, a ewe and a lamb.

'Share out the spoils, wolf,' said the lion, when it was time to eat.

'God has already done so, O king,' said the wolf. 'You are the biggest, so the ram is for you; the fox is the smallest of us, so the lamb is for him; I am midway between the two, so the ewe is for me.'

The ram, of course, would be old and tough, the lamb tasty but very small.

The lion was furious, and cuffed the wolf so hard with his paw that one of his eyes popped out. The wolf lay down and sobbed bitterly.

'You divide the spoils, fox,' said the lion.

'God has already done so, O king,' said the fox. 'The ram is for your breakfast, the ewe is for your lunch, and the lamb is for your dinner.'

'You cunning rascal,' said the lion. 'Who or what taught you to give such fair shares?'

'The eye of the wolf!' said the fox.

VARDAN

The Priest and the Widow

The priest stole a cow belonging to a widow and concealed it in the stable at the back of his house.

The widow found out what had happened, and said to the priest:

'Father, my life is at an end. Let us go into the stable, and hear my confession.'

The priest ran off and led the cow out of the stable, through the house, through the porch of the church, and into the aisle.

Then the widow said:

'Father, it is not right and proper to confess in a stable. Hear my confession in front of the altar.'

The priest ran off again and hastily led the cow up the aisle, stationed it by the altar, and drew the curtain.

When the widow entered the church with the priest, she went straight to the altar, and drew back the curtain.

'Why, you rascal!' she cried. 'I always took you for a cow! Who taught you to celebrate Mass?'[1]

VARDAN

---

[1] In Armenian churches the secret part of the liturgy is celebrated at the altar behind a drawn curtain, the equivalent of the Greek and Russian Orthodox iconostasis.

198

The Place of Sacrifice

A hawk swooped down upon a dove and seized her.

'Do me no harm!' cried the dove. 'I am an offering unto the Lord!'[1]

'An offering to the Lord ought to be on the altar, not flying around in the sky!' retorted the hawk.

And he killed and ate her.

MEKHITHAR

Insincere Greetings

A wolf came to the top of a hill and looking down, spied a flock of sheep.

'Peace be upon you!' he called.

The bell-wether looked up.

'Brothers,' he said. 'A wolf is a wolf! Though he preach the gospel, run for your lives!'

VARDAN

The Cow and the Ass

A widow had a cow, and her stepson had an ass. The stepson stole fodder from the cow and gave it to his ass.

The widow prayed to God for the death of the ass, but it was the cow that died.

'Alas, O Lord!' lamented the widow. 'Can you not tell the difference between a cow and an ass?'

VARDAN

The Bargain

A man prayed to God.

'If you send me one hundred silver pieces, Lord,' he said, 'I will spend ten of them on oil for the church lamps for you.'

Shortly afterwards he found the sum of ninety silver coins.

'How great is your wisdom, O Lord,' he cried. 'You have already subtracted your ten!'

VARDAN

[1] See Leviticus 1:14 and 5:7, Luke 2:24.

Trust

A baby would not stop crying.

'If you do not stop crying now, I shall throw you to the wolf!' threatened its nurse.

The baby did not stop crying. A wolf chanced to be passing at the time, and hearing the nurse's threat, waited by the house, ready to take the baby when it should please the nurse to give it to him.

Dusk fell, the baby slept in its cradle, and it was very late at night before the wolf finally returned to his den, with nothing to eat.

'Why are you such a failure?' scolded his wife.

'I trusted the word of a woman,' said the wolf.

OŁOMPIANOS[1]

The Debtor's Couch

An old man in the imperial city of Constantinople incurred debt upon debt. His debts mounted and mounted, but his various creditors never met, and the old man slept soundly in his bed at nights, caring nothing. When the old man finally died, the vast amount of his debts became public knowledge throughout the city, until the Emperor himself heard of them.

'So many debts, and yet he slept without a care in the world!' exclaimed the Emperor. 'Fetch me the bed he slept in, for it must be a worker of wonders!'

VARDAN

Self-assured Ignorance

A man was once asked:

'Have you ever seen a bath?'

'Of course I have!' he replied. '*And* tasted its flesh!'

'What does it look like?' they asked.

'It's got the same sort of horns as a pig,' he said.

They looked at each other.

'This man has not only never seen a bath,' they marvelled. 'He's never seen a pig!'

VARDAN

[1] The author of a collection of fables preserved in Armenian, mentioned for the first time by Grigor Magistros, *c.* 990–1059. The name *Ołompianos*, *Oghompianos*, seems to be a distortion of Greek *Olympios* 'dwelling on Mount Olympus' (in Thessaly), and is probably intended as an epithet of Aesop, possibly born in near-by Thrace, just to the north. The above fable, and *The Lion in Love* (p. 201), may both be found in Aesop (see *Aesop's Fables, a new translation by V. S. Vernon Jones. With an introduction by G. K. Chesterton and illustrations by Arthur Rackham*, William Heinemann Ltd., 1912, pp. 89 and 172).

The Hedgehog and the Stoat

A stoat pestered the hedgehog to entrust his son to his care, so that he might bring him up.

'Then we shall be very good friends, I assure you,' he said.

At long last the hedgehog was persuaded that it was the right thing to do, and he agreed.

'It is however very difficult to embrace your little son,' said the stoat. 'Could you not remove all those prickles, which prevent me from caressing him as he deserves?'

The silly hedgehog pulled out all the prickles from the back of his son, and handed him over to the stoat—who gobbled him up at once.

MEKHITHAR

The Lion in Love

A lion was dazzled by the beauty of a certain maiden, and approaching her father, asked for her hand in marriage.

The man was very frightened, but not entirely out of his wits, for he thought he saw a way out.

'I should be very glad to have you as my son-in-law, lion,' he said, 'but my daughter would be terrified at the sight of your powerful claws and huge teeth. It would be better if you could get rid of them before you come to court her.'

The lion, blind with love, ripped out his claws and teeth, and then returned for the girl. But being now quite defenceless, he was stoned to death.

OŁOMPIANOS

Envy

A king knew that two of his warriors hated each other, each eaten up with envy of the other. Summoning one of them, the king said:

'Ask of me anything you will, and I shall give it to you, with one proviso: I shall give your comrade double.'

The soldier thought for a while, then said:

'I would beg you to put out one of my eyes.'

Whether the king complied with this request, and put out both the eyes of the other soldier, is not recorded.

VARDAN

Pearls before Swine

A great and benevolent king kept a favourite pig within his palace, ordering his courtiers to treat it with reverence and respect. He placed a golden ring worth a thousand gold pieces or more in its ear, and clad it in a priceless silken cloak embroidered with gold thread and a robe of fine white muslin. The next morning the pig went into town and rolled about in the mud, ring, cloak, robe, and all.

VARDAN

The Wolf's ABC

Once upon a time some men captured a wolf cub and wrote down the alphabet to teach it to read and write.

'Say "*A*",' said the teacher.

'Ass,' said the wolf.

'Say "*B*",' said the teacher.

'Beef,' said the wolf.

'Say "*C*",' said the teacher.

'Sow,' said the wolf.

'Say "*D*",' said the teacher.

'Deer,' said the wolf.

'Say "*E*",' said the teacher.

'Eat,' said the wolf. 'But hurry, or they'll all get away!'

VARDAN

The Priest and the Bandit

A bandit once seized a priest, and made to kill him. But great strength was sent to the priest from above, and he overcame the bandit, and thrashed him soundly according to his deserts.

'Why do you beat me so?' gasped the bandit. 'Are not you priests always saying "Peace to every man" and such?'

'I am thrashing you so that every man may be able to live in peace, and you, an evil doer, are no friend of that.'

MEKHITHAR

The Fox and the Partridge

A fox seized a partridge between its jaws and prepared to eat it.

'Thanks be to God,' cried the partridge, 'who has summoned me to his kingdom, and will free me from all earthly ills! Fox, before you eat me, render thanks unto God for your good fortune!'

The fox relented, raised his eyes to Heaven, and prayed:

'I thank thee, almighty God, for the good things that thou hast prepared unto me.'

As soon as he opened his jaws, the partridge flew away.

'What a fool I am,' said the fox. 'I should have eaten first, and given thanks afterwards!'

VARDAN

The Good Soldier

A brave warrior, already lame in both legs, went to war.

'Where are you going, you unfortunate fellow?' asked one of his comrades. 'You will surely be killed, being unable to run away!'

'In battle, comrade,' replied the other, 'the thing to do is to stand and fight and conquer, not to run away.'

VARDAN

The Peacock and the Eagle

A peacock, displaying his splendid feathers for all and sundry, was greatly praised. The praises went to his head, and he began to think how he could become king of the birds. Some of the wiser birds warned him of listening to flattery, and sought to remind him that kings owed their thrones to their birth. He would not listen to them. The king of the birds, the eagle, learned of the peacock's ambitions, and swooping upon him, put him and his whole family to flight. Many of the other birds seized the opportunity to snatch away his fine feathers, and stripped him bare. So that not only did he fail to become king, but he lost all of his much praised beauty as well.

MEKHITHAR

The Eagle and the Arrow

An eagle was soaring high in the sky, when an arrow struck him in the breast. As he fell, he looked at the arrow, feathered with eagle plumes.

'Woe is me,' he cried. 'I am the cause of my own destruction.'

VARDAN

The Price of Dignity

The other animals appeared before the lion.

'In all respects you behave as a prince, Your Majesty,' they said, 'save for one thing: when you hunt, you act like a thief, for you slink about, and cover your traces.'

This the lion did at their expense, and they sought a way to hoodwink him, and so escape the danger.

The perplexed lion, seeking to preserve his dignity, and to act as a prince in all things without exception, ceased to hunt his prey stealthily as in the past, and went about openly, his head held high. The other animals could now see him coming, and save themselves, while he grew very thin.

MEKHITHAR

203

The Hermit and the Horse

A certain hermit arrived tired and hungry in a town and asked for food, but in vain. As he left the town, he saw a horse, belonging to a certain prince who dwelt there. He took the horse to the next village, and sold it for a single loaf. It was not long before the prince found him.

'What sort of fool are you, hermit,' he cried, 'to sell my valuable horse for a mere loaf of bread?'

'Do not scold so, prince,' replied the hermit. 'Did not Christ himself say, "Freely receive, and freely give"?'

VARDAN

The Priest and the Birds

At Easter all the birds came to the priest to confess their sins and to receive absolution. The goshawk and the cormorant came with them.

'We know of no sins we have committed, father,' they lied, 'except perhaps that we have eaten a few frogs and mice.'

The priest angrily sent them away without absolution, calling them unclean.

The two birds flew off, swooped on some clean and tender young birds and fledgelings, and offered them to the priest.

'You have nothing to confess, my children,' said the priest, receiving them gratefully. 'These birds were old, and have hardly any feathers left.'

And he absolved them.

MEKHITHAR

St. George and the Fox

A fox was swimming across a river, when it was caught by the swift current and started to drown.

'St. George! St. George! Help me!' cried the fox. 'If you save me, I'll burn an ounce of incense in your honour!'

St. George hastened to the scene and dragged the fox out of the river. Safe on shore, the lately terrified fox recovered in the shade of a rock, and began to complain.

'What is the world coming to?' he exclaimed. 'When the saints lived in the flesh on earth, they went around in carts and on horseback and caused the world much weeping and wailing; but then they underwent tortures and suffered martyrdom, and were beloved of the Lord. Now you have to offer them a bribe before they will lift a finger to help you!'

As he talked, the rock he was sitting under began to slip.

'St. George! St. George! Help me!' cried the fox. 'If you save me,

I'll burn one and a half ounces of incense in your honour!'

St. George took pity on the fox, and held back the rock until he had got away.

Recovering from his fright, the fox began to grumble again.

'There you are!' he said. 'It is a scandal! Where am I going to get incense from? Am I a tradesman? Am I a shopkeeper? No, St. George will have to do without!'

As he talked, a group of hunters suddenly appeared, and set their dogs on him.

'St. George! St. George! Help me!' cried the fox. 'I *shall* find the incense! And I'll sacrifice a lamb in your honour!'

This time no help came. The dogs fell upon the fox, harried him hither and thither, until he faltered and fell, and was seized by them, still calling upon the saint. The huntsmen took him, flayed him alive for his fine fur, and cast the rest of him away.

Then St. George appeared.

'You deceitful dog!' he said. 'You are naked, and covered in blood, but you shall never be a martyr, for you have broken your oaths, and shall die unabsolved!'

VARDAN

PROVERBS

If a poor man eats a chicken, either the chicken is sick, or the poor man.

If a poor man says a cat has eaten lights, he is not believed; if a rich man says a mouse has eaten iron, he is believed.

Choose the nail to suit the plank.

A camel is not watered with a spoon.

A man cannot clap with one hand.

When a dog is tired of life, he lies at the door of a mosque.

A forced rose gives no scent.

When coarse and fine fetch the same price, woe to her who spins fine.

There is one father's blessing which is worse than his 'son of a dog!' (*when he is dying*).

The cat who wears gloves will catch no mice.

Where there are no horses to be had, mules too are dear.

One does not pour cold water into hot soup.

A fly may fall into a king's goblet.

I come from church, and you give me a sermon?

He who is too fond of swimming ends up in a fish's belly.

Carpets are not made for the sake of the flea.

If you are blessed with intelligence, keep it to yourself.

A plump lamb deserves a sharp knife.

In a hanged man's house none talk of rope.

Tired hands, restful heart.

Small wit, active feet.

You cannot draw a straight line with a crooked ruler.

What is sport for the cat is death for the mouse.

A mouse in the claws of the cat has no time for squeaking.

A partridge's egg is not found under a hen.

Near a fire there is no need of a flint.

If a horse jumps well, they praise the rider; if a sword cuts well, they praise the hand.

Fish in the sea fetch no price.

If hair had power in it, goats would be prophets.

The goat has a beard as well as the priest.

A traveller's departure lies in his own hands, his return in the hands of God.

A wine shop is not founded on one grape.

If a house has two mistresses, the floor will not be swept.

In the time it takes for the fat to grow thin, the thin have given up the ghost.

Kiss the hand you cannot cut off.

First become known as a lamb; then turn wolf, and eat.

One has to knock on seven doors for one to open.

The mouse dreams dreams which would terrify a cat.

The mouse is small, but he dreams big dreams.

Do not burn down the house to catch a mouse.

When a dog goes into the water, he will not swim until it comes up to his tail.

Gold will shine in mud.

He who says what he likes will hear what he does not like.

If you would kill a dog, declare him mad.

A tree which bears fruit will not want for water.

Satan's sandals are soon worn out.

One cannot make a blancmange of onions.

Spit and wipe your nose with your fingers a thousand times, but once in your life set a good example.

If the right edge will not cut, the left one will.

When the apricot's ripe, the mouth will open.

They asked the fish, What news of the sea? Much news, but my mouth is full of water, it said.

Man is of earth, not of Heaven.

It is better to ruin a church than to break a heart.

The church was completed, but for the dome.

He who gives nine will give ten.

What good is a golden bowl if used to spit blood in?

Ask a donkey what gifts it has, and it lifts its tail and brays.

I know many songs, but cannot sing.

A fool spoke, a wise man believed.

One does not pay the coachman when only half way.

The world is black in the eyes of the blind.

They read the gospel to the wolf. Hurry, the sheep are getting away, he said.

Say 'broth', and the fly will come from Baghdad.

They spat in the face of the man without honour. It is raining, he said.

A lie has short legs.

He who fears wolves should not walk abroad at night.

How does the wolf know that mules cost money?

The poor man wants bread, the rich man wants everything.

The words of the rich man are ephemeral, those of the poor man are not heeded at all.

If you have made friends with the raven, your perch is in the house of the Turk.

A near neighbour is better than a distant friend.

An old friend will not become an enemy, nor an old enemy a friend.

There is a friend for the heart, and another for the belly.

A friend looks at your head, an enemy at your feet.

The camel looks down on the groom.

The horse and mule quarrelled, and the ass was trampled underfoot.

A goat is dearer to a goat than a flock of sheep.

A hungry man will eat the soft parts of a stone.

The wolf longs for a foggy day, the thief for a cloudy night.

When the cat's away, the mice dance the saraband.

He who catches fish will get his clothes wet.

A cut of the sword will heal, but not a cut of the tongue.

He who steals a needle will steal a camel.

He who sails the ocean will not drown in a brook.

Temptation does not announce its coming.

When the cart has broken down, there are many to show one the way.

A priest will not eat cake every day.

Though sin be a sable fur, do not put it on.

By the time the dried fruit was soaked, the patient had died.

The serpent pitted himself against the dragon, and was torn into a thousand pieces.

One cannot hold two water-melons in one hand.

He who runs after two hares will not catch one.

He who descends into the well at the end of another's rope will remain at the bottom.

A man must clean his own carpet.

If they crack a nut in India, *she*'ll come out.

He who rises in anger will sit down the worse.

A red cow will not cast its skin.

The serpent changes its shirt, not its nature.

A hen may be ugly, so long as she lays eggs.

Fruit will not keep in a boy's pocket.

Black heart, white teeth.

He who is bitten by a speckled snake will shy at a speckled rope.

A donkey which has been to Jerusalem forty times will still be a donkey.

The donkey knows seven styles of swimming, but seeing the water forgets them all.

Be a mountain ne'er so high, one day a road shall cross it.

He who finds room for his feet will find room for his bottom.

He eats lamb with the wolf, and cries 'Alas!' with the shepherd.

A sweet tongue will charm a serpent from its lair.

Shun water which neither babbles nor roars.

The fool gives, the wise man takes.

He was born seven days before Satan.

He takes everyone who says 'Good morning' to be his friend.

No one will call his own yoghurt sour.

The frying-pan will not say its bottom is black.

Every man will praise his worthless son and his boss-eyed daughter.

They invited the donkey to the wedding. Either you have no salt, or you need someone to carry the water, he said.

He laid down the gospel, and took up the tambourine.

A fair name is known from Van to Tiflis, a fair face from house to hammam.

There is a name for it, but the thing itself does not exist.

The world calls you 'Sir'; you know your own status.

God save the dumb from the wicked.

Sleep comes to the wounded, but not to the hungry.

Full belly wins no honours.

Tall in stature, short in wit.

The cat could not catch the mouse. I offer it to my grandfather's soul, she said.

The cat could not reach the meat. It is Friday, she said.

The chimney is crooked, the smoke rises straight.

The fool threw a stone into the well, and a thousand wise men could not get it out again.

The fool asked a question, and forty wise men could not find an answer.

The thieving cat sits on the old woman's lap.

An ox breaks a leg in Daghestan, and there's trouble in Koghb.

A long tongue makes for a short life.

The goat which escapes the wolf ends up at market.

On a rainy day there are many to water the chickens.

Lost property has many claimants.

What the eye sees is surer than what the ear hears.

Not every cloud brings rain.

The fool's bread is in the smart man's belly.

Seven priests baptized a boy, and christened him Mary.

That which you put in another's cup will come back in your own spoon.

If you dig a pit, be sure to dig it your own size.

The sound of a distant bell is sweet.

They said to the mouse, Why are you so small? For fear of the cat, he said.

Fine house, ramshackle town.

He did not know the dead man, but cries 'Woe is me!'

There is water where there is no bridge; there are bridges where there is no water.

Satan works evil on Sundays.

Satan does not go to weddings himself, but he sends his slippers.

They told the monk, Your son is dead. I have no son, but it is very bad news, he said.

What does it matter to a blind man if candles are dear?

Pass in front of a horse, and behind a dog.

He who speaks the truth must have his horse at the door and a foot in the stirrup.

If Satan is eating garlic underground, *he* knows about it.

Hump rocks with the wise, but do not eat bread with a fool.

What use is soap to the black man, or advice to the fool?

It is better to be reduced to tears by a wise man, than to laughter by a fool.

No sooner is the chicken hatched than it flies to the perch.

The crow tried to strut like a peacock, and forgot how to walk like a crow, or a peacock.

They took the camels to be shod, and the frogs too lifted up their feet.

With one lame donkey he joins the caravan.

I went to Hamadan, and flew seven furlongs on the way.
—Hamadan is a long way off, but a furlong is near at hand, so come on, fly!

They were selling brains at an auction, but he preferred his own.

The pot said, My bottom is made of solid gold; the ladle said, Where do you think I come from?

They asked the frog, Why are you always croaking? I am pleased with the sound of my own voice, he said.

The worker in linen will not agree with him who works in silk.

If he has a cartload of chick peas, he calls God Theo.

The boaster will have no middling skills.

You will get a straight answer from a fool.

If he has to make a needle, he demands a hundredweight of steel.

She has no shift for her back, but she wears a rose in her hair.

There is one, and he is worth a thousand; there are a thousand, and they are not worth one.

They took the fool to a wedding. It is prettier here than in our house, he said.

Acknowledgements

The translator would like to acknowledge his debt to the many Armenian scholars by whose efforts a vast amount of Armenian folk-lore material has been collected and preserved, and particularly to the publications of the Academy of Sciences of the Armenian S.S.R. The medieval fables have been selected from Prof. N. Marr's edition of the fables of Vardan of Aygek, *Sbornik pritch Vardana*, St. Petersburg, 1894–9, and the Mekhitarist edition of the fables of Mekhithar Gosh and Olbmpianos, Venice, 1842. The proverbs are selected from A. T. Ghananalian's extensive compilation, entitled *Aratsani*, Erevan, 1960, scientifically based on earlier smaller collections of proverbs current in particular regions and published in various journals. The folk-tales are translated mainly from the dialect versions reproduced in I. Orbeli and S. Taronian, *Hay zhoghovrdakan heqiathner*, [Armenian popular tales], abbreviated as *APT* in the footnotes, vols. I–V, X, Erevan, 1959–67. *Loqman the Wise*, originally recorded by Sargis Haykuni in Turkish Armenia and first published in the *Eminian Azgagrakan Zhoghovatsu* [Emin's ethnographical collection], vol. II, Moscow-Leningrad, 1901; *The Red Cow*, first recorded in Maku, N.W. Persia and published by E. Lalayan in *Margaritner hay banahiusuthean* [Pearls of Armenian literature], vol. III, Tiflis-Vagharshapat, 1914–15; and *The Liar*, originally recorded in a village in the province of Ayrarat and published by T. Navasardiantz in *Hay zhoghovrdakan heqiathner* [Armenian popular tales], vol. III, Tiflis, 1884, have, owing to the unavailability of the original Armenian texts, been translated here from the Russian versions in Ya. Khatchatrian, *Armjanskie skazki* [Armenian folk-tales], 2nd edition, Moscow-Leningrad, 1933. *The Nightingale Hazaran*, originally published in G. Sĕrvandztiantz's collection *Manana*; *The Beardless, the Lame, and the One-Eyed Thief*, originally published in E. Lalayan's *Margaritner*, vol. II; and *Badikan and Khan Boghu*, originally published in G. Sĕrvandztiantz's *Hamov-Hotov*, have also been retold from their Russian versions in Khatchatrian's *Armjanskie skazki* and have previously appeared, with two other Armenian tales, in *The Peasant and the Donkey, Tales of the Near and Middle East*, ed. H. M. Nahmad, Oxford University Press, 1967. The translations are meant to be as close to the original Armenian as is consistent with acceptable English style. Nothing has been omitted from the tales selected, with one exception: the pogrom of the *dénouement* of *The Forty Thieves' Apprentice* (p. 111) has been greatly reduced in scale, for even mythical kings must not be allowed to set children too bad an example, especially when they are presented as otherwise just. A few phrases and epithets have occasionally been added to make the story-line a little clearer, or to enliven passages that appear rather bare in translation. Reciters of oral tales are apt to nod from time to time and to omit to mention important details early enough on, a harmless ellipsis in that most of their natural audience will have heard a version of the story already. The oral reciter also has the advantages proper to the spoken word, namely the ability to vary intonation, volume and speed, to pause for effect, and to illustrate his tale with eloquent physical expressions and gestures; the writer needs a few more adjectives and adverbs.